Daniel's Beetles

Tony Bianchi

Daniel's Beetles

Seren is the book imprint of
Poetry Wales Press Ltd
Nolton Street, Bridgend, Wales

Explore thirty years of Seren books at
www.serenbooks.com

ISBN 978-1-85411-544-7

Adapted by the author from his Welsh-language novel *Pryfeta*,
published in 2007 by Y Lolfa

A CIP record for this title is available from
the British Library

The publisher works with the financial assistance
of the Welsh Books Council

Published with the financial support of Cyfnewidfa Len Cymru /
Welsh Literature Exchange

Printed by Bell & Bain Ltd, Glasgow

BOOK ONE

The Entomologist

1. Excerpt from a biography

North Shields, September 1964

Daniel Robson takes hold of his mother's hand. She looks down at him and smiles.

'*Fory byddi di'n chwech.*'

She smiles again, willing a response.

'Six years old, Daniel. *Whech mlwydd oed.*'

Daniel doesn't reply. Instead, he draws the fingers of his free hand along the top of the stone wall that runs alongside the pavement.

'Don't hurt yourself, *bach*,' she says, in English, to make sure he understands. The boy examines the small granules on his finger tips. His mother reverts to Welsh.

'I wonder what presents you'll get.'

After walking the two hundred yards from their house to the cemetery, Daniel lets go of his mother's hand and runs ahead.

'Don't get lost now.'

As Daniel and his mother enter between the black iron gates, most of the cemetery remains obscured by the high trees and dense undergrowth. The gravestones, crooked and sooty, the pious angels, the pillars, the urns, the whole paraphernalia of another age's death have long ago yielded this territory to the ivy and the weeds.

'*Paid ti mynd yn rhy bell nawr, Daniel!*'

A single tarmac'd road runs from the entrance to the open area at the top of the cemetery, where the war dead are buried. Another, narrower way, more path than road, runs across the main thoroughfare. Where the two meet there is a circular flower bed overlooked by four wooden seats. Within the segments created by these arterial routes there are scores, perhaps hundreds of lesser paths. These are the routes mourners would once have used to tend the graves of loved ones, to take fresh flowers, to clear leaves in the autumn, perhaps to give the marble a scrub. They were, without doubt, well used, the graves here being so tightly packed together, the interments in each family plot so numerous. Today, under the dense canopy of trees, it is difficult to make out where these capillary paths lead, except into the darkness.

This is their appeal to Daniel. Because, through his frequent visits with his mother, the tiny, overgrown paths have already inscribed detailed maps in his memory. Although he is not yet six, he knows ways which cannot be seen, not even by his mother. Having run past the flower garden, having held the water tap for a moment, as he always does, in his left hand, having glanced back over his shoulder to make sure his mother is following, Daniel slips through a narrow gap in the hedge.

'Don't go too far, Daniel... *Bydda i'n ffaelu cadw lan.*'

But his mother knows exactly where Daniel is going. She squeezes through the same gap, holding up the hem of her skirt so that it doesn't snag on the thorns. At once her nostrils are filled with the pungencies of wild garlic, damp earth and rotting leaves. Although there's been no rain for days, it is still wet and slippery here, under the shade of the trees, and she must tread carefully so as not to trip over a root or the concealed kerb of a grave. She sees her son snatch another glance backwards before taking an abrupt turn to the right. Only his blonde hair, caught by the occasional finger of sunlight, is visible now above the ragged bushes.

'*Sa f'yna, Daniel bach...* Wait for me.'

But Daniel has already reached his destination. When his mother catches up with him, he's standing on tip-toe, fingering one of the rectangular stone tablets which have been set, in orderly rows, on the inside wall of the cemetery. She realises it is the first time he has reached this, the lowest row of tablets, and smiles. Daniel is a little short for his age.

'Well done, Daniel... *Ti'n tyfu'n grwtyn mawr.'*

'What's it say, Mam?' he asks, in English.

'*Nac wyt ti'n cofio, bach...*? Try to remember.'

'Say the story again, Mam.'

And his mother tells him the story, exactly as she does on each of their visits here, on sunny afternoons when she's finished her household chores or her shopping or has had enough of being in the house or, as now, when she feels the need to clear her mind before her husband returns home.

'What were the ships called, Mam?'

The mother underlines the name with her finger.

'Friendship *o'dd un.*'

And moves to the next tablet.

'*A* Stanley *o'dd y llall.'*

'Which ones were the babies, Mam?'

The mother reads two of the inscriptions, the names, the dates of birth.

'There's too many, *bach. Alla i ddim 'darllen nhw i gyd.'*

'This one, Mam... This one.'

The mother takes her son's hand.

'Come on, Daniel,' she says. 'We've got to go home now, or your dad'll be back before us.'

⋆

A birthday party. The cake and jellies and sandwiches are standing on the formica-topped bench in the kitchen, ready to be carried out to the garden. There, in the middle of the lawn, a small rectangular table has been laid. The white tablecloth, the plates, the knives and spoons shine under a bright sun. There are five chairs, one set at the head, the others on either side.

Inside the house, the mother looks for Daniel.

'*Ble rwyt ti, bach?'*

Daniel is sitting on the window seat in the front room, looking through the pictures which his father gave him yesterday to put in his scrapbook. Some footballers, some cars, but mainly ships. He practices the names of those he can remember.

'A...pa...pa... Apapa.'

Apapa

He puts each picture to one side and turns to the next.

'O...lym...pi...a... Olympia.'

Every now and again – when he hears a bus stopping or a car door being slammed shut – he looks out to see whether anyone is coming. Once, he sees his brother, John, crossing the road to catch the bus to Newcastle. Because John is too big to go to a six year-old's birthday party. Then he returns to the pictures.

'What's this say, Mam?'

Daniel's mother tells him to put his pictures away, because his friends will be here any minute. But he persists.

'What's this say, Mam?'

The mother takes the card and turns it over.

'SS Canberra, *bach. Mae SS yn meddwl "steam ship". Llong stêm.*'

'Canberra... Can...be...rra.'

Daniel takes the card back and places it on the pile at his side.

'And this?'

'Golden Grain Tea, *bach.* The picture came with a packet of tea.'

'And this?'

Daniel takes out a picture somewhat larger than the others. His mother doesn't need to turn it over.

'You should remember that one, Daniel.'

Daniel looks up at her, expecting a fuller answer.

'That's where your dad's spent the last two months.'

The mother looks out through the window.

'Trebartha, *bach,* Tre...bar...tha.'

She turns the word around in her mouth, thinking how Welsh it sounds.

Daniel starts to tidy his pictures. And for a few seconds both mother and son are absorbed in their own thoughts. When the shout comes from the kitchen, it takes their breath away.

'Mary! I'm away out to clear the gutter.'

The mother wants to shout back. She wants to tell him that Daniel's party is due to start shortly, that the other children are about to arrive, that working on top of a ladder in the garden is going to spoil things, distract people, make her anxious. But she shouts these things in her mind only. She half turns towards the door.

'Take care.'

And in that second, the mother, who is also a wife, is unsure whether she should follow her husband and offer to help him in the garden, or whether she should stay with her son and prepare for the party. Because of this dilemma, Daniel's next words come to her indistinctly, as though from a great distance.

'Not coming.'

Daniel finishes tidying his pictures, squaring the pile on the window sill, one side at a time. He gets down from his seat.

'What...? *Beth wedest ti, bach?'*

'They're not coming.'

He lets the words out in a dry monotone, without looking up, so that his mother, her ears still ringing with her husband's brusque announcement, fails to register that anything significant is being said. She turns back towards him.

'Pam, bach? Why do you say that?'

And then she sees the tight lips, the little creases at the side of the nose, the little old man's face she'd laugh at sometimes, thinking it 'old-fashioned', now seeing it only as odd, beyond her ken. As he walks past her, she reaches for his arm, but he pulls free and makes for the door.

'Why, Daniel, why?'

He replies without turning back.

'Him.'

⋆

Tea in the garden. A birthday tea. Daniel is kneeling on the paved path which stretches from the back of the house to the high hedge separating the Robsons' garden from its neighbour. Behind him is the lawn with its table and chairs. In front, running the length of the path, is a narrow border filled with clusters of fuchsia, geranium and phlox. Near the hedge there is also a small bed of jibbons which Daniel's mother grows to put in salads and sandwiches. Were he to turn and raise his eyes at this moment, Daniel would see his father reach the top of his ladder, or as near to the top as he needs to go, and pull a plastic bag from his pocket. But Daniel sees none of this, because his eyes are fixed elsewhere.

Daniel bends down until his face is within six inches of the earth. In his right hand, between finger and thumb, he holds a small stick. Slowly, and skilfully for one so young, he uses this to turn a black beetle on its back. The beetle wriggles furiously, recovers its footing and tries to make its escape through the undergrowth. Before it can do so, however, Daniel traps it with his left hand and repeats the experiment. Getting the same result as before, he loses interest and starts poking about elsewhere amongst the leaves and clods of earth. A woodlouse comes into view. Daniel turns this creature, too, on its back. To his surprise, it makes no attempt to escape but instead rolls itself into a tight little ball, as still and lifeless as a stone. Despite prodding it with his stick and rolling it from side to side, there is nothing he can do with it. He turns his attention to a ladybird which has alighted on a leaf just above his head. And this is when he hears his mother's footsteps.

'*Dyma ni*. Let's have a nice party, shall we, just the two of us?'

She carries the sponge cake ceremoniously to the table and calls on her son to come and sit down.

'Soon as we start eating, you'll see, they'll turn up, bet you they will, *gawn ni weld, ife?*'

He looks blankly at her. To console him, she cuts a slice of cake and puts it on the plate at the head of the table. Both Daniel and his mother know that it isn't normal to cut the cake at the beginning of a party but they know, too, that this is not a normal party. So he rises from his knees, wipes his hands on his shorts and takes his place at the table.

'We'll light some candles inside afterwards, if you like... There's too much of a breeze out here.'

Daniel studies the portion of cake on his plate.

'I'll get the sandwiches now,' she says, stating the obvious, needing to say something. 'And then you can open your presents.'

She wipes her hands on her pinny and turns back towards the house.

'Back in a minute.'

As she approaches the back door, Daniel's mother glances up at her husband, who is now filling the plastic bag with dirt and leaves and twigs from the gutter. Once she has returned to the house, Daniel picks up his piece of cake and begins to eat it. He does this methodically, starting at the thin, inner end and working his way towards the outer wedge. This he divides into two segments and devours each in a single mouthful. He pauses to lick the cream from his fingers. A minute later, as he swallows the last of the crumbs, he puts his plate to one side and smoothes the tablecloth, as best he can, with the palms of his hands. When he is satisfied that the table is neat and tidy again, he sits back, wondering where his mother has got to. He would like a drink, because it's hot, because he always has a drink with his tea. He glances over at the border and wonders whether he has time to look for more insects, just until the drink comes, but decides that wouldn't be right, his mother would be cross, because the party has already started, the cake has been cut. So he looks back at the cake, the remainder of it, which his mother has left in the centre of the table. He reaches over, grips the edge of the plate between fingers and thumb, and tries to draw it closer. But it is awkward, and heavy, too, even for a boy who has just had his sixth birthday. So he must get up from his chair and use both hands.

'Daniel!'

Now that he has the plate in front of him, he sits down again and turns it around until the gap in the cake – the gap left by the piece he has just eaten – is facing him. He looks at it and furrows his brow.

'Daniel!'

As Daniel contemplates the cake, his father reaches over towards the end of the gutter where it joins the down-pipe. His left foot is still on the ladder but he has had to move the right to the bathroom windowsill in order to gain a few inches. He keeps his balance by holding the gutter in his left hand but does not feel secure enough to put both feet on the windowsill, as it would then be difficult, he calculates, to return to the ladder. Despite his best efforts, he remains a yard or so short of his goal. And if someone were to see him at this moment – a neighbour, perhaps, or even his wife, although Mary is often reluctant to offer her husband advice – they would no doubt suggest that he get down from the ladder and move it just the necessary few feet that would enable him to reach the end of the gutter without difficulty or danger. But there's no-one there. No-one but Daniel.

'Daniel! Go and get your mam, will you? Right away, Daniel. D'you hear?'

Daniel, however, is preoccupied. Having pondered a while, he has concluded that the cake cannot be made whole again. This is a painful realisation. Indeed, so acute is his disappointment that he even regrets eating the piece his mother gave him. He could have placed it in the gap and no-one would have been any the wiser. So acute, in fact, that he starts to get cross with his mother for cutting it in the first place. The gap stares at him. He scowls back at it.

Then, as quickly as it came, the scowl lifts from his face. Daniel takes a knife and begins cutting the rest of the cake, using firm, confident thrusts, his left hand pressing down on his right to give it extra force, to make sure he cuts through both layers to the plate underneath. He counts each cut in turn, 'One, two, three, four, five...' and turns the plate carefully each time so that the pieces will be of equal size. Except that cutting is not quite the right word for what Daniel is doing, because this is one of those old-fashioned children's knives, rounded at the end, with a blade designed only for spreading, not cutting. And although he tries his best to cut neatly and precisely, as he has seen his mother do on countless occasions, the cake is quickly reduced to a heap of shapeless fragments, crumbs scattered about the table, on Daniel's lap, even on the lawn at his feet.

'Get your bloody mother, will you!'

Daniel doesn't understand why this has happened. In his own mind he has done everything necessary to create a display of neat, uniform pieces, to get rid of that unpleasant gap, to restore some propriety to his tea-party. And in his own mind, the cake is still, in fact, whole. It's something else that's at fault. The knife. The plate. Or the friends who haven't turned up to eat the pieces provided for them, as Daniel himself has done. Something's to blame, that much is certain, but not the cake in his mind. No, this mess has nothing at all to do with that perfect, round, indivisible cake.

'Ah...'

And all he has to do, to get rid of this offence to his special day, is to give the plate a small but firm push with the back of his hand. Even though it seemed so heavy before, one push is all that is needed and the cake falls to the ground, plate and all. Daniel looks at it. Purses his lips. Marvels at how the plate has performed a somersault in the air and fallen on top of the pieces of cake, so that it rests at a tilt. At how other fragments have sprayed outwards, over the grass. He continues looking, until a little shiver inside him makes his arms tremble. And at first he likes this feeling, is excited by it, because somehow he is bigger now, he has done something of consequence. But then, as the shiver moves to his stomach, be begins to feel a little sick. So he gets up from his chair and makes as though to return to the insects.

And it must be at this moment that he hears the sound of the ladder scraping against the wall, because suddenly he looks up towards the roof of the house, shielding his eyes from the sun with his hand. In front of him, slightly to the left, he sees the ladder careering noisily against the neighbour's fence. The plastic bag follows, but on a different trajectory, and making what is, after such clatter, a rather mocking *fwap* as it hits the ground. It is only then that Daniel notices his father, hanging by his right hand from the gutter, gasping and spluttering, his feet dancing wildly as they seek the absent ladder. Sees him lunge with his other hand, wrap it around the gutter so that, for a moment, he is quite steady, he is perfectly perpendicular, almost as though he had placed himself in that position deliberately, a kind of party stunt to impress the guests. And hears, less than a breath later, a strange dry sound, creck, creck, as the rusted metal bends and breaks, slowly, and then not entirely, just enough to cause the father's hands to lose their grip, first the left hand, then the right. And he hears the cry, and then an unexpected sound, an impersonal sound, like a bag of chippings falling on the concrete path. Then another cry, cut in half.

Daniel's gaze now turns downwards, because his mother is running out through the back door, saying over and over, in a voice of muted beseeching, 'No, no, no, no, no.' So that, seeing his mother in such distress – in greater distress even than when his father calls her bad names and makes her cry – Daniel can only shout out at the top of his voice, not knowing what language he's speaking, *'Wy'n flin, Mam.* I'm sorry about the cake. Please, Mam, *wy'n flin am y gacen. Mam! Mam!'*

2. On the Phone

Cardiff, August 2000

'Sue? That you, Sue?'

'Yes.'

'You OK, Sue?'

'Yes.'

'You sure?'

'Yes, I'm sure. Why shouldn't I be?'

'You sound... You sound a bit...'

'A bit what? I sound a bit what?'

'Don't know, just ...'

'I'm OK, Dan.'

'You looked tired yesterday... When we got back...'

'It was a long day, Dan. A long journey.'

'Yes, but...'

'You didn't look that great yourself.'

'No, I'm sure... But you're OK now, are you?'

'Yes, Dan, I'm OK.'

'The girls were worried about you...'

'For God's sake, don't go on. I'm alright.'

'OK... Sorry...'

'Somebody's at the door, Dan, I've got to go... No, no-one you know... Yes, perhaps... But I'm busy, really busy... Yes, right through the week... No, Dan, I don't want to go to the reading group... No, there's no point asking again. The last thing, the very last thing I want to do now is go to the reading group. Do you understand? Do you hear what I'm saying?'

3. Translating Wallace

The Indians of the Amazon are less fastidious in their tastes, for while turtles, alligators, lizards, snakes and frogs are all common articles of food, some species of insects and other Annulosa furnish them with their greatest luxuries. The first is a great-headed red ant, the Œcodoma cephalotes. It is the female of this destructive creature that furnishes the Indian with a luxurious repast. At a certain season the insects come out of their holes in such numbers, that they are caught by basketsfull. When this takes place in the neighbourhood of an Indian village all is stir and excitement; the young men, women and children go out to catch saübas with baskets and calabashes, which they soon fill; for though the female ants have wings, they are very sluggish and seldom or never fly. The part eaten is the abdomen, which is very rich and fatty from the mass of undeveloped eggs. They are eaten alive; the insect being held by the head as we hold a strawberry by its stalk, and the abdomen being bitten off, the body, wings and legs are thrown down on the floor, where they continue to crawl along apparently unaware of the loss of their posterior extremities. They are kept in calabashes or bottle-shaped baskets, the mouths of which are stopped up with a few leaves, and it is rather a singular sight to see for the first time an Indian taking his breakfast in the saüba season. He opens the basket, and as the great-winged ants crawl slowly out, he picks them up carefully and transfers them with alternate hand-fulls of farina to his mouth. When great quantities are caught, they are slightly roasted or smoked, with a little salt sprinkled among them, and are then generally much liked by Europeans.

It is eight o'clock in the morning. I am sitting at the window of my flat in Pontcanna, a cup of coffee in my hand, watching the heavy lorries go by, feeling the tremors. *At the Cutting Edge. Timber and Building Supplies.*

The translation into Welsh of the major works of Alfred Russell Wallace – *A Narrative of Travels in the Amazon and Rio Negro, The Geographical Distribution of Animals, Contributions to the Theory of Natural Selection*, the autobiographical *My Life*, and so on – has been my ambition since I was a university student and conceited enough to consider such a project within my grasp. He was, of course, a hero of mine well before that. I've no doubt it was unusual for a teenager in the seventies to adopt as his role-model, not merely a scientist, but a venerably bearded scientist who had died even before his parents were born. But that is what I did. Whilst my school friends repaired to the Vetch to cheer on Toshack and his Scousers, or shared a cigarette on Mumbles beach, it was my pleasure and privilege to turn to the mountains. To catch the bus up to the higher reaches of the valley, perhaps, and roam the slopes of Fan Gihirych which, on a clear day, I could see from our house in Pentrepoeth. Or, when I had sufficient time and pocket money, to venture further afield, to Cwm Nedd and Cwm Dulais, where I could follow in the footsteps of the great man himself.

Apart from my passion for Wallace and my desire that his works be translated intro Welsh, I cannot claim that my qualifications for the task are especially robust. I refer, of course, to my linguistic, not my scientific, qualifications. Without wishing to be boastful, I believe my publications in the fields of biodiversity and entomology compare well with my peers. But translation is a different matter entirely, particularly when one aspires to recreate, in another tongue, the voice of one of our greatest naturalists. And yet, as soon as I embarked on the project, I realised that there were, at the very least, some elements in my scientific training which could usefully be transferred to my new labours. Above all, perhaps, the single-mindedness: the concentrated focus and attention to detail. Yes, and also a certain humility, a recognition of the need, as far as is possible, to observe without being observed: the ability to make oneself invisible. Because, as I discovered, the translator, like the scientist, is at his best when he resembles a pane of glass: one is unaware of his presence until some little blemish – a mere scratch, perhaps – interrupts the perfect transparency. It is the business of both to reveal the original, nothing more, nothing less. The mediator, the collector, the dissector must, ultimately, stand to one side, out of sight.

As I say, I have no formal qualifications in translating. Nor, I fear, have I accumulated much practical experience in the field. It is true that, from time to time, Ahmed in the Publications Department asks me to supply copy for some leaflet or other. I might also, on occasion, help our full-time translators write captions and hand-outs, to ensure accuracy and consistency of usage. And then, of course, there's the Edward Llwyd Society. I receive requests from this quarter, too, mainly concerned with the naming of species that have yet to receive a Welsh baptism, so to speak. This, however, is all rather piecemeal work: a matter of selecting the correct term, of matching picture to text, of digging out striking case studies, and the like. I am never called upon to write what you might call 'prose'. And 'prose', properly considered, requires one to wrestle, not just with the subject at hand, but with all sorts of other questions, too: questions of style, of syntax, of register and so on. And while I have a tolerable grasp – a passive understanding, you might say – of these questions, a mere understanding by itself does not equip one to be a practitioner. And that, I'm afraid, is the end of my *curriculum vitae* in this regard.

No, not quite the end. I can add one other item. For my own amusement, whilst I was studying for my degree, I would devise

Welsh versions of those mnemonics which students use to remember unwieldy slabs of information. Things like *King Phillip Called Out Fifty Good Soldiers*, which helped us recall the major biological categories, *Kingdom, Order, Class,* and so on. But as no-one studied Biology through the medium of Welsh, these little seeds of mine fell upon stoney ground. And perhaps, in retrospect, they were never much more than frivolous devices for assuaging the tedium of lectures.

Today, three days after returning from Northumberland, where I was born, Wallace fulfills a purpose similar to that of the old mnemonics. He is a distraction. He keeps the unpleasant images at bay. The intrusive thoughts, as Sue calls them. The girls, back at their own home now, ringing to ask, is everything OK, is Sue feeling alright? The memory of that absent-minded peck on the cheek with which Sue said good-bye, her eyes not meeting mine, already looking at the car, making her escape. Her voice on the phone, cold, offering me nothing. And that voice in my head still, its admonishment, its indifference. Wallace helps me subdue that voice, permits me to put it in my bedside cupboard and close the door for a while.

★

I heard Wallace's name for the first time when my mother took me to stay with Wncwl Wil at Bryn Coch. John, my brother, had left home by then, so it was just the two of us. Wil was my mother's uncle, not mine, but I still called him 'Wncwl'. In fact, as far as I can recollect, he was 'Wncwl Wil Bryn Coch' to everyone in the family, whatever their degree of kinship. Although not especially old, his mind, or the better part of it, 'had gone off over the mountain with Anti Magi', as Mam would say. This Magi, Wil's wife, had recently died and as my mother was the only widowed relative within a hundred miles, it fell upon her to put Wncwl Wil's affairs in order before he moved to a care home in Pontardawe. I don't recall seeing him after this visit, and I can't say that I saw that much of him even at Bryn Coch, because he was largely confined to his bed at this stage, and because illness and old age and their attendant drudgeries were anathema to twelve-year-old boys such as myself.

In its own right, Bryn Coch was not a romantic or beautiful spot. Wil and Magi had failed to produce an heir, so the farm itself had been idle for years. An air of creaking dereliction permeated the place. The close was dense with weeds and at night I would hear slates fall from the roof of the cowshed: not because of the wind, but rather through their own unbearable weight, their inability to hang on any longer. On its eastern side, the land bordered the busy road to Neath. There was no view worthy of the name.

And yet, in that bright flower of my adolescence, and despite its many imperfections, its dilapidation, Bryn Coch was everything to me. On its western side, behind the farm, and far from the din of traffic, flowed Afon Clydach, and there, on its wooded banks, I spent the whole of that short, hot, magical summer. This was, again, to the dispassionate observer, a retreat of quite meagre proportions. But at the time, and to one reared in a cramped terrace, it offered horizons beyond imagining. This was no Sunday afternoon outing to the Gower, no tea-and-Victoria Sponge weekend with Mam-gu at her own, even tinier terrace in Llanelli. Going to Bryn Coch was for me not just a change of location but a voyage of discovery. There, you might say, I found my own proper habitat, the habitat to which I was properly fitted by disposition but from which, owing to some dreadful accident of birth, I had somehow been sundered. It was like going home.

My chief delight at Bryn Coch was to clamber down to one particular shaded pool in the river, where I would hunt for beetles and spiders and other scuttling creatures that sought shelter there amongst the stones and tree-stumps. Having found them, I would proceed to identify them with the help of the *Observer's Book of British Insects and Spiders*, a volume my mother had given me as a birthday present. I vividly recall the surge of excitement whenever I succeeded in matching the wriggling specimen in my jam jar with one of the pictures in the book. *Whirligig (family Gyrinidae), usually found only at the surface of the water.* And there it was, the whirligig itself, twitching and gyrating precisely as it was meant to. 'I had never before experienced anything so much resembling death itself,' said

Wallace, describing the swoon of bliss into which he fell after discovering a new and exceptionally beautiful butterfly in the Amazon basin. That little river near Neath was, indeed, my own Amazon.

However intense the pleasures of insect-hunting on the banks of the Clydach, however, it is likely that I would have remained a mere hobbyist were it not for one particular circumstance. Wncwl Wil had ventured downstairs on one of his 'walking days', as my mother termed them. Every now and again he would summon strength from somewhere and declare to whomsoever was present that he was about to 'go out and tend to the fowl' or 'bring the cows in for milking' or set about some other task which it had been his custom to perform in times gone by. And it was quite painful to witness the confusion, the incomprehension, the shock on his face, then, when he realised that there was no such work to be done, that there were no cows, that, in fact, there was little enough left of the cowsheds themselves. Once, he came down screaming blue murder that some Mr Critchley was 'trying to break in to steal the mare.' None of us had any idea who Mr Critchley might be, or why the mare should have strayed into the house, but I can tell you candidly and soberly that the look in Wncwl Wil's eyes was as frightening to me as if there had, indeed, been a horse thief in the house, yes, and a horse as well.

Be that as it may, Wncwl Wil came into the kitchen one afternoon in his old work clothes – his cap, his muddy wellies, his grey mac – and saw one of the jamjars which I used to carry insects back to the house for further observation and identification. I believe there was a caterpillar in it, and some leaves. Uncle Wil looked at the jar and said. 'There was a chap here the other day. He was catching beetles, too. Young chap by the name of... by the name of...' He didn't remember the name, and in any case it was his Da'-cu had let him in, because he himself had been out at the time. Yes, dipping sheep down in Ca' Gwaelod or else, perhaps, fighting in the War, he couldn't be sure now. But, said Wncwl Wil, the chap had left some old papers in the cupboard, *rhyw hen bapurach*, and it was high time he sent them back, yes, he'd have to do that today, soon as he found the address. And he told me to go and ask Magi if she'd please get them packed up ready because she was better than him at packing things, at getting them neat and tidy. And Mam would have to tell him, then, 'Magi can't do it today, Wil. Magi's gone.'

But he would sometimes become confused and say Mari, not Magi, because the two names sounded similar, and perhaps because there was, in fact, a Mari in the house at the time. (Mari is my mother's first name.) And it is curious, in retrospect, how he could 'remember' things which had happened long before he was born, and yet failed to recall the death of his wife only a few weeks earlier. At other times, he seemed to make light even of that death. He would sing a jingle to himself: "Our dear Magi's dead now, her body lies beneath, Her soul is in a wheelbarrow, bound for smokey Neath." Or was that Mari, too? I don't remember. Both, perhaps.

I found no papers in the cupboard. What I did discover, beneath the dust and the spiders' webs, between the family Bible and yellowed copies of the *Farmers' Weekly* and *Neath Guardian*, were a little booklet entitled *Materials for a Fauna and Flora of Swansea*, an issue of the *Zoologist* journal, dated 1847, and a thick blue tome whose spine bore the words, *My Life: a Record of Events and Opinions*. The author of this last title was one Alfred Russell Wallace: a genial, bearded gentleman of advanced years, judging by the photograph on the frontispiece. As I say, the cupboard exhaled dust when I opened the door; to all appearances, its contents were equally dry and unappealing. And yet, in a way, this somehow added to their mystique. By some trick of the juvenile imagination, I saw not Wncwl Wil's old papers, but rather a horde of rusty chests, awaiting one such as myself to open them and lay bare the treasures within. (I must stress here that I did not regard my appropriation of these items as, in any sense, an act of theft. Wncwl Wil was adamant that they should be disposed of. And I, at least, was an appreciative recipient.) So, whilst my mother sought to assure her uncle that everything was in hand, that the parcel was ready for posting, I happily became the boy hero, prising open the locks and hinges.

We had to go to Glamorganshire to partially survey and make a corrected map of the parish of Cadoxton-juxta-Neath. We lodged and boarded at a farmhouse called Bryn-coch (Red Hill), situated on a rising ground about two miles north of the town. Here we lived more than a year, living plainly but very well, and enjoying the luxuries of home-made bread, fresh butter and eggs, unlimited milk and cream, with cheese made from a mixture of cow's and sheep's milk, having a special flavour which I soon got very fond of. A little rocky stream bordered by trees and bushes ran through the farm, and was one of my favourite haunts. There was one little sequestered pool about twenty feet long into which the water fell over a ledge about a foot high. This pool was seven or eight feet deep, but shallowed at the further end, and thus formed a delightful bathing place.

I am unable, today, to convey fully what this passage meant to me, how tall I suddenly became, how brightly the world shone. These were Wallace's own words, in his own autobiography, recording his sojourn at Bryn Coch – yes, Wncwl Wil's Bryn Coch, my own Bryn Coch – only a few months before he departed for the Amazon. To say that the dark pool became for me thereafter a place, not only of discovery, but of mythological grandeur, is greatly to understate the matter. Before, I was an eager footsoldier on the outer rim of Elysium; now, I supped with the gods themselves.

And yet, in another sense, Bryn Coch became smaller, too. Because Wncwl Wil's farm, for all its wonders, was merely the bolt-hole from which Wallace set out to explore a much wider world. My pool had received his blessing, yes, but in so doing, had become, not an end in itself, but rather a kind of baptismal font, its waters preparing me for new departures. It was no longer sufficient simply to steal a glance over my hero's shoulder as he rocked by the fireside in his temporary lodgings. It now behoved me to follow the path which the great man himself had opened up for me. For both of us, Bryn Coch could only be a starting point.

That is why, over the next three years, my own little Amazon grew, acre by little acre, as I traced Wallace's forays into the adjacent valleys and sought out the specimens he had discovered there. The *Adelosia picea* in Glyn-y-big, the *Aplotarsus quercus* 'by the road near Crinant', the *Mathinus minimus* in the woods at Aberdulais, the *Trichius fasciatis* 'on a blossom of *Carduus heterophyllus* near the falls at the top of Neath Vale', and so on. Whenever I was fortunate enough to sight one of these creatures in the designated location, on mountain slope or river bank, I would declare its name to the assembled reeds and sedges, precisely as though I were a priest baptising a new-born child. And I truly believe that my pleasure on such occasions could scarcely have been less than that felt by Wallace himself when he stood in those very same places and named his creatures for the first time. For, like Wallace, *I was bitten by the passion for species and their description.*

At this early stage in my entomological career, I would capture my specimens in a net, examine them, record them and then let them go. I had neither the space nor the equipment to do more; nor, perhaps, had I the appetite. Indeed, I had been quite perturbed by some of the tales I had read about the early pioneers in the field and their rapacious practices, and John McGillivray was the subject of more than one boyhood nightmare. (It was this same McGillivray who used a rifle to catch the first known specimen of *Ornithoptera victoriae* Gray, an enormous butterfly that lives in the tree canopy, beyond the reach of even the most zealous collector.) Wallace himself was little better, of course: such was the spirit of the age. In time, I came to appreciate that these acts of apparent despoilation were the heavy but unavoidable price to be paid for the acquisition of knowledge. Where would our National Museum be without them?

I was compelled to name my specimens in English: at that time, it didn't occur to me that I had any choice in the matter. As names go, they were charming enough: the Rosy Footman, for example, the Round-winged Muslin, the Satin Lutestring, the Gothic Wainscot, the Heart and Dart, and so on. And in Latin as well, of course, following the standard classification procedures which I had by now learned from the textbooks. But even in this early period, my inability to acknowledge these creatures in my mother tongue, and then to talk about them, to write about them, without changing language, was a source of niggling discontent. As time went by, it began seriously to erode the pleasures of recording and classifying. But it was this same discontent, I believe, which ultimately spurred me on to begin translating the works of Alfred Wallace into Welsh. Did not the *chwilen fwgan* and the *cleren fustl* deserve a christening according to the rites of their own habitat? And if no-one else was willing to meet this obligation, then I myself would have to step up to the mark. But also, perhaps, I fell prey to a more grandiose desire: the desire to imagine that the splendid, many-coloured butterfly that Wallace discovered in the Amazon forests had been captured for the very first time in the net, not of the English language, but the Welsh. To imagine a different, more capacious, more wondrous past.

As I have said, I am not a translator by profession and the task of turning Wallace into a Welshman has been a demanding one. The main challenge, however, has little to do with words or, at least, with matters of naming and terminology, with which I am reasonably familiar. It derives rather from the need to establish what I believe they call the correct voice, the appropriate register. With striking that combination of precise scientific engagement, infectious enthusiasm and a certain Victorian fastidiousness, which tells us, quite as clearly as its plumage betrays the magpie, that this is Wallace and no other.

Mae Indïaid yr Amazon yn llai cysetlyd na ni yn eu harferion bwyta. Er bod crwbanod y môr, aligatoriaid, madfallod, nadroedd a brogaod i gyd yn fwydydd cyffredin iddynt, ymhlith y trychfilod a rhai o'r Annulosa eraill y mae eu prif ddanteithion i'w cael. Y pwysicaf o'r rhain yw'r morgrugyn pengoch, Œcodoma cephalotes.

If you read Welsh, perhaps you can judge whether this captures something of that voice, that spirit. I am still unsure. I showed my very first efforts to Sue, hoping for constructive comment. Critical, perhaps, but constructive. *'Hidlo gwybed, Dan,'* she said. It is a Welsh expression. I'm not really sure how best to translate it into English, whether there is an equivalent idiom. It means 'sieving gnats'. I'm sure you get the drift.

I must go and see my mother.

4. Déjà Vu

There are no windows in the long corridor. No natural light, no shadows either. A uniform electronic glow fills the entire space, day and night, throughout the year. It is accompanied by heavy and equally immutable odours of gravy and boiled cabbage. I ring the bell and open the door with my own key.

'Mam!'

I pause a moment and cough. Silence.

'Mam!'

'Helo...? Ti sy' 'na, Dan?'

'Ie, Mam.'

My mother lives alone in a retirement flat within easy walking distance of my own flat. I call by two or three times a week, to make sure she's coping, to keep her company. Sometimes, particularly in the summer, we go out together for a walk but it is now mid-autumn and there are wet leaves everywhere, making the paths slippery, and Mam has already had one nasty fall this year. She is sprightly enough, however, for her age – she will be eighty in two months' time – and she still does all her own shopping. In fact, I am sometimes anxious that she is perhaps too independent for her own good. She spurns all offers of help from her neighbours and is less than keen to accept favours even from her own family.

'Shwt mae'r hwyl, Mam?'

'Is Sue with you?'

As I enter the small lounge, I can see nothing but her legs and feet, protruding from the easy chair. The chair faces the window, enveloping her, and you might be uncertain, to begin with, whether it is my mother who has shrunk or the chair that has grown beyond its proper size. Everything else, however, is as it should be. This is a little doll's house, and my mother has adjusted herself in order to meet the requirements. The chair is merely a stray relic from some house of giants long abandoned.

'She's working, Mam. Did you go down for coffee this morning?'

My mother never goes to the coffee mornings, so I know it is futile to ask. She can't abide all those cackling busybodies, she says. She means others such as herself, of course, because they're nearly all widows here, their husbands having abandoned ship long before them.

'You've already asked me that, Daniel.'

But my mother's greatest problem is that she believes that everything she sees and hears has happened before.

'No, Mam, I haven't.'

'Yes... Just now...'

'I've only just arrived, Mam.'

'No, Daniel, I'm certain. I know what you're thinking, but this time I'm certain.'

My mother is also certain that the man who came to replace the television last week had called the week before. Is outraged that televisions should break down so often. And then, since she's thinking of televisions, that they broadcast the same news, day in, day out. The same accidents, the same murders, the same fallings from grace. 'What do they do that for, Daniel? Mm?' As though it were my responsibility to kick the newscasters back into motion, to prevent the innocent from being butchered twice. *Paramnesia* is the name for it. A kind of eternal *déja vu*. A never-ending omnibus edition of your least favourite soap opera.

'You been out, Mam?'

'Yes... Went to fetch a loaf and a piece of cheese.'

I have already seen the two full bottles on top of the dresser.

'And a tin of ham. Yes, and ...'

'And the bottles, Mam...? You didn't carry those back yourself ..?'

We both look at the sherry bottles.

'Nice young lad in the off licence... Offered to bring them round... If it gets too much... You know...'

Why does she buy two bottles at a time? Why buy any, when I can now see, bending over and opening the door of the wooden cupboard, that there are already two unopened bottles there? There is a mound of toilet rolls in the spare bedroom, too. (She has run out of space in the bathroom itself.) And I don't know how many writing pads and envelopes she has squirreled away in various drawers and cubbyholes, even though she rarely writes to anyone these days. Even though, by now, there are few alive to whom she could write.

'But Mam, I've told you, I'll do your heavy shopping... You just need... You just need to...' I draw a deep breath. She is not listening.

'Don't you find it dark here, Daniel?'

She is looking through the window.

'It's the tree, Mam. The big ash tree outside, casting a shadow. The leaves will be falling, soon enough, you'll get more light then.'

Because, although my mother thinks that everything has happened before, she does not necessarily remember those things that actually do happen, that happen repeatedly, are part of the warp and woof of her daily life. So this exchange – an exchange for which I know the entire script – is for my mother a departure into new and perilous territory.

'And those big black birds, flying across the window... Do they live in the trees, Daniel? Why are the birds so much bigger here?'

She means the crows. She always means the crows. Although they may be rooks. In any case, they are unexceptional creatures. Why they appear so big to my mother, so frightening, I cannot say: perhaps it is the effect of the cataracts which are now dimming the sight in both her eyes. Perhaps she just needs an object on which to pin her abstract fears.

'They wouldn't have nested... I mean, he wouldn't have let them... Are you listening, Dan?'

'Yes, Mam, I'm listening.'

'He wouldn't have let them nest so close to the house, I mean, to the old house, not before... I mean, that's one thing he... That's one thing you could say about... about...' She is talking about my father. I must resist the temptation to complete her sentences, which she often leaves dangling in mid-air.

'Yes, Mam, you're right. He wouldn't.'

'You remember when you broke the window in the back?'

'John broke it, Mam.'

'Mm?'

'John, Mam. Not me.'

And my occasional corrections derive less from a desire to establish the truth than from a hope – vain, I'm sure – that she may remember next time, that there will be less risk of disagreement and unpleasantness.

'What?'

'I said, John… It doesn't matter.'

'Good with his hands, see.'

She is satisfied with the image she now holds in her mind of my father's hands, mending the broken window. She settles back in her chair.

'Push that stool under my feet, will you, Daniel?'

I do as she asks. Then I go to the kitchen to make myself a cup of tea and pour my mother a sherry, pausing for a moment to check the cupboards, to make sure that she hasn't imagined the bread and cheese and ham.

'Thank you, *bach.*'

On my return, I change the subject. Did the girls visit over the weekend? Did they talk about our holiday? Did John phone? Has she seen anything good on the television? Formally speaking, you might say, the outcome is the same. Following this or that thread, she will swear that she has seen every episode of *Pobol y Cwm* before, that the children *did* tire her so much with those old stories, the same stories as the time before, and why, Daniel, why do they always tell me the same stories? Formally much the same, therefore, but less troubling. Irritation is, after all, more bearable than fear, for all concerned.

But this time, I have a question to ask which is not altogether part of the ritual, which is, in fact, a real question with a real purpose behind it. And this is why I had inserted my little query about the girls and our holiday together. Now you may think me culpable for asking it, even a little calculating, a little devious. But there we are. If you were in my position, if you'd seen the coldness in Sue's eyes, heard the indifference in her voice, I venture that you would do the same.

'You know last week, Mam, when I phoned you, when I phoned to say when we'd be back…'

'Last week?'

'Yes, last Friday.'

'Last Friday?'

'Yes, just before we came back from…'

'The girls saw a seal. That's what they said. Saw a seal up by Holy Island.'

A promising start. She remembers that we've been on holiday. And to prove to me how well she remembers, she takes a little blue notebook from the table, places her spectacles on her nose and thumbs through the pages.

'Sykes Cottage Embleton. Leave Saturday, back about 6. Phone number 01244376.'

'That's it, that's it. Good. Now then, do you remember…'

'Bolam we'd go.'

'What?'

'When you were little… We'd go to Bolam… It was full of frogs… in the lake… And newts...'

'But when I phoned...'

'They wouldn't live long, mind, not once you'd taken them out of their… you know… out of their…'

'No, they wouldn't, that's right, Mam, but when I phoned, last Friday, to say when we'd be back, and I put Sue on to the phone, to have a chat, to say hello, to let you know what we'd been doing…'

'Sue?'

'Yes, Mam, Sue. Do you remember talking to Sue? Do you remember what she said? She said something, didn't she, Mam? Something important.'

'Something important?'

'Yes, and I missed it. Because I was looking after the girls. But I could hear her, I could half hear her. What did she say, Mam. What…'

'No, I remember, now.'

'Yes?'

Silence.

'What, Mam? What do you remember?'

'I remember you asking me that before. I do. I remember you asking me yesterday. And don't you go saying it's one of those things again, because it's not, not this time. I remember, see. I remember it all. I was talking about those birds and then you started asking me about… about ….'

'About Sue?'

'About Sue… And I know what you're going to say next…'

'Yes, Mam?'

'It's on the tip of my tongue, it is, it's just coming back to me now… I'll have it in a minute…'

5. Concerning the pinning of insects

Even as a schoolboy, I knew that the Monarch was the most splendid of all the world's butterflies, the bravest of all its migrants, and that some day I would greet it, not in a book, not pinned to a card in a museum, but in the glory of its own habitat. Cherishing that dream, I was content, in the meantime, to make do with less regal specimens. All, to my mind, were part of a larger progress, inching me towards my ultimate goal. A strange notion, but such are the enthusiasms of young boys.

Sometimes, as I have already said, I would pursue these specimens in the upper reaches of our valley, where Alfred Wallace himself had wandered a century and a half earlier; where, however desultory my actual sightings, I felt at least that I was communing with the great man's spirit. But perhaps, in the enthusiasm of my recollection, I exaggerated the frequency of these outings. The truth is that I had insufficient funds to venture very far and, in any case, public transport did not penetrate to the most interesting of Wallace's haunts. More usually, therefore, I would visit sites closer to home. By a stroke of luck, these locations, and particularly those nearest the sea, transpired to be amongst the richest in Wales. Indeed, I know now that they are far superior to those we more generally associate with Wallace. It is important to remember how laborious it was, in his day, to cross the inhospitable marshes and heaths that separated the Neath valley from the coast. Even for me, in the late 1970s, I often decided not to waste time and money catching the bus back and forth from Morriston, and stayed instead with my grandmother, who lived in a little terraced house on the western edge of Llanelli. From there, it was only a short bike ride to the very best of these habitats.

Yes, it was a convenient arrangement, and I look back on this period with a degree of nostalgia, perhaps as a craftsman contemplates the days of his apprenticeship, however straitened his circumstances might have been at the time. Is this not how memory filters our experience, keeping the bright grains, discarding the dross? Which is no bad thing because I know, on more careful reflection, that my sojourns at Ebenezer Street, Llanelli were not the idyll which I would have wished them to be. Mam-gu had lived without human company for many years and solitude had not treated her kindly. Although it would be inaccurate to say that she lived entirely by herself. With her dwelt a small mongrel bitch called Blackie, who was as fat as Mam-gu was thin. My grandmother would speak to this creature all day long. It was with her, not her grandson, that she chewed over morsels of village gossip, the state of her hip or her back, and the minutiae of her shopping list. And, strangely enough, it was through Blackie that she directed her efforts to discipline me. 'Daniel knows he's not to shift from this table until he's eaten all his dinner, doesn't he, Blackie?' 'Ten past nine, Blackie! Doesn't he know it's after his bedtime?' I was small for my age and sometimes I could swear that Mam-gu saw before her, not a twelve year old boy of quite independent and mature character, but another dog, a stubborn, intractable little mut whose will needed to be broken. 'Spoilt by his mam, see, Blackie.' Mam-gu reserved her indulgence for her pet. She smiled only rarely. Her face was thin and wrinkled. Not the cute wizened apple of the fairy tales. Just wrinkled.

Wrinkled and boney. Yes, Mam-gu was as thin as a rake, as they say, and little wonder, considering how little she ate. Indeed, so meagre were the rations eked out at Ebenezer Street that I was forced to bring my own provisions so that I should not pass out from hunger. As thin as a rake, they say, but that's not right. A scythe. She was as thin as a scythe, and just as bent. Mam-gu suffered badly from what she called 'the rheumatics' and walked with a stoop – a stoop tilted slightly to her left – using a stick. This stick, which I think of now more as a rod, accompanied her everywhere. She used it to change the channel on the television and if she needed her cigarettes first thing in the morning, or a cup of tea, and couldn't get up because of her infirmity, she would use it to hit the floor or the wall to attract my attention. Once, I saw her hobble into the back yard, cursing like a tinker, and bludgeon to death two large beetles which Blackie had inadvertently freed from my secret storage box in the disused coal-hole. (I dared not tell Mam-gu about this box because she harboured an extreme distaste for all insect life. Indeed, I kept it a secret until her dying day.) Nevertheless, despite these difficulties, I did my best to knuckle under, to do odd chores around the house, to obey the injunctions of the rod. And in time I believe we established a kind of *modus vivendi*. Without a doubt, the arrangement served me well in my entomological pursuits.

I have no desire to try the lay-person's patience by enumerating even the highlights of this period. Suffice it to say that I succeeded in identifying twelve of the nineteen species of snail-eating flies which inhabit the dunes at Pembrey Forest, that is, the species which I could distinguish with the help of a simple magnifying glass. This achievement was something of a feather in the cap of such a young, aspiring entomologist as myself and it led, I have no doubt, to my later, professional interest in *diptera*. I was also fortunate enough to sight, on the peat bogs by Llannon, several specimens of the rare harvestman, *Sabacon viscayanum*, a species previously considered to be a recent migrant but which is now acknowledged, because of the remoteness of Llannon from other possible habitats, to be a full-blooded native. Another cause for celebration was my discovery, at Burry Port, of the carabid, *Panageus crux-major*: a striking creature in black and orange livery, once common throughout south Wales but now, alas, restricted to these few acres.

But whilst these adventures, and others, gave me great delight, the most memorable of all – and I use this word advisedly – was the discovery of a Leaf-miner of no special distinction called *Timarcha tenebricosa*. I regret, however, that no joy attaches itself to this capture or its aftermath. It is memorable only because it marked a rite of passage in my apprenticeship. I must explain here that this was the time – around fourteen years of age – when I began to collect my first specimens. In so doing, I was taking the first tentative steps on my journey as a serious, committed entomologist. I do not claim that these steps were any different from those trod by many, many thousand others in my profession before and since. Nonetheless, first steps, small though they may be, must not be taken hurriedly or without due diligence. Perhaps I ventured too soon. Be that as it may, I believe I did my best under unfavourable circumstances. I could find only one relevant title at Swansea's Central Library: H. Oldroyd's *Collecting, Studying and Preserving Insects*. I studied this closely, and with growing dismay, for it seemed, according to Mr Oldroyd, that not even the least ambitious dabbler in the insect world could indulge his interest without first acquiring a bewildering array of sweep-nets, beating trays, poosters, killing jars, aspirators, glues, pins, chemicals and other arcane paraphernalia. Even the ink to be used on the identification labels had to be carefully chosen and procured.

Lacking such equipment, or the money to purchase it, my tools were necessarily of a crude and makeshift kind. I adapted sweet containers – small plastic ones scrounged from the corner shop – to serve as both collecting and killing jars. The boxes I used to store my specimens were gathered in a similar way. Those made for walking boots were best, in my experience, being sturdier and rather bigger than common shoe-boxes. I could fit at least four of the smaller insects in each of these, together with their identification cards; more room was needed, of course, for the larger beetles and butterflies, while each of my prize specimens was allocated a box of its own. My net was a pillow case, held open through sewing into it a steel wire, both ends of which I then inserted into a cane. Although I congratulated myself at having fashioned such an ingenious contraption, it was, in fact, a highly deficient tool, as limp as a pocket handkerchief, and I caught few specimens with it, despite sweeping for hour after hour through the grass and the reeds and the heather. I was somewhat more successful with the *coleoptera*, in particular the non-flying varieties, which could be ushered into the killing jar using only a small stick.

By the time I was fourteen, too, my skin was a good deal thicker than it had been a year or two earlier. Wallace would have approved of this, I'm sure. I had cast off any 'affected' sentiment I might once have harboured towards invertebrates and begun to see them in their true light. How did I achieve this maturation, this suppression of a misplaced but, I believe, quite typical squeamishness? Well, I knew already, of course, that Nature could be a cruel mother, to use the anthropomorphic idiom of common parlance. At home, the cat frequently brought in her offerings of mice and small birds, some still wriggling and squealing. I had, at least on television, observed the ways of the spiders, gobbling their offspring. And wasn't I witness to the daily carnage above the Farteg and Allt-y-Grug, as buzzard and hawk swooped on their prey? The lesson I learned from such experiences was simple and consistent and does not, I think, need further elaboration.

My greatest difficulty lay in procuring suitable chemicals. Extemporising a collecting net or storage jar is one thing. 'Making do' with inappropriate chemicals is quite another. Of course, it was out of the question for a boy of my age (I was too short to deceive anyone on this score) to buy ethyl alcohol at the chemist's. And I dared not ask my mother, who was already deeply suspicious of my 'little hobby', as she disparagingly called it. Faced with this dilemma, I did for a time experiment with other killing methods. I tried, for example, to suffocate specimens in a small plastic bag. This met with little success, however, perhaps because of microscopic perforations in the plastic which I could not detect, perhaps because so little air was needed to keep them alive. I tried to drown them in water. Indeed, I succeeded in doing so, but was unable to dry them out afterwards without breaking legs and tearing wings. For a while, I kept the specimens in a sealed box under my bed thinking that, sooner or later, they would expire through lack of nourishment. This, too, was largely a futile exercise. The creatures made so much noise, thrashing and scratching about in their confinement, that it was I, not the insects, who suffered the greater privations, losing a large part of three nights' sleep. I feared, also, that my mother would find them and tell me off for giving house-room to such odious guests. I beseeched her not to come in to my bedroom, in case she disturbed my paperwork or knocked over a box or a jar, but I frequently detected the signs of her hoovering and dusting. I even began to do my own cleaning, so as not to give her a pretext for trespass. I believe that this sudden concern for cleanliness – a trait that ran counter to every known norm of teenage behaviour – caused my mother even more anxiety than the insects.

In the end, and ironically enough, it was the hoover I had to thank for resolving this problem. Yes, and for creating another in its place. Because, as I was putting it back one day in the cupboard under the stairs, where it lived amongst the tins of paint and rolls of old wallpaper, I spied two glass bottles. One of these was full of a transparent, colourless liquid; only a few drops remained in the other. I had seen them before, no doubt, but without realising their significance. Each bore the label: *Carbon Tetrachloride* DO NOT INHALE FUMES, together with other warnings of a similar nature which I no longer remember. I'm sure the liquid in question was nothing more exciting than carpet cleaner, dating perhaps from the time we moved into the house. But its provenance was of no interest to me. I needed to know only one thing: that I must not, on any account, breathe its noxious vapours. This is the liquid for me, I thought. I pulled out the cork of the nearly-empty bottle and held it tentatively under my nose. I breathed in, just a little sniff. I breathed again. And I was rather disappointed that its smell was not more unpleasant, more acrid, as befitted, to my mind, a poison worthy of the name, a poison akin to the ammonia and hydrogen sulphide and other foul-smelling substances of my school chemistry lessons. Unlike them, this solution smelled sweet, with just a hint of lavender, and reminded me of Mam-gu's bathroom. I found it hard to believe that anything which resembled an old lady's soap, even if that old lady were my grandmother, could harm the smallest and feeblest of our fauna. But what could I do but persevere?

The following Sunday, after a productive day of collecting, I returned to Pentrepoeth eager to get to work. I had captured nine specimens that morning from the dunes at Pembrey and took great care to bring all of them home alive. There had been ten, but I was forced to discard a tiger beetle – a highly predatory little monster with secateur-like mandibles – for fear that it would savage and devour the others. These nine included, I think, a robber fly, a couple of butterflies, and a variety of beetles. Amongst the latter, as I mentioned earlier, was a handsome but otherwise unremarkable variety of Leaf-miner. In anticipation of this moment, I had already placed a layer of cotton wool on the bottom of the killing jar. Using a drinking straw as a pipette, I now deposited upon it a few drops of the Carbon Tetrachloride. Without delay – I was anxious that the fumes might dissipate and lose their power – I set about transferring the insects from the collecting bottle. In the absence of more sophisticated equipment and to ensure that they did not escape, I had no choice but to decant my whole motley collection, unceremoniously and in one fell swoop, from one bottle to the other and clamp down the lid as quickly as my trembling fingers would allow. This was a rough and ready procedure, which I'm sure distressed me no less than my captives. The butterflies, as one would expect, caused the greatest commotion, hurling themselves around in all directions, and it was no mean feat to get both of them into the bottle without causing serious injury. But, in the end, they bent to my will.

The aromatic solution was more potent than I had anticipated. Within a minute or so my creatures lay still and lifeless, except for the tiny twitch of a leg here, the quiver of an antenna there. The butterflies, after their vigorous struggle, were the first to yield, perhaps because they found the carpet cleaner to their taste. (Butterflies taste with their feet.) And as my specimens gave up the ghost, one by one, I proceeded to prepare the identification labels, as follows.

Plateumaris braccata

Fforest Pen-bre
SN 005 413

Collected in the reeds with a net

8.8.1974

D. Robson

The next task was to mount them. I had already fixed squares of white polystyrene to the bottoms of four of the shoe boxes, to take the pins, which I had borrowed from my mother's sewing box. In light of my inexperience, I judged it prudent to begin with the largest and sturdiest of the beetles. This, as it happens, was the Leaf-miner. I followed the instructions in Mr Oldroyd's book as best I could, proceeding cautiously, step by step, first placing the insect in position on the card, then extending the legs and then, most importantly, locating on the thorax the precise muscles between which I would have to push the pin to ensure a tight grip. Easier said than done. The cuticle was hard, very hard – unlike human beings, an insect wears its skeleton on the outside – and I felt at one point that I might need to fetch a hammer to complete the job. Nevertheless, after some minutes of fiddling and fumbling, I managed, somehow, to drive the pin home. I then pressed it through the card, on which I had already written the details of my find, and into the polystyrene.

And that was that. I had mounted my first specimen. More remarkably, I had done so without mishap and without doing harm either to the beetle or to myself. I contemplated my handiwork. I studied the legs, with their strong, intricate joints. I marvelled at the thick abdomen, its metallic gleam putting me in mind of the body armour of some medieval knight. I turned the box around. I looked at the beetle from the front and the rear, from above, from each corner, indeed from every conceivable angle. And when I could devise no more ways of viewing my creation, I got up and poured myself a glass of dandelion and burdock, as a reward for my success. I sat down again, taking small sips, savouring the fizz on my tongue, savouring the moment too, drawing it out, my head swimming from the day's exertions and anxieties, my heart still pounding. There it was, the Leaf-miner, standing resplendent in its display case, the very first exhibit in my collection, the Daniel Robson Collection of Rare Beetles and Butterflies, Pentrepoeth, Morriston, Swansea, Wales. And I swelled with pride.

Having finished my drink, I put the cover back on the box and placed this at the bottom of the wardrobe where, I supposed, it would not be vulnerable to interference from my mother or indeed anyone else who might happen to come in to my room. And I moved on to the next beetle. Another two hours passed by in this manner before I had mounted all my specimens and stored them, too, in the safety of the wardrobe. When finally I crawled into bed I was, of course, exhausted and my head and eyes ached from so much concentration. But I was filled, too, with a deep contentment. And if this contentment was less intense, less visceral than the excitement I'd feel on discovering a new insect out on the marshes or the dunes, it was nevertheless a more rounded, more grown-up emotion. It was the contentment of one who had found, not just a curious insect, but his course in life and who knew, at least for the time being, that this was all he desired. I had come of age.

The following afternoon I came home from school a little earlier than usual. I was rummaging in my duffle bag for the house key when I heard the scream. One short scream. I ran upstairs and found my mother standing in the middle of my bedroom, trembling from head to toe. The box lay on the bed in front of her, without its lid. '*Beth nest ti iddo fe?*' she said. 'What have you done to it?' And again. And again. In the box, the Leaf-miner had somehow revived and was doing its frantic best to escape. It couldn't, of course. It couldn't run, it couldn't even crawl, because it was still firmly impaled on its pin. It could only spin on its axis like a Catherine Wheel. Click like a needle on an old record. *Cer-rick, cer-rick, cer-rick.* I stared at it, entranced and horrified in equal measure.

'It can't feel anything, Mam.'

Pinning an insect for the first time

The Entomologist

6. Our Reading Group

'So, Dan. Good holidays? Good insects?'

'Good holidays, Ozi, yes. Good insects, no. Not especially. Nothing that you'd... You know...'

'And Sue? Sue's fine, is she?'

'Yes, thank you, Haf. Busy, of course. As per usual...'

'Send her my love.'

'I will, I will...'

'Be good to see her again. Get her to call by some time, Dan, will you? We miss her.'

'Thanks, Sonia, I'll tell her you're... But you know how it is, what with work...'

It was Thursday yesterday. Thursday 11 September. The second Thursday in the month. And in the evening we met, as usual, to discuss books. Now I must warn you at the outset, before you jump to conclusions, that we are not by any stretch of the imagination a learned group, so please don't expect intellectual acrobatics from me or anyone else or you'll be sorely disappointed. This is no false modesty. I have a degree in Biology, of course I do, my job at the Museum requires it. The others have their skills, too, their certificates and diplomas, their CVs, their apprenticeships and what have you. What I mean is, there isn't a literature degree amongst us. Scarcely an A-level. We are spared the preenings of that particular gaggle.

On the other hand – and I shouldn't pre-judge you on this matter – this may well come as a relief. If so, I am glad. Indeed, I have begun to think lately that it is precisely this lack of intellectual pretension that is our most attractive attribute. Let me explain myself. We discuss books, yes. We discuss Welsh books, we discuss English books, we even, on occasion, discuss Brazilian and Chinese books. But that, unless I am much mistaken, is not what you would call the *raison d'être* of our group. The pretext, yes, but not the purpose. I cannot at the moment find the right word, the right phrase, to describe exactly what that purpose is, but it will come to me, I'm sure, there's no rush. In any case, we, its members, know very well what that purpose is without having to give it a name. I believe this is self-evident, otherwise why, after three years, would we still bother to turn out, month after month?

Whatever the word might be, it has something to do with this: no-one feels under threat. We do not, for example, fear reprobation because we haven't, perhaps, read the latest Booker short-list, the latest Nobel laureate no, nor even the latest Eisteddfod winner. We are not embarrassed because we cannot employ modish jargon. We are not scorned for admitting that we tried and tried but just couldn't get past chapter three.

'Ha! You don't even like books, Dan.'

That's what Sue used to say. It was an overstatement, of course, and a mischievous one at that. But, despite herself, I think that she may have captured a deeper truth. After all, one need not be an alcoholic, nor an afficionado of the brewing arts, simply to enjoy a night out in the pub. We forgive each other our failings, our occasional slowness to understand what is new and difficult, our middlebrow taste. In a word, we are ordinary. And perhaps that is the word I am looking for. We are readers who celebrate the ordinary, who seek to appreciate what is common to us all.

You may be surprised to learn that Sue, at the outset, would accompany me to these meetings. I found particular pleasure in this, again not so much because of the activity itself – I have already forgotten many of the books we discussed – but because it demonstrated our status as a couple. We were acknowledged by others. It was also a treat, perhaps over a meal at The Italian Way, or in bed on a Sunday morning, to argue about the merits of this or that character, about whether such-and-such a plot was credible or not. Often more of a treat, if truth be told, than the act of reading itself. I cannot claim that such occasions were particularly frequent. Indeed, they are vivid, perhaps, precisely because of their infrequency. Owing to her shift work (Sue is a nurse, caring mainly for old people) and the taxing nature of that work, and the fact that she lives in Splott, Sue and I do not see as much of one another as I would wish. In addition, I am forced to acknowledge that, despite her initial keenness, despite my continuing best efforts, despite the evident rewards which the meetings bestowed upon the others, they afforded Sue small satisfaction, and even that small satisfaction diminished over time. This was perhaps only natural. For one such as myself, deprived of the company of all but my microscope and specimens for most of the day, the group provides a link with the outside world, a bridge to humanity. Sue, bless her, is at the beck and call of that world day in, day out. A tranquil retreat is what she seeks, not further stimulation.

But there was, I fear, more to it than that. At times – and I don't deny that I can be over-sensitive about such things – at times, Sue seemed somewhat dismissive of us, even a trifle antagonistic. After a while, I began to feel uneasy when she was present, fearful of what she might say or do. This is a dreadful admission, and I do not make it lightly. But Sue can be touchy at times, even a little intolerant. The evidence is there, in her own words. 'I spend half my life with needy people,' she said after attending her last meeting, 'and I don't want to spend my leisure time with them as well.' I translate as accurately, as fairly, as I can. '*Anghennus*' is the word she used, which means 'needy', no more, no less: that is, lacking in some necessity, wanting of care, with a certain suggestion of incapacity, perhaps even of indigence. I knew at the time, of course, that it was the pressure of work talking. She was merely reacting retrospectively, as it were, to the insatiable demands of some poor, demented patient. Be that as it may, I thought it best not to prevail upon her to return, believing that she would, in time, relent and feel the need of our company once more. As I say, Sue, though of a caring and generous disposition, can be a little impetuous, and people of that sort, in my experience, are best left to recover their equilibrium without interference from others, even from loved ones. With hindsight, I am compelled to ask myself whether, perhaps, she was not a reluctant participant from the outset. To ask myself whether, indeed, I rather bullied her into coming in the first place. No, not bullied. Chivvied. Cajoled, perhaps. In any case, I must guard against such traits: they are unworthy of me.

Sonia's house was the venue for last night's meeting: a sweet little terrace in Rhiwbina Garden Village, although the lounge was perhaps rather *too* little for a gathering such as ours. Indeed, we had to bring in high stools from the kitchen for the latecomers. The faithful six were there: Haf, me, Ahmed, Phil, Ozi and Sonia. '*Hen Daps A Phâr O Sannau*' is my mnemonic for this particular grouping, for which an English equivalent might be 'Hot Dogs and a Pair of Stockings'. ('Hot Dogs and a Pair of Silk Stockings' when Sue was present.) And yes, you would be entirely within your rights to raise your eyebrows at this device, for a mnemonic is, I admit, scarcely necessary for such a meagre number. I was fortunate enough to secure one of the two easy chairs: I should not have enjoyed perching on one of the high stools, like a moth on a pin; and, to be honest, neither should I have much enjoyed sharing the sofa with Phil.

We had a lively enough discussion about Goronwy Jones's latest novel and lamented the dearth of humorous material of this kind in Welsh. Haf read out her favourite passage, at which we chuckled politely. But, with due respect to the teller, a funny story is never, I fear, quite so funny in the retelling. We then turned our attention to *Northern Lights.* Now, I make no bones about it: I have little sympathy with the genre, with its far-fetched tales of monsters and talking animals and the like. An entomologist knows only too well that the real world is so much more complex – yes, and so much more remarkable, too – than such flights of fancy. But our children had seen the film and some of the glitter had rubbed off on to the parents, too, no doubt. Nia, my younger daughter, was herself a fervent disciple.

So there we were, discussing *Northern Lights* or, in some cases, perhaps only the film of *Northern Lights*, although we all had the book open on our laps. Those of you who have read the one or seen the other will not be surprised to learn that we spent some time pondering the nature of the *daemon*. We asked ourselves, for example, why a child's *daemon* should constantly change its character, from one animal to another, whilst that of an adult should remain unchanged. We had a stab at understanding the exact function of the cord that connects each *daemon* with its host. We hunted in the text for an explanation of why severing this cord should lead to the death of both parties. And so on and so forth. So much hot air, if you ask me, because not a single one of these notions has the least basis in reality. I am glad to say that we then turned to a more personal engagement with the story. Yes, and this, too, I believe, is part of the group's strength and sustenance. We are ordinary, but we are also individuals, willing to share our diverse experiences of life.

'How about you, Phil? asked Sonia. 'Which animal would *you* like to have as your *daemon*?'

Now you may think that this did not take us far away from those fanciful notions which had so recently irritated me. In fact, you may conclude that we were simply pursuing the same folly by different means. You may agree with Sue that a question such as this has little to do with the book. If that is the case, I can only tell you what I told her. Sue, I said, you miss the point entirely. No-one's coming to test us at the end of term. And who will admonish us if we wander a little from the syllabus? What penalty will we incur? But by then she had no interest. As I say, that's how our group works, and that's what Sue failed to grasp. I tell you this because you need to understand it for yourself, otherwise you will end up as sad as Sue is today.

'I don't like animals,' said Phil, drily. Which is his privilege. He was perhaps not the best choice to open the discussion and his cynicism soured the atmosphere a little.

The greatest disservice that Sue rendered us, of course, was to tar us all with the same brush. It is possible that one of us, and one alone, had rocked her cage. I'm sorry, I'm mixing metaphors now, please bear with me. Yes, it is possible that there was but one offender, and that Sue then took against the group as a whole simply by association. Phil. Phil would be the likeliest culprit, if one needed to be found, although I can't remember her ever picking him out for special disapproval.

'I love swans,' said Sonia, as she refilled our glasses. As host, she no doubt felt responsible for restoring our *ésprit de corps.* 'For their fidelity, you know… Mind you, I'm not sure whether a swan is too big to be a *daemon*.'

There is, of course, nothing needy about Sonia. Nothing whatsoever. And that is all there is to say on the matter. Except, perhaps, this. Her husband was putting the twins to bed when I arrived last night, and that is the sound that comes back to me now, as I sit here in my flat, a sound that danced so easily and brightly around that sweet doll's house of contentment, the sound of babies crying, of a father soothing. It brought a smile to my lips, which you might even call a smile of nostalgia. Yes, nostalgia, not envy, because nostalgia smiles from a distance, and I assure you I do not wish to return to such scenes, to such obligations. But for the others? For Haf? Yes, for Sue herself? Ah! Who knows whether Sonia's domestic bliss did not stir deeper emotions? *Tell me, Sue, does Sonia make you jealous, does it hurt you inside to be childless when you see her, when you come to the group and hear the babies crying?* How could I possibly ask such questions?

'And you, Ahmed?' said Sonia. And I thought, yes, that's a better choice. Gentle, courteous, self-deprecating Ahmed.

'In a way,' said Ahmed, 'I already have my *daemon*.'

How could you find fault with Ahmed, Sue? And how could you find fault with his story?

'I lost my brother way back, when I was little more than a baby. Yassuf. His name was Yassuf. I have no memory of him. Nothing. Not even a picture. But they say you can never separate twins, not really, not even when one of them dies. Not even when they've never known each other. I cannot say. My father would sometimes call me Yassuf. Perhaps that's got something to do with it. But he's still with me, here, inside somewhere. My brother Yassuf is still with me.'

For me, of course, this was familiar territory. Ahmed is a colleague at the Museum and we have shared this and much more during our years there. Although I must say that he delivered the old story with an emotional charge that was new to me. I should tell you that he occupied one of the high stools as he spoke. It is not impossible that this had something to do with his uncharacteristic eloquence. That he felt, somehow, in such a position, that it behoved him to address us all. A mere fancy, perhaps. I say no more. I am sure you would have been impressed, Sue. Moved, even.

And yet, as I consider these matters at leisure, as I chew over in my mind those bitter little morsels that Sue has spat out during the past weeks and months, I am forced to conclude – and the notion is at once intriguing and unnerving – that perhaps the others were not the problem after all. That Sue was not especially bothered, for example, by Haf and her ingratiating smile, that she cared not one jot, beyond a momentary annoyance, that Phil occasionally wiped his nose on his sleeve. That, in short, I had turned some minor irritants into pretexts, into excuses, for maladies much closer at home. That, in reality, there was no problem other than myself, and never had been.

I apologise. I really don't know why I've prattled on so much about our reading group. It has little to do with the story I'm about to tell you and I shall not return to it more than once or twice throughout the course of these pages. Sue. That's it, I was telling you about Sue, I was trying to puzzle out why she'd taken against us. But there is only one real, compelling reason why I should bring up the matter of the reading group at this point, and it has nothing to do with Sue, nor with Ahmed, nor indeed with any of the others. What stirs the memory today, what captured my curiosity last night, was the unexpected appearance of a new member. Her name is Cerys. She arrived half an hour late, just as we were drawing our discussion of Goronwy Jones to a close and lamenting, in somewhat grave terms, the dearth of laughter in Welsh prose, so we had no opportunity to engage her in small talk, to learn something of her history. She is a woman in her mid-thirties, I would say, and there is nothing at all remarkable about her appearance except this: she is blind. That much was evident when we saw Sonia take her by the arm and guide her into the room. It was confirmed, then, when we saw her eyes. These were in constant, unseeing motion. One moment they would stare at the floor, the next at the window, and then, to my great surprise, at my own eyes, so that, briefly, I felt that I had been mistaken all along, that she'd fooled us somehow, or perhaps that some miracle had happened. Until, of course, the eyes resumed their restless wandering. I offered her my easy chair and went to sit on one of the kitchen stools. She beamed a smile at us as she sat down and received ours in return, but to what end? And we were all, I am sure, asking ourselves the same unspoken questions. Why is she here? How will she read the books? And also: how shall we communicate with such a person, a person who can see neither smile nor frown, nor any of the other myriad expressions on which we rely to get us through the day? A strange question, this, considering that Cerys's hearing and speech were clearly unimpaired, but not, I believe, an unimportant one, because communication, I'm sure you will agree, consists of so much more than words.

'*Croeso,* Cerys. Welcome to our reading group.'

I must admit that, during our discussion of the *daemon*, we did, all of us, steal an occasional glance at our new member. The sighted assume a right to scrutinise the unsighted, I think, if only because they know they cannot be subjected to the same imposition. And the freedom to examine someone closely, without let or hindrance, is a privilege so rare – yes, even amongst lovers and close relatives – and, I dare say, so exquisite, that it is difficult to resist the temptation when it presents itself. God forbid, of course, that we should reveal our little weakness to other members of the sighted faction. Just the odd glance, therefore. A sly, surreptitious peek, here and there, now and again. To have a better look at how that blue jumper clashes with those lilac trousers. To wonder at the light brown hair, cut into a short, anachronistic, schoolgirl bob, so that you wanted to tie a ribbon around it, to make the picture complete. To study the face, quite round, although not fat: structurally round, you might say. And quite animated, too, although, after a while, you noticed that it tended to follow its own, idiosyncratic rules, wholly oblivious to the faces around it, with their smooth Mexican waves of smile, frown or surprise. And perhaps the make-up had been over-applied to the lips and eyes. There was a little smudge of lipstick by the side of her mouth. Why wear make-up at all? But then, once the decision is made, it's not surprising, is it? All of which, of course, enlisted our sympathy, I have no doubt. Our admiration, too. And in me, at least, a desire to help: a somewhat patronising desire, no doubt, because of what account, her ill-matching clothes, her smudged make-up? But a sincere desire, nonetheless. To welcome her fully into our company. To make her feel at home. Hot Dogs and a Pair of Crimson Socks.

'And which animal would you choose, Dan?' asked Sonia.

I needed no time to reflect.

'The Monarch. *Danaus plexippus*. The most magnificent of all butterflies,' I said, from my perch on the stool. For who else could so fittingly become my life partner but the butterfly that chose my birthday to make its first ever visit to Wales? 'The sixth of September, 1876,' I said. 'My very own birthday.' That chose Neath as the destination for that visit. Yes, Neath, as though this, the finest of all butterflies, would happily go far, far out of its to pay homage to the great Alfred Russell Wallace, king, patron saint, exemplar of all would-be entomologists. 'Neath, of all places,' I said. Which always evinces a little chuckle.

And I believe that Cerys, in particular, was pleased by this answer because she smiled and said that was splendid, that the Monarch was an inspirational *daemon*, that she could not possibly think of one nearly so fine.

7. An e-mail from Cerys

Only a few of the Museum's insects are on public display: most of the collections are stored out of sight, in the basement. Here, too, is my own room. I say 'my own room', although this is not strictly the case: my position here is not sufficiently exalted to warrant such a privilege. 'My room' is also home to over one hundred thousand beetles. These are British beetles, in the main, and are housed in alphabetical order in uniform rows of drawers which stretch from floor to ceiling, both in the middle of the room and across two of the walls. My desk is in the corner furthest from the door, beneath the high window. (The window is high because most of the room is below ground. Many of the other rooms – those at the centre of the Department – have no windows at all.) I also share the room with two pipes. These are as stout as ancient oaks and resemble the pipes you might see in the engine room of an ocean-going liner. For here, in the basement, lie the heart and intestines of the Museum's heating system.

I am busy examining an Australian spider beetle when the porter rings to say that Sue is waiting for me at the rear entrance.

'Sue?'

'Sue.'

'Sue James?'

'Sue James.'

Now Sue is an infrequent visitor at the Museum. She has, after all, little cause to come here. She is also impatient of the red tape. The Museum operates strict security measures. No-one is permitted to wander its corridors unaccompanied. Indeed, no-one may gain admission without first being photographed and registered. Even Sue, whose connection to me is well known, who is readily recognised by the doorman, must submit to these rigours. 'Do they think I want to be a specimen in one of your collections?' she said, the first time. Sue dislikes fuss. And this is why I am forced to put my spider beetle to one side and make my way to the porter's office.

Sue reads the surprise on my face.

'I hope you don't mind, Dan.'

'Not at all… Lovely to see you...'

And although it is true that I am pleased to see her, we walk back to my room in silence, or rather, to the staccato accompaniment of Sue's shoes, striking the tiled floor. Yes, I am pleased to see her, of course I am: I have seen little enough of her in recent weeks. But when we reach my room, I am still searching for words. She is carrying a boxfile under her arm. I am confused.

'Your hair, Sue… Your hair's changed.'

'It's shorter, Dan. I've had it cut, that's all.'

The new hairstyle has hardened her face, exposed it, made it look more clinical. Perhaps this was her intention. To cultivate an image more in keeping with her profession. With her age. This is dangerous ground. I must tread carefully.

'It looks smart.'

'Smart?'

'It… It suits you.'

She smiles. And with that smile, the hardness melts a little. I venture a modest kiss, a gentle embrace around her waste.

'It's really nice to see you, Sue… I'm sorry about…'

She places her hands on my shoulders, lets the palms rest there, just a second, and ever so lightly. And in that lightness, in that butterfly touch that is really no touch at all, I know that Sue's mind is elsewhere. That she has not come to see me but is here on some other errand entirely.

I try to fill the gap. To hold all this at bay.

'I went to see Mam last night.'

'And how is she?'

'O, just the same… Thinks that everything has happened before.'

I should like to say, 'And she's hard work, too, Sue, as always.' But I refrain. Sue would merely think me pathetic. Doesn't she have to cope with this and worse, much worse, every day of her working life? And in any case, Sue gets on with mother. They are two women, after all, so they have a head start. At the very least, they can share their scorn for men. Yes. And perhaps Sue is a little more patient than me. Is *at liberty* to be more patient, you might say, because my mother is not *her* mother, because she does not carry the burden of belonging. So I refrain.

'You've just got to be patient with her, Dan.'

'Yes, yes, of course.'

'It's not her fault.'

'No, no, I know that.'

So they get on. Always have done. It was Sue who cared for my mother when she first moved to Cardiff. (Had it not been for my mother's illness, Sue and I would never have met.) Unaccountably, given the circumstances, my mother trusted Sue from the outset. Trusted her strength, perhaps, her authority, her way of getting things done and dusted and out of the way. Because my mother, like Sue, has always hated fuss. Perhaps she liked the comfort of Sue's hand on her arm, too, her readiness to smile. All of these things count. But mostly, I think she liked Sue because of her lack of fuss. 'Well, there's not much the matter with you, Mari, is there?' And my mother would believe it, just because Sue had said it. (Sue called her 'Mari' right from the start. I thought this a little forward but my mother seemed as pleased as punch.) Come to think of it, I'm sure her height was a factor, too, because Sue is tall, for a woman, in particular for a south Walian woman. Which is odd, because it was precisely this that made me nervous when we first met. I confess that I have not yet become fully accustomed to holding the hand of a woman taller than myself. A silly conceit, I know, for there is scarcely an inch of difference between us.

So you could say that my mother borrowed from Sue a portion of her fortitude. And this was indeed a valuable prop as she settled in to her new home, as she began to explore the highways and byways of her new neighbourhood. She had someone at hand who knew the way, who could take her arm and help her avoid the kerbs and potholes. I speak figuratively, of course. In fact, Sue did little, in a practical sense, other than give my mother a few memory tests: who was the Prime Minister, what was the capital city of France, what was her mother's maiden name, and so on – and then, when she answered correctly, tell her how good she was, how *exceptionally* good, for her age. 'You know more than I do, Mari.' My mother was in her element. By the end of the session her paramnesia was scarcely more than a minor inconvenience. Against the odds, it must be said, Sue gave her back something of her old self.

I must, however, record a slightly sour note. More than one note, perhaps, although each voiced a similar concern. Now then, I should stress that my mother was not at all reluctant to reminisce about her childhood days. She had a vivid recollection of every stick of furniture which (from her lengthy descriptions) must have been crammed forcibly into the little Llanelli terrace where she had been brought up. She could see in her mind's eye each flower in the garden; she could hear the voice of every visitor who would call by on such-and-such a day, on such-and-such an errand. And she would happily regale Sue with their life stories, the sad little twists of fate they had to endure. Strangely, however, she would hesitate before recalling my father's name. '*He* doesn't remember, Nurse,' she said, casting a dismissive glance at me, as though to imply that mine was the deficient memory, not hers. So that I had to explain that my father had died at sea when I was still a small child. Sue was wise enough to let the matter rest and turn to other, less contentious subjects. Where was my brother born? What were the names of our pet animals? What was the date of my birthday? Neutral questions. Because Sue was well versed in the unexpected twists and turns of the senior mind and she was not in the least perturbed by any of my mother's enigmatic pronouncements or stubborn silences.

I, too, derived not a little comfort from these exchanges, partly because they raised my mother's spirits but also and, I believe, chiefly, because this unfussy, matter-of-fact woman had, as it were, taken up a portion of my burden. At least, that is how it felt. Sue had, in some sense, become a mother to my mother. And I warmed to her. I have no wish to be mealy mouthed in this matter, so I shall say it: I found her gentle authority attractive. No, not worthy – at least, not *merely* worthy – but actually attractive. Yes, of course, I admired the thoroughness and practised competence of her care, but I positively delighted in the way that care was embodied in her person. In the way she would draw her chair closer to my mother, moving hand, arm and leg with such graceful economy in order not to disturb her patient's repose. In the way she would bend forward to speak to her and, in so doing, expose an inch, only an inch, of nape beneath her dark hair. In the way she would tie her hair back in a butterfly clip: a playful touch, this, which leavened the image of duty and diligence.

And so, when Sue finally got up to leave, at the end of my mother's memory tests, at the end of her rambling reminiscences, when the last drop of tea had been squeezed from the teapot, I took her to one side and asked her – quietly, so that my mother couldn't hear – whether we might meet again. 'To talk about what I can do to help her... To ask you about other support services... Perhaps some books, or ...' She seemed bemused, even a little taken aback – I am not sure whether by the invitation itself or because, as a rule, sons rarely display such concern for their mothers. 'I've really done as much as I can,' she said. 'Your mother will need to see her GP if there are any problems. That's what normally happens.'

These words, understood at face value, were as forthright a rebuttal as I might have expected. Sue was ever one to speak plainly. Simplicity, directness are of the essence when addressing old people. The habit has no doubt infiltrated her more general discourse. I cannot fault her for it. And yet, behind these words, between them, tucked away in the little crevices, I sensed something rather less dismissive, something which invited me to explore further. Because words, in my experience, resemble doors. Most are locked shut. Keep out, they say, politely but firmly. And then, quite out of the blue, you hear the sound of a key turning. 'That's what normally happens,' said

Sue. Only a little push, then, and the door opens. 'Ah!' I said, my eyes cast downward in resignation, 'That's a pity... Yes, a great pity... You have been such a support...' And the key turned one further notch. 'Well... I suppose....'

The following morning, over coffee in one of the cafes in Pontcanna, Sue explained the exact nature of paramnesia and offered a cautiously optimistic prognosis. There was no reason, she said, why the condition should worsen unless, of course, my mother suffered another stroke. 'Be patient,' she said. 'Take her for a meal... Take her shopping... She'd like that, I'm sure.' And although none of these suggestions appealed greatly, they were delivered in a way which helped quell my anxiety. To understand even the ravages of ageing, and to understand them factually, with compassion yet without sentimentality, draws their sting somehow. In addition, and to my continuing surprise, there was something exquisitely sensual – yes, I still cringe to think of it as such, but it is without doubt the correct word – in the way Sue conjured the more arcane terms of her profession, her gentle Pembrokeshire Welsh caressing each one, rounding off their corners, smoothing their hard edges.

'Tea?'

'No, Dan. Sorry.'

Sue offers her explanation for what I know already.

'I need to...I've come to use your photocopier.'

'Ah!'

'The one in the clinic's broken. I won't be five minutes.'

I am innocent enough to imagine that, perhaps, after the elapse of those five minutes, once she has her papers in order, we might then enjoy a little of each other's company. Because Sue, as I have already intimated, is prone to unexpected bouts of petulance when things fail to run according to plan. No, you would never guess it, not from the way she dealt with my mother, but then, a person is always more than their job. That goes without saying. Or less than their job, of course. Yes, I suppose that is possible as well, at times. So I nod, to convey my understanding, my support.

'We'll go over to the canteen then, shall we? Or for a little walk in the park, perhaps? It's surprisingly mild for the …'

'No, no, Dan, that's the point… I need to take these papers straight back to work.'

'Ah!'

Yes, that is the point. I have misunderstood. So I raise my hands to acknowledge the fact, a little gesture of 'So be it'.

'I'm working, Dan.'

Of course she's working. So I proffer a smile. I nod sympathetically.

'There's no need to be like that, Dan.'

'Like what?'

Because, I assure you, I did nothing but smile and nod and make that little gesture with my hands.

'You know what.'

And there you have it. Yes, unexpected bouts of petulance, of irritation. Having won the argument, she offers a consolation prize.

'We'll have time to ourselves over the weekend.'

And what can I do but accept?

'Well, yes, thank you, Sue… I look forward…'

Thank you? Yes, that is what I say. Thank you. Meaning, how good of you to grant me such a favour. How unworthy I am. But what choice do I have?

I know what you are thinking. You are thinking that Sue and I are an unlikely couple. Well, it is true that our relationship blossomed slowly and somewhat hesitantly. I ascribed this fact, at the outset at least, to my exaggerated desire to make an impression, to present myself in a virtuous light. You may be surprised to learn that I was, at the time, a little unsure of myself in the company of women. Yes, it is true. In the wake of my divorce I had come to the conclusion that I was unattractive to the opposite sex. I mean physically unattractive. And perhaps, to the superficial observer, of a not entirely attractive temperament, either. My spirits were low, you understand. I had a poor opinion of myself. So, when I met Sue, it seemed to me that I had precious little to offer her except my virtue. Good behaviour, I thought, might compensate for my lack of more conventionally appealing attributes. I therefore made something of a display of the little kindnesses I would show my mother: fetching her tea, asking about her rheumatics, examining the contents of her cupboards. I even went so far as to read some of the standard textbooks in Sue's field of work – books of quite impenetrable density and tedium with titles such as *Cognitive Gerontology* and *The Neuropsychology of Ageing* – so that we should not run out of topics of conversation, so that Sue should not think me overly frivolous. I would set about quizzing her, then, about the trials and tribulations of her daily routine, about her intractable patients, about their distressing habits. And I would declare, repeatedly, my boundless admiration for one who had dedicated her life to such a noble and challenging cause. But above all, I believe it was my readiness to listen that brought us closer together, for this is, I'm sure, a virtue in short supply amongst those whose company she must share day in, day out. At the very least, I believe that she came to approve of me. I passed muster. And that is no small matter. I held on to the hope that approval might, in due course, be a step towards friendship and then, with perseverance, to something more intimate.

Anxious that I might, at times, be at risk of appearing abnormally preoccupied with Sue's work, I would sometimes shift the conversation to my own profession. This was not easy. There is, after all, little common ground between mental illness and entomology. In any case, Sue displayed scant interest. Quite the contrary, in fact. 'Insects? I've had it up to here with insects,' she said, somewhat scornfully, when I first broached the subject. And told me about an old woman in her care who was forever complaining that 'the ants are eating me alive' and scratching so much that her arms and stomach were red raw.

But I persevered. I had little option. After all, and despite what I have said already on this issue, there is no doubt that, in my own case, my profession and I are as one. Know my work, and you know the worker. And after a while – indeed, after several false starts – Sue began to react more favourably to this change of tack. Why? I cannot say for certain. We spied a little caterpillar on one of our walks in the park. 'Did you know that a caterpillar has two hundred and twenty eight muscles in its head?' I asked her. She put the creature on the palm of her hand and watched it curl up. 'Have you counted them all yourself, Dan?' she said, with a smile. Yes, it was a slightly teasing smile, but I could tell, at the same time, she was impressed by the secret riches of this miniature world. 'You see that wasp, Sue?' I asked her. 'It lives for a day. It will not, it cannot, be alive tomorrow.' And the May Fly. 'A mere five minutes, Sue... Think of it... Five minutes to find a mate, have sex and lay her eggs... Only five minutes!' I would blush then, seeing her laugh. And her laughter would increase, in turn, at the sight of my embarrassment. That is when Sue's mood would soften, would loosen. Yes, perhaps that is the explanation for her change of heart. I offered her something – an innocence, perhaps, a naïveté – to set against her all-too-adult obligations.

And who can say that it was not this initial bashfulness of mine, too, that prepared the ground, quite fortuitously, for what followed? Yes, who can say? But I believe there is some truth in the hypothesis because, when finally we came together, Sue would address me as she might do a young child. 'And what would little Daniel like to do now, then?' Sometimes she would actually call me the *crwtyn bach*, just as my mother once had done. 'What's the *crwtyn bach* getting up to now, then, I wonder?' Her playful side would then come to the fore: the side I had already half glimpsed in the butterfly hair-clip, in the banter she employed with my mother. And so it was, piece by piece, step by step, and with the help of the occasional bottle of Merlot, that this playfulness extended its reach well beyond hair accessories and droll turns of phrase; indeed, extended itself so remarkably that I found it difficult to believe how such contrary tendencies could dwell within the confines of a single person.

'Talk dirty, Dan. Talk dirty.'

I cannot tell you how much of a shock this was, after weeks of chaste exchanges about old people and insects, and after feeling just a trifle guilty, too, that I had perhaps taken advantage of Sue's good nature, her caring instincts. And how mortified I am still when I remind myself of these times.

'*Gwaedda fe ma's*, Dan. Shout it out!'

I am wiser now, of course. I know that Sue is not two people, after all, merely a rather devious one. I know that this was how she got her own way: that, in fact, she had been treating me like a little child from the outset, sometimes bossing me, sometimes teasing.

'Shout it out, Dan, there's a good boy.'

Always a mute lover by preference, I did my best to obey. Which, to be brutally honest, made me perform with a great deal less conviction than might otherwise have been the case. There it is. I have said it. And perhaps that was another fly in the ointment.

I envy the mantid its efficiency in this regard. It would not be so fussy. Would that be better, Sue? Would you prefer it if I were a mantid? Because the mantid can tup for all his worth even whilst his mate gnaws away at his chin, his eyes, his head. It matters not one jot to him. Indeed, his brain is really a bit of a nuisance: he copulates a great deal better without it. More energetically. More passionately.

Bite my head off, Sue. Bit by bit. The eyes first. You'll see, then. You'll see how everything will come right then.

Time for the two of us, she said. Just the two of us. An evening. (A night, perhaps?) A chance to have another go.

When I look again, Sue is busy teasing out a sheet of paper which has got stuck in the photocopier. She tears it free, scrap by little scrap.

'Bloody thing...'

I help her dispose of the pieces which, by now, are scattered across the table and the floor. She looks at her watch. Curses again. I decide that now is not the time to plan our evening together. Instead, I sit down at my desk and resume work. In this way – my default position, you might call it – I hope to remind her that I am still a dutiful and industrious individual, deserving of her approbation. I turn to the computer and open my e-mails.

Two messages have arrived during the past hour. One is from Sue, asking whether she might come over to use the photocopier. I kick myself for not having checked my messages earlier: it would have saved me much trouble and embarrassment. A company rejoicing under the name *happinesstheexperience.com* has sent the other, together with an attachment.

'At last.'

By now, Sue has got the photocopier working again. I seize the opportunity.

'Tomorrow?' I say it as nonchalantly as I can, perhaps a little too nonchalantly, too cryptically.

'Mm?'

'Tomorrow night, Sue... I thought, perhaps, if you fancied it, we could go out …'

'Out?'

'For a bite to eat.'

'That would be nice.'

Yes, it would. Very nice. And I am about to say as much. But this is when I open the email from *happinesstheexperience.com*.

Hello Dan

It was fun meeting you the other night and talking about books etc. Sorry my own contributions were not quite up to scratch. I'm looking forward very much to next time. Your house, isn't it? Better still.

Ahmed passed on your email address. Said you sometimes do translation work. So I thought, maybe you'd be interested in the attached. Nothing very creative, I'm afraid, just the usual PR stuff. To publicise our new centre in Cardiff.

Let me know if you're interested and I'll send you an order.

Best wishes
Cerys Fortini

I am taken aback. 'I'm looking forward very much to next time.' I read the words again. Try to capture them in her voice, Cerys's book club voice. Try to get their proper flavour. Because this is, indeed, a strangely effusive thing to say, given the brevity, the tenuousness of our acquaintance. I seek alternative explanations. Could it be merely an exaggerated courtesy? A gesture from one seeking new friends in a strange city? Yes, that. Or else, to take a more sober view of the matter, might it be no more than business protocol? A dab of oil to get the wheels of commerce moving. I am, I admit, hopelessly jejeune in such matters. There is, I notice, no x at the end.

'You busy, Dan?'

I tell Sue that I am preparing a description of an Australian spider-beetle. But that this particular specimen, far from being antipodean in origin, actually hails from Cardiff Bay.

'Mm.'

I tell her that the cellars of Butetown have lately been invaded by rats. That the Council has used warfarin to exterminate these vermin but that the poison has been mixed with a particular kind of flour, to achieve a greater spread, to make it more palatable. And the flour, from foreign parts, is infested with greedy little spider-beetles.

'Mm.'

I tell her that it is the beetles, not the rats, that must now be brought under control.

'Mm.'

Mm? And I think, Is this not, then, a mission of some purpose, of some virtue? A project of some social benefit? An endeavour which merits more than your indifferent 'Mm'?

I look again at the e-mail. What does she mean by 'Better still?' *'Your house, isn't it? Better still.'* I curse the brevity of emails, their ritual breeziness, the fact that you can get away with this sort of throwaway comment, unchallenged. I'm surprised it's not punctuated with LOLs. But, as I say, there's no x either. What, after all, does she know of my house? Unless, of course, she lives in this neighbourhood. Because, if she does, my house would certainly be more convenient than, say, Sonia's in Rhiwbina. Doubly so, given that she cannot see. Is that what she means? So that she is merely expressing a functional preference. A neutral, clinical observation. My *house*. Not *my* house. Is that where I should put the stress? On the place, not the person?

'They're bad news, spider beetles,' I say. 'Really bad news.'

'Mm,' says Sue.

On the other hand, it is to me Cerys has come for her translation. Yes, for some reason she has eschewed all real, qualified, *bona fide* translators and entrusted this not insignificant task to a mere tyro in the business. Odd, don't you think? Does she, perhaps, expect favourable terms? And why, when all is said and done, does she not translate the document herself? Because she's blind? Surely not. Because she's illiterate? Her Welsh is sound and idiomatic. If she can write e-mails she can surely translate. Only two small blemishes let her down: a missing circumflex on the word 'tŷ?', when she refers to my house, and her misspelling of Ahmed's name. But these hardly count. And in any case, how many of us bother to correct our e-mails? It is true that the message seems to cool somewhat towards the end, but I may simply be imagining this, having already, as I say, sensed a no doubt chimerical intimacy in the opening sentences.

'And the book?'

'Book?'

'The one about that madman who ran about the place shooting parrots? How's it coming along?'

'Ah! Fine, Sue. Yes, it's coming along fine. Slowly but surely.'

I open the e-mail attachment. It contains the English-language text for a leaflet advertising a variety of what one would call, I suppose, party accessories – fancy hats, masks, stilts, plastic skeletons, juggling balls, clown shoes, coloured ribbons, itching powder and the like. And then a brief and enigmatic reference to some 'entertainment services' about which no further details are given. (Yes, I look for them. Because, for some reason, I am curious. So perhaps this laconic leaflet has worked its cheap magic after all.) It is all a puzzle. And as for the name, *happinesstheexperience.com:* it is quite beyond me what such tawdry geegaws have to do with happiness.

Annwyl Cerys

Thank you for your e-mail. I'm glad you had a good time the other evening. Pity it's only once a month, isn't it? I hope the new books are to your liking. I chose them without reading them, I'm afraid. And anyway, taste is such a personal matter, it's impossible to predict how others will react, even to one's very favourite titles. Do you have any favourites, I wonder? I shall be delighted to translate the document. Your work looks very interesting.

'Got anywhere in mind?'

'Mm?'

'To eat.'

'Somewhere close. The Spice Tree, perhaps.'

Do I dare?

'We could walk back to my place then.'

'Sounds OK to me.'

And it sounds OK to me, too. I delete the message and start again.

Annwyl Cerys Fortini

It was a pleasure to meet you the other evening.

Thank you for offering me the translation work. It will be ready by the end of the week, if that is acceptable. Please find my terms in the attachment.

Regards
etc.

8. Dinner with Sue

Ahmed likes collecting improbable facts with which to amuse us. He is, after all, our Publications Officer: facts are his currency. When the brand name, 'Coca-Cola', was first translated into Chinese, he said, pictograms were chosen that best approximated the sound of the original name. Yes, the sound, and the sound alone: the great corporation was interested only in targeting the consumer's ear, believing, in its American innocence, that it could convey the real thing, and nothing but the real thing, without picking up any loose debris on the long and tortuous route from Atlanta to Shanghai. No, not the merest speck of dust. The sounds they chose were: ke-koo-ke-lah. After manufacturing several million labels and signs, the corporation was informed that this close approximation meant: 'Eat the wax lizard'. This is what Ahmed told us.

Last night was not a success. It was my fault entirely. I believed, like

Coca-Cola, that my words, being well-intentioned, would therefore be well received. I miscalculated. For words, as we have seen, can conceal all manner of hooks and barbs and spikes of which the speaker has not the slightest inkling. This was a great pity, as I had tried my best to avoid topics which might sour the occasion. From the moment we entered the Spice Tree, I said not one word about work or my mother or our holidays or the reading group. I didn't even mention Ahmed and the business with his brother although I was curious to know her professional opinion on this matter. I should have liked to run through the daemon nonsense with her, too – she would, I'm sure, have been as dismissive as myself. But no, I wasn't taking any chances. I put not so much as a toe in any of these potential quicksands.

Things went swimmingly for an hour or more. We talked quite cheerily about this and that – the latest reality shows on TV, the barbarity of Cardiff city centre on a Friday night, the behaviour of dogs in Llandaff Fields, and so on. I told her how I was advised by a friend to carry a stick whenever I went for a jog, lest I be mauled by some corgi or Jack Russell. I told her how, armed in this fashion, I immediately attracted a veritable pack of the monsters, who chased me the length of the park and barked and jumped around me in the most menacing manner. 'Ha! It was the stick they wanted, Sue! Just the stick!' She laughed at this. We both laughed. We proceeded, in similar vein, to count the number of violent deaths inflicted upon the inhabitants of *Coronation Street*. Sue reached nine before giving up. I, of course, being older, having a longer memory, had no difficulty in exceeding this number. I counted twenty-two, although I'm sure even this figure is far short of the true total, as my first memory – of Valerie Barlow electrocuting herself on a faulty hairdryer – dates from no earlier than 1971 or 1972. Sue quite got into the spirit of things and had great fun mimicking the accent, rolling her head from side to side, 'as they do up there', she said, 'especially the girls in the factory.' And I had to plead with her to keep her voice down, because the other customers were beginning to stare at us. She then began to talk through her teeth, like some third-rate ventriloquist, but without lowering her voice at all, no, not a single decibel. 'No-on' 'll know who's sheeking now, 'ill ey, if I talk dike dis?' And asking me then to pass her a 'hohadon'. After a full-bodied Rioja, our taste-buds still zinging with ginger, capsicum and missal spices, how ready we were to laugh away our cares.

Indian food is a perfect accompaniment to such inconsequential yet sweetly sensual conversations. It abjures the linear plot of the British meal. Its delight, rather, is to follow its nose, its tongue, its fingers, along the paths of much less predictable pleasures. Last night, I truly believed that Sue and I had begun to find a new taste, also, for each other. For the first time in weeks we behaved like lovers. And despite my earlier discomfort, I was pleased that others would see us as such, would hear us, too. I felt that their witness would somehow make this reclaimed contentment all the more real, more lasting. I told Sue what a nice evening I was having. She smiled. I told her how important it was to set aside time for ourselves. She nodded. 'Very important, Dan,' she said. 'Very important.' And I suggested, only in passing, and without making an issue of the matter, that one of the major problems in my marriage, as I now reflected upon it from the perspective of a wiser middle age, was that we – that is, my wife and I – had not been able to spend sufficient time together.

That is all. I had no desire to pursue the question further. As I say, these were merely idle comments tagged on to what was intended to be a restatement of my affection for Sue, my appreciation of what we had together. These things are not easily said. And perhaps the alcohol was partly to blame. I have noticed before that Sue has a tendency to become a little emotional when she drinks. Be that as it may, what I said then was that my wife and I spent so little time together mainly on account of the children. No, not the children as such. Rather on account of our having children so early in our marriage. Yes, that was it. And the burden of this comment, for me at least, was simply to underline how much more fortunate were Sue and I. Our relationship had been given time to breathe, to put down roots, to stand on its own feet. That is what I meant, no more, no less. But she looked perplexed. So I elaborated a little. And perhaps that was my error, for I too was beginning to succumb to the effects of the wine. I said that our relationship had more room to breathe, it could put down proper roots, &c., &c., because my children had reached a more convenient age. Yes, 'convenient' is what I said. 'For want of a better word,' I added, then. But the damage was already done. I said more. I said I was much in her debt for the way she had befriended them, had enlisted their trust, even their affection. 'They look on you like a big sister,' I said. But her ear had snagged on that one word. 'Convenient.'

A long silence followed. Sue retired to the ladies and, when she returned some minutes later, her eyes were red. 'Have you been crying?' I asked. 'Has something – has someone – upset you at work?' Followed by more silence. 'That's when the stress comes out, you see,' I said. 'When you begin to relax. At the end of the day.' This, of course, was pure speculation on my part, and of what use was speculation to Sue? Neither of us said a word for a full two minutes, neither of us drank a drop of wine. I could do nothing but search her face for some clue as to what was wrong, whilst she, in turn, could do nothing but stare at her hands. I glanced nervously at the tables on either side, suddenly aware that those benign witnesses whose attentions I positively welcomed only minutes before could no longer be relied upon. Would they not assume, under the circumstances, that it was I, the man, who was at fault? For is not that the meaning of a woman's tears? At which point Sue drew a handkerchief from her sleeve, wiped her nose and looked me squarely in the eyes: 'You don't understand, Dan, do you? You haven't got a fucking clue.'

Did I understand? Well, evidently not. But I was not to be allowed to languish in my ignorance. Didn't I realise, Sue said, that she would sacrifice everything to have the children of whom I had spoken so slightingly? 'So slightingly?' I asked. But she paid me no heed. 'I'm thirty-five, Dan,' she said, through her tears. 'I am not in a position to be bothered by the inconvenience of children.' I tried to console her, but she didn't want my consolation. I apologised for being insensitive. 'I'm not worthy of you, Sue,' I said. And I meant this quite sincerely. It is true, after all, and I have said as much on many occasions. But she didn't want my self-pity, either. That's what she said. 'Self-pity, Dan. Nothing but self-pity.' Which wrong-footed me, rather, so that I was unsure where to turn next. I mumbled a little. I said, perhaps not entirely coherently, that I still felt guilty about the divorce and the children and I agreed, yes, I agreed readily that I must break out of my present rut, that I must… But no, that wouldn't do, either. 'It's not you we're talking about here, Dan,' she said, and became quite animated. 'Don't you get it? I don't give a fuck about your ruts or your conscience. I'm talking about me, Dan. Me. Where do I stand in all of this? Where, Dan?' She paused for a moment. Perhaps to wait for an answer. But I had no answer. At least, no answer that I was yet aware of, no ready-made answer. 'Between your conscience and your convenience, perhaps. Eh? Is that where I stand?' And she got up and left.

Having discovered their faux-pas, Ahmed said, the Coca-Cola corporation undertook a survey of more than forty thousand alternative pictograms. Ultimately, they discovered the combination, ko-koo-ko-lay, which means 'happiness in the mouth'. So similar to the first effort, and yet so different. Ahmed believes it to be superior even to the original, which of course has no meaning at all beyond its familiarity. I agree with him.

I am in no position to review forty thousand alternative formulations of my feelings for Sue. However, after last night's bitter reversal, I know that something must be done. My first act this morning, therefore, after I got out of bed, was to send Sue an e-mail. (I judged that a telephone call would be a tadge premature.) Not to apologise, of course, nor to offer any words of mitigation. Sue had made it perfectly clear that, to her, all such stratagems were just so much hot air. No, I made no reference whatsoever to my own travails, but stated, simply, candidly, that I took what she'd said last night to heart and, if I were given another chance, I should commit myself entirely to making up for any lack of consideration I had shown. Somewhat vague, you might think, a little blurred around the edges. But then I know quite well that nothing will satisfy Sue except one, simple, unambiguous and immutable declaration of intent: 'Sue, my love, I want us to have a baby.' And such a declaration is not, I am fairly certain, likely to be uttered. It is two o'clock in the afternoon and I have still received no reply.

9. On the Web

I have asked Nia and Bethan to call around today. I had originally intended to take them to town for a bite to eat, and then perhaps catch the bus down to the Bay for a walk and an ice-cream on the Quay, if the weather were fine enough. And see a film, perhaps, in that ghastly new multiplex. I wasn't altogether sure. What do teenager girls normally do on a Saturday afternoon? How could I know? But they'd already arranged to see some friends and couldn't make it until mid-afternoon. (Different friends, of course, and in quite different locations. Strict segregation of age-groups is fundamental to their sense of identity. I knew that much.) When, exactly? They couldn't say. They'd come as soon as they were able. I shall make them a meal. 'Salving your conscience, is it, Dan?' That's what Sue would say, forgetting that we had just spent our holidays with them. 'Ah! So generous with your time, Dan. A whole week every year.' That's what she'd say then. And perhaps I'd pluck up courage to muster a modest retort. 'Well, their mother isn't complaining, anyway.' But she has an answer for everything. 'No, Dan, I know, mothers *don't* complain. They just get on with it.' I can't win.

In this empty, indeterminate period, while I wait for the girls to arrive, I find myself in front of the computer again, seeking a more satisfactory explanation of what it is, what precisely it is, that Cerys does for a living. I open her message. I scroll to the bottom. There is a web address. *www.happinesstheexperience.com.* I click.

A circle appears. A small, blue circle on a white background. It stands there, motionless, for a few moments, then grows until it fills the whole screen. In the centre of the circle, letter by letter, words emerge and disperse. I can grasp only a few of them because the letters move so swiftly, so randomly. The permutations multiply. The letters flow back and forth between the words, a torrent of exclamations, ejaculations, exhortations. *Rally* is transformed into *thrill, reach* into *achieve*, *bmx* begets *xtreme, xcitement, xcel*! Pictures surface, one, two, three, four… then dive and swoop, a child laughing, a couple kissing, and an old woman – yes, an old woman, I'm sure, except that she is wearing a Robin Hood outfit – an old woman is firing an arrow from her bow, *twang!* and the arrow, I would swear, hisses directly towards me. I even raise my hand to protect my face, I pull my head back in instinctive recoil. The screen, or rather the illusion of the screen, breaks into a thousand splinters, and each splinter becomes a flower, yellow, red and blue in turn, until the display freezes and a command appears in bold copperplate.

CLICK HERE TO FIND YOUR GOAL!

I click. A page opens, filled with flags. Many are unfamiliar to me, but there is the Red Dragon, in the bottom row, between the Japanese sun and the Turkish moon. I click again and a drop-down menu appears. I click the first item, Kite-flying, which in Welsh is *Barcuta*. (For the list is in alphabetical order.) A girl and a boy run through a

Flying a kite

sunny field, pulling behind them a pink kite with a long tail. It rises high into the sky. Improbably high. At the same time I hear a familiar voice – Frank Lincoln, perhaps, or R. Alun Evans, or some other stalwart of radio or television – offering me, in seductive, velvet tones, *the greatest gift you ever received*. And a pause, then, whilst the boy and girl gaze at the kite, still floating obediently in the sky. *Freedom*. Another pause. *That rare freedom that only flying a kite can bestow on body and soul. View our extensive selection at Tŷ Dedwydd.*

But I have no interest in flying kites. I return to the menu and consider the other options. *Bungee Jumping. Canoeing. Climbing. Dancing. Drama. Juggling. Sailing.* I click *Bungee Jumping*. And see another kaleidoscope of words.

Nirvana

Mecca

heaven

and hell

where everyone's

twisted

BUZZING

magnetic

on to it!

The Welsh has disappeared. I'm not sure why, to begin with, but the reason soon reveals itself. A young man stands in the middle of the screen. He has fair hair, a rich bronze tan and a toothy white smile. He speaks Australian. The name Howie is emblazoned on his shirt. As the camera pulls back, it becomes clear that Howie, if that is what he is called (for it might, of course, be merely a logo), is standing on a tower, a high metal tower. A rope is tied around his left leg. He is ready to jump. Are we ready, too? It is Howie's voice that asks. His legs bend.

Wooow, radical road hip, man, adrenaline eldorado, shitting boulders.

He looks at me. Smiles. Waves.

Act cool, Howie, act cool. Hey, this is legendary madness, man, wow! wow! wow! what the hell am I DOING here?

He steadies himself.

OK, Houston, OK, countdown, countdown... three... two... one... and TAKEOFF... Holy shit!

He jumps.

AAAAARRRWWWWWYYYYYAA....

The same clip plays itself over and over again. The jump, the yell, the rebound. The jump, the yell, the rebound.

I linger awhile. No, I have no interest in bungee jumping. Indeed, I have even less interest in bungee jumping than I had in kite-flying. But I am distracted for a while by Howie's colourful effusions. Or rather, I should say, by the demands they would present a translator. Because this is Australian, not English. And it is bungee-Australian, too: a quite particular and arcane variety of that dialect. I do this for no good practical reason, you understand: Cerys has not asked me to translate any of this material, and I should certainly baulk at the task if she did so. It is merely an instinctive reaction. If you have ever been employed as a translator, you will understand what I mean. The brain has become so used to shifting back and forth between one language and another, like a shuttle on a loom, that it continues to do so long after the day's quota of linen has been woven. It sees random scraps of text – road signs, advertisements, and the like – it hears inconsequential snatches of conversation in the pub and it is compelled to set about recasting them. Now, then, how would he say that if he were, say, a garage attendant in Llangefni? *If she* were a library assistant in Ammanford? Because the translator, the truly dedicated, hard-bitten translator, abhors the loneliness of a single tongue.

So I set about Howie's monologue, for no reason other than that I cannot help myself. But the challenge, as I say, is formidable. What is 'radical road hip' in Welsh? What is 'legendary madness'? I have the words, but not the meaning. And I think to myself, who or what would Howie be if he were a Welshman? It may be a meaningless question, of course – a category error, I think they call it. I trust that *happinesstheexperience.com* intend to translate this page – after all, bungee jumping is in essence no more than kite-flying in reverse – but I do hope that Cerys doesn't expect me to do the job. The tower is 300 feet high. Each jump costs £50, including the video. That is my kind of translation.

I bypass *Ogofa,* as I am prone to claustrophobia, and even virtual caving is not something I wish to sample. And then, between *Pêl-droed* and *Rygbi*, quite unexpectedly, I see *Pryfeta*. This is, I think, a curious pastime to bracket with football and rugby. But as I open the page in question, I realise that the translator has taken liberties with the terminology. '*Pryfeta*', in common parlance, is what a sheep's flesh does when it is crawling with maggots. I can almost hear Wncwl Wil's voice as he contemplates the poor animal, shaking his head: *'Dan bach, mae hi wedi pryfeta'n ofnadw.'* Because *pryfed* are vermin. But it can, too, denote the pursuit of, the preoccupation with, even the study of, insect life. *Pryfeta*. Yes, a more colloquial, idiomatic term for the discipline of entomology, the dissection of *pryfed*. If you don't understand Welsh, I'm afraid you will have to take this on trust. In any case, as I click the page open, it is clearly this that the translator has in mind. The Welsh has now been restored and the picture is a good deal more agreeable than its predecessor.

What's in the net today, children?
Click HERE to find out!

I click again and another menu appears. *Buwch Goch Gota. Ceiliog y Rhedyn. Cleren. Chwannen. Chwilen Ddu. Iâr Fach yr Haf. Morgrugyn...*

I click on *Morgrugyn*. And am disappointed to discover that the page has nothing to do with ants. It is dedicated, instead, to promoting a computer game called SimAnt, for sale at the knock-down price of £12.99. I turn to *Chwilen* and find a black beetle of sorts, a creature which is both much more and much less than a beetle could ever be, starring in its own game, *Bad Mojo*, only £15 a throw. And then the *Butterfly Hunt*, with not a single butterfly in sight. I venture no further, because these are not insects at all. They are prosthetics. And I have no wish to seek my entertainment disguised as a bug.

I am about to close down the site when I hear the voices of Nia and Bethan at the front door. They are quarelling. That much is obvious even before the bell rings. I cough as I approach the door, to save our mutual embarrassment. The bickering stops, which is a good thing, of course, except that it encourages me to think that the cross words might have had something to do with me. I open the door. They dispense with greetings and small-talk. Bethan has bought a CD – I don't catch the name of the group – and she makes straight for the lounge, where I keep a portable CD player. She asks me, in passing, whether this is OK, but it is a ritual gesture only. Bethan is fourteen. She puts the CD on and lies back on the sofa.

As I go to the kitchen, to get their drinks, to switch on the kettle, Nia calls from the study. At eleven years old, her voice still rings with innocent enthusiasm. She is sitting at the computer. '*Gawn ni fynd, Dad?* Can we go to Tŷ... to Tŷ Ded...'

'*Tŷ Dedwydd, bach.* Yes, of course we can.'

10. Drama in Tŷ Dedwydd

'Is *that* it, Dad?' said Nia on our first visit, doing her best, poor thing, to affect excitement

For all its name, Tŷ Dedwydd is a glum-looking building. (The name translates, I am embarrassed to say, as something like 'House of Felicity'. 'Happy House' would do, perhaps, but has unfortunate connotations.) It is located on a new industrial estate on the eastern fringes of the city between the River Rumney and the sea-marshes. To reach it, you must follow Lamby Way past the refuse tips, fork right onto New Road and turn left up the Avenue – and there it is, at the far end, between a double-glazing factory and a cleaning products warehouse. Unit 6b. A huge aluminium cube, its bland uniformity is punctuated by only a few small, square windows. There are no logos or signs, save for the name, in red perspex letters above the door – **TŶ DEDWYDD** – and beneath it, the website address.

'It's a dump,' said Bethan.

Early days, I thought. Give it the benefit of the doubt. 'It'll be better inside. Bet you it well.' Because how could it not be?

I had been in this locality many times before, over the years, primarily to dispose of unwanted furniture on the nearby tips. I also came here in a professional capacity one particularly hot summer – '92 or '93, I forget which – when the residents of Tremorfa were complaining about the flies in their neighbourhood. I helped Simon, our expert on *diptera* at the Museum, with the initial field work and identification. They were, in themselves, nothing remarkable – a mix of cluster flies (*Pollenia rudis*) and common flies (*Musca domestica*) – but their numbers were troublesome. Millions were killed that year. They were not mourned.

But it must have been some time since my previous visit, because I could see, whilst driving along Lamby Way, that great changes had taken place. A large part of the refuse tip was now carpeted in grass and shrubs, creating a smooth green mound which might easily be mistaken for an Iron Age fort. A lake had also been constructed. Beyond this, however, and out of sight of the main entrance, the tip still lived and breathed. Even from here, at Tŷ Dedwydd, I could smell its sour exhalation. I could see the gulls circling overhead, hear their screeches.

'Yes, it'll be much better inside.'

The girls became regular visitors at Tŷ Dedwydd during the following weeks. Nia took the lead because, although the younger sister, it was in her nature to do so. 'I'm going to be Tracey Beaker this time,' she would boast – or 'Violet', or 'Gemma', or some other character from one of her favourite books. At least, that is what I took to be the case: I am not, for obvious reasons, as familiar with the girls' reading habits as I once was. Nia would ask me, after each visit, and much to my consternation, whether she was old enough yet to be Dunk's special friend, or Simon's or Lee's? Could she do a gig with Beyonce Knowles? None of this surprised me. As I say, she is an extrovert little creature, much given to displays of gratuitous joy and sadness. The drama workshops at Tŷ Dedwydd could not have suited her better.

Bethan was less impressed. 'I'm not Nia, Dad. I'm fourteen, for god's sake. Get real!' Somehow, and without any help from me, she found alternative diversions in the Tŷ Dedwydd café: watching DVDs, playing video games and hanging out with other girls, it seems, from the little she has been willing to tell me. As I am no more than a *chauffeur* in this business, the activities of both are something of a mystery to me.

The visits are not cheap. Nia's workshops cost me £15 a go and woe betide if Bethan doesn't get an equivalent enhancement in her pocket money. It is also a bit of a *potsh*, as we say, crossing the city, then idling away two hours or more until the girls' activities are finished. Until recently, I would occupy myself by taking a walk around the refuse tip. No, it cannot be described as a picturesque location, and yet it is not without its attractions. Indeed, for a brief while, when I first explored these barren acres, I felt a little echo of the excitement that once accompanied my childhood adventures. From the bottom of The Avenue, I could squeeze through a hole in the fence and follow the path along the bank of the Rhosog Fach – a not insubstantial stream that had previously escaped my attention –

and emerge, in due course, at the sea-wall. In clement weather, I would make my way over to the big gates at the back of the site and then spend a pleasant ten minutes or so chatting with one of the men employed to gather up the stray scraps of paper that are blown here by the wind. It is an exposed spot. More often than not, however, I was deterred by the rain or the smell and I would have to return to the artificial hill. Now that the days are shortening once more – it is mid-September – I shall soon have to devise alternative diversions.

Yes, it is a bit of a *potsh*. But at least one good thing has emerged from the House of Felicity. It has brought the girls and me closer together, and this at a time, in the normal course of events, when girls tend to retreat into their shells. I am grateful to Tŷ Dedwydd for this much. And I am grateful to Cerys for opening the door.

*

It is seven o'clock on a Friday evening. Nia and Bethan are in Tŷ Dedwydd, while I sip a pint of SA at the Six Bells in Peterstone Wentloog. Gwynllwg in Welsh. Llanbedr Gwynllwg. It is unnaturally quiet. I have, over the weeks and months, tried other pubs in the locality. The Carpenters. The Monkestone. And, for a quite terrifying five minutes, the Rompney Castle Hotel. But this, the Six Bells, is the most pleasant. The least unpleasant. This and the Royal Oak.

If Sue and I were to be reconciled, of course, I could go to her house. I came within a whisker of doing so last Friday night after a swift pint in the Oak. Indeed, I left the pub early with that in mind. I walked up to her door, stared for a full minute at the bell, at Sue's name underneath, written in her own neat hand. At the window, then, where I could see the gleam of light between the curtains. But that is as far as I could go. Because what was there to say? It is a difficult business, preparing a conversation in advance: you can learn your own half of it, have it word perfect, but of what use is half a conversation if your interlocutor does not follow your prompts, or indeed goes off on a tangent, establishes new terms of reference? So I did nothing. I have received no response to my e-mails, to my phone messages, to my texts.

This evening, therefore, I am in the Six Bells, not the Oak. It offers fewer temptations. Unfortunately, it also offers few comforts. Two young couples enter, full of Friday night high spirits and I am suddenly overcome by the malaise of the lone drinker. Billy No-mates. That's what they're thinking. That's what I'm thinking myself. I have brought a copy of the *Echo* to hide behind. It is a sad little prop. I scan the television pages for the third time. I scrutinise the small ads, trying to look as though this were a perfectly reasonable, even rewarding, use of my leisure hours. And when I have exhausted these gambits, I look at my watch, down the remnants of my pint and smile a friendly 'good night' to the barmaid, who will understand, from these actions, that I am not a lone drinker by conviction, no, indeed, I must depart this very instant because my next rendezvous beckons.

It is half past seven: much too early to fetch the girls. But what is there to do? It is already getting dark outside. A chill wind batters the *morfa*. There's rain in the air. I drive back, as slowly as I dare, towards Lamby Way. In the distance, I see the gulls circling the tip, their white wings catching the last glimmers of sunlight.

When I reach Tŷ Dedwydd, the lobby is heaving with children: some waiting for their parents to take them home, others enjoying a short break before resuming their workshops. Two furry bunnies hop expectantly in the corner. There is also a mouse, a long-nosed witch with a pointy hat, and a cluster of children dressed in Victorian work clothes – caps, breeches and clogs for the boys, white smocks for the girls. In such company, it is I, an interloper from the real world, who feels out of place. For a moment, so large is the crowd, and so busy, that I am unable to move from the doorway.

It is now eight o'clock. I know that I still have another half hour to wait before Nia's workshop finishes. I know, also, that it was a mistake to come here so early. And you might say, well, the Six Bells offered fewer temptations, but of what use is a pub in which I cannot bear to spend more than twenty minutes? Yes, and it is not appropriate, I think, for an adult male to be wandering about in a place like this, by himself, in the gloom of an autumn evening. So I am glad when a member of staff appears and shepherds the children back to their respective rooms. I make my way to Reception and ask about

Nia's workshop. Much to my relief the girl recognises me. She looks at her computer and tells me that Nia's workshop is due to finish in half an hour. Which, of course, I already know, but that is not the point. I am not seeking information, I am simply confirming my right to be here. She says, would I perhaps like to wait in the café? And I must explain to her that my elder daughter is enjoying the company of her friends there and it wouldn't do, would it, for a father to barge in unannounced and embarrass her in such a way? No, I say, thank you, but I am happy waiting here, in the lobby.

I sit down and look around me. At the comings and goings. At the mothers and fathers, arriving in their ones and twos. At the children, telling them their adventures. At my watch. At the bilingual leaflets, in their wire racks: the very same leaflets that I translated some weeks ago. At the little administrative rituals being performed by the girl at Reception. And then, at the television screens, five of them, mounted on the wall behind the reception desk. I see these for the first time – not just the first time this evening but the first time in all my visits here. Perhaps they have just been installed. Or perhaps it is because they are silent, merely moving pictures, not drawing attention to themselves. No, I am early, very early. That is why I see them this evening.

So, since I still have some minutes to endure, I consider the televisions in turn, moving from left to right. There, on the first screen, are the familiar children with their kite, running through that field of eternal summer. The next screen shows the view a pilot would have if his aircraft were skimming across the surface of the sea: no, not the pilot, but rather a camera tied to the aircraft's wing, as there is nothing to be seen of the cockpit or indeed any other part of the aircraft itself. I feel dizzy. And next to this, on the third screen, something quite different. Children in costumes. A mouse here. Two rabbits there. And the quality of the picture more grainy, less composed than either the aircraft or the kite. I look again. At the mouse. At the rabbits. And I realise that this is, indeed, something wholly different.

'You're showing them… the workshops… on the screen?'

The girl at Reception nods.

'Live? I mean, now… as they're happening?'

She nods again and tells me that here, on Screen 3, *The Gruffalo* is being enacted. That *Horrid Henry and the Stink Bomb* is to be seen on 4. That the last screen shows Chance House. 'Your daughter is in Chance House.'

'I see.'

'In Studio Five.'

I study the screen. I don't see Nia at once. Or, at least, if I do see her, I fail to recognise her. Most of the children – half a dozen or so, altogether – have their backs to the camera and their clothes make them look unfamiliar. Not that the clothes are unusual in their own right, but they are adult clothes, or at least adult in style, if not in size. A nurse's uniform. An old man's cap, and the figure beneath it bent, leaning on his stick. An old woman, too. And her daughter, perhaps, because she's holding her arm. The younger woman wears bright red lipstick. All have their backs to the camera. Both they and the camera are now looking across to the other side of the room, where a boy is standing alone. He wears a long jacket which seems, at first glance, to be made of some soft, shiny material. Only after further inspection do I realise that it is not the material of the jacket itself that I see but rather other pieces of material, scores of them, which have been attached to the jacket. Each has the same silvery sheen. Ribbons, I think. As though a hundred ribbons have been sewn on to the jacket. Except that they are too substantial to be ribbons. Too alive.

'Chance House, you said?'

The girl explains that Chance House is a house in a story by – no, she doesn't remember the name of the author, but the book is called *Feather Boy.* She looks through her papers. Would I like her to find out who the author is? There's probably a copy here, somewhere, if she could only lay her hands on it. But I say, no, thank you, because I am now too preoccupied by the picture on the screen. Yes. And that is the explanation, of course. Feather Boy. The jacket is not adorned with ribbons at all, but with feathers. A feather jacket.

And everyone is looking at him now. Because the boy with the feather jacket is climbing onto a table. A long, sturdy wooden table, of the kind which might preside in the kitchen of some old farmhouse. First, he steps up onto a stool, steadies himself, then climbs onto the table, right foot, left foot. Feather Boy. He stands there in the middle of the table, waiting.

'So they're acting the story…?'

The girl tells me – I can see the name on her badge now: Yvonne Walker – and Yvonne tells me that Cerys has chosen excerpts from the book. Has adapted them for performance. Highlights, she says.

'Cerys?'

'Cerys Fortini.'

I don't see Cerys on the screen. She is no doubt directing the children from behind the camera. Yes, that is the conclusion I draw, even though I know it to be impossible. Because how could someone blind…? But at this point one of the group breaks free. A boy. And this boy, unlike the others, is dressed as a boy, not a man. He runs towards the table. After a few paces, however, he stops suddenly, turns and walks back to his starting point. Why? Without sound, I cannot tell. He does the same again. Runs. Stops. Walks back. And again. Whilst all the time the Feather Boy stands motionless on the table.

As the scene unfolds for the fourth time, I see the old woman – the old woman who is really a child – turn her face to the camera. No, not to the camera, because her eyes do not quite meet mine. She turns her eyes towards Cerys. Yes, I am certain of it now, Cerys is standing there, near the camera, out of sight. And she turns much too quickly to be a real old woman, despite the wig, despite the baggy cardigan. She turns and I see… I see Mam. I see her old green cardigan. A corner of a hankey sticking out of one of the pockets. I see her white blouse with the pink embroidery on the collar. The woollen skirt. The hand bag. The necklace. I see my mother. I see Nia.

The boy runs across the room. This time the other boy, the one on the table, the Feather Boy, is ready for him. He raises his wings. No, not his wings. This is a boy. He has no wings. He raises his arms. His feather arms. He bends his legs. I think, perhaps Cerys will call a halt, as she has done before. That the running boy will return to his place, the Feather Boy will get down from the table, the scene will conclude. But she doesn't. Even though there is no sound, I know she doesn't, because no-one is looking at her now, all eyes are fixed on the Feather Boy, raising his arms, bending his legs.

And I know what is going to happen next. I know that nobody will stop it. That I am the only one that can stop it. That I must stop it.

11. A Word about the Monarch

Ahmed told us about Coca Cola, so I told him about the Monarch.

The Monarch, I said, has visited Wales on only four occasions during my lifetime. At least, that is how many times it has been seen by people who knew enough about butterflies to recognise what they saw and to be sufficiently exercised to inform the authorities. The first three passed me by. In 1968 because I was too small. In 1981 because I was too immersed in college affairs. And 1999 was the year of my divorce. Which left 1995. And in that year, the year of golden opportunity, I should, by rights, have caught at least a glimpse of my elusive quarry. It was surely my due. I missed it by what, in the wider scheme of things, was less than a hair's breadth. I missed it utterly.

Beyond the Atlantic, I told Ahmed, this miracle was an annual event. The days shortened, the wind's blade sharpened, and tens of millions of these splendid creatures knew it was time to up sticks and head south. Two thousand miles separate Canada and Mexico – barren miles for the most part, with scarcely a meadow or a garden or a leafy glade to provide refuge for the brave migrants. But the Monarch has a compass – an ancient, inner compass, its finger pointing eternally towards the equator – and it will follow that compass with unswerving determination until it reaches the Promised Land. That, at least, is the story, the myth. And it is not so far from the truth, as stories go. But it errs in one respect. Because the Monarch does, in fact, swerve. Indeed, one small but quite definite and specific swerve has become an integral part of its annual pilgrimage: a little twist that is as deeply engraved on its memory's map as the long flightpath towards the sun.

Having crossed Lake Superior, without rest or sustenance, the Monarchs, every one, take an unexpected turn to the east. They then proceed to a point which, as far as the human eye can tell, has no distinguishing features, indeed is no point at all. Here, they take another turn and resume their original course. What is it that the eye cannot see, that triggers such behaviour? Some entomologists say that this zig-zag allows the Monarchs to bypass a gigantic ice-flow: an ice-flow that disappeared, in its corporeal form, over twenty thousand years ago but which still looms, ominous and frightful, in the butterfly's collective memory. Geologists, on the other hand, maintain that here, by the great lake, in the earth's youth, there was once a great mountain, the highest this continent has ever seen, before or since. No, Ahmed, I am not convinced by either explanation. Personally, I tend toward a much more pragmatic view. I believe that what might once have been a memory, be it of ice-flow or mountain or some quite other obstacle, itself now utterly lost and forgotten, has turned into a habit. It is the habit that is remembered, then, from year to year. Habit is the greatest master of all.

Whatever the true explanation for the Monarch's deviation, without it not a single specimen would ever visit these shores. For in taking that diversion to the east, in turning its sights towards the Atlantic, the creature puts itself at the mercy of the wind. And if that wind, then, should be a particularly brisk westerly, it has no option but to resign itself to a long, hazardous and unintended voyage above the ocean wave. In an average year, most will tire and drown. But 1995 was not an average year. In the wake of Hurricane Marilyn, a flow of warm air blew across the Atlantic, swift yet without turbulence, allowing the Monarch the easiest of passages. And this is no tall story. It is a fact, well attested. We have the photographs, the witnesses. After only four days the Monarchs arrived, none the worse for their adventure.

Where did they arrive? Well, Ahmed, I'll tell you. Some were spotted in the Scilly Isles. And then several more in Cornwall. So surely, we thought – and by 'we' I mean members of the Glamorgan Butterfly Group – it was not too much to hope that a few might make it across the Severn Estuary. They had done so in the past, they would surely do so again. Habit, you see. But it is the devil of a job to predict where a butterfly will come to ground. Over fifty of us waited diligently at diverse locations along the coast, all the way from the Gower in the west to the outskirts of Newport in the east. Alas, as far as we know, only one of these specimens made it to Wales that year. It was seen recharging its batteries on a Michaelmas Daisy in an unremarkable suburban garden in Penarth. I, at the time, was a mere mile or two away, at Lavernock Point. As I say, a hair's breadth, in the larger scheme of things. Within an hour, it had disappeared. And that, I'm afraid, is par for the course in these matters. Another couple of days and not a single specimen remained in the whole of Britain.

So then, Ahmed, the Monarch is a rarity in these parts. But it is not an illusion, a mere myth. Unlike the *daemon,* for example. And its journey across the Atlantic is anything but a game. So I live in hope. I shall, I am sure, have other opportunities to welcome it to our shores. Perhaps before too long, because it has been some years now. Yes, you could say it is long overdue. But then, as I say, prediction is a devilishly difficult business. And when did wishing for things ever make them come true?

12. Cerys Learns to See

I am sitting in Cerys's office. She picks up the remote and points it at the television.

The video shows a boy, dressed in a jacket of feathers, preparing to jump off a table. A woman's voice issues directions from somewhere off-camera. 'You've got to bend your legs…' A rope is tied around the boy's waist. It stretches upwards, to the ceiling, perhaps, but this is out of view, so I can't say for certain. The rope tightens. The boy jumps. Flies. Yes, for a moment, it appears that the boy actually flies. And it is at this very same moment, between flying and landing, that another boy runs towards him, shouting, shaking his right fist. The remaining children rush forward and make a circle around the two boys. They, too, shout and gesticulate. Some are dressed as adults. One of them, now at the rear of the group, mimics the hobble of an old woman.

Because of the shouting, and because a small television monitor can show only a segment of the action, it is only gradually that I become aware of another commotion emanating, not from the children's performance, but from a different source, somewhere out of sight. The sound of a door, slamming open. Of someone tumbling over chairs. Shouting, 'Don't...' And the shout stopping abruptly, unfinished. By now the children are no longer looking at the two boys. For some reason which cannot yet be fathomed, they have turned away from both the Feather Boy and his adversary and are facing the camera. A man's head comes into view, only the head to begin with, then his shoulders. His straw-coloured hair is dishevelled. The sweat shines on his face. Despite this, despite his physical exertions, he is as pale as a ghost. He stares at the boy with the feather jacket. The boy stares back at him, open-mouthed. Everyone is silent.

Nia was hopping mad. Of course she was. 'You showed me up in front of all my friends... Why, Dad? Why?' And, hand on heart, I couldn't tell her why, I could only say, 'I'm sorry, I'm sorry,' and mutter some lame excuse about how I had walked into the wrong room. 'I was looking for the Gents, Nia! Can you believe it? For the Gents!' And I changed the subject. I praised her hobbling old woman. I told her what a brilliant idea it was to borrow Mam-gu's clothes. But to no avail.

'And what will Miss Fortini say?' That is what she asked me last night, in the car, as we drove home.

Yes, indeed, what *would* Miss Fortini say? I slipped over to Tŷ Dedwydd today, to find out. Yes, and to apologise. And also, perhaps, if I could find the words, to explain. Or, at least, to offer something by way of mitigation. My efforts had not satisfied Nia, I know, but that was a different matter. I would say 'Health and Safety'. Cerys would surely appreciate that. She might be cross, but she would understand. Except, of course, that to cite Health and Safety might imply a certain negligence on Cerys's part, which was not my intention. So no, I thought, best revert to the wrong door explanation. But something. I had to say something. Because it wasn't acceptable, simply to walk away, to see the boy with the feather jacket land on his feet, to mutter a swift 'Ah!', a peremptory 'Sorry', an incoherent

'I thought… I thought…', and then walk away. I blush even to think of it.

The lobby was full of giggling schoolgirls when I arrived and it took me some time before I spied Cerys standing at the desk, talking to the receptionist – not Yvonne, but some other, unfamiliar girl. I waited at a polite distance until there was a lull in their conversation. 'Hello, Cerys,' I said, in as clear and unflustered a voice as I could muster. Then, 'It's Dan here,' to make sure she knew who I was, where I was standing. And perhaps I said this rather too loudly, too pedantically – it was a difficult calculation, you understand, in the midst of such squeals and titters – because everyone turned in my direction. Yes, not only Cerys and the receptionist but the schoolgirls, too, or a good number of them, no doubt believing me to be the master of whatever proceedings they were about to engage in. They all turned, capturing me in their gaze, like a rabbit in headlights. It is a tired simile, I know, but it will have to do. I have little experience of describing such events.

'I mean… Do you have… Is there somewhere…'

To my surprise, Cerys took my arm and led me away. This is a paradoxical statement, I know. She took my arm, just as I would expect a blind person to do, in such circumstances. But I had not expected her to lead the way. She did this quite unerringly. She negotiated the busy corridors, she reached for door-handles, she pressed the correct buttons in the lift.

'My office is on the second floor. We'll get more peace there… If that's OK by you, Dan…?' She said this with a humility, a tentativeness, that was disarming. And I knew that I had already lost the initiative. This is not a complaint. I had no wish to retain whatever initiative I had mustered, because it had been a wearisome task mustering it in the first place, and as far as I was concerned, I was well shot of it. So, as I say, this is not a whinge, a protest. It is simply to say, once more, that another's humility can have an unexpectedly disabling effect, particularly when one is expecting a more brusque, a more frosty response.

Cerys's room was small, bare and rather dark. Only its lower half was illuminated, and that quite dimly, through two small internal windows.

'I admire what you did last night, Dan.'

'Admire?'

'I agree with you, Dan. A blind person cannot be left in charge of children.'

I should have liked to disagree with her, in recognition of her candour, her civility. To show that this wasn't what I'd meant at all. But how could I? For it was precisely what I had meant.

'I owe you an explanation, Dan. I apologise for not giving you one earlier.'

'An explanation?'

'I'm not blind.'

Cerys raised her head. And for the first time, in the grey half-light of that room, in that grey industrial estate off Lamby Way, she looked at me with a glimmer of recognition.

'At least, not in the way you think.'

Yes, she looked at me, but I did not return her gaze, thinking that this would be an affront to her affliction.

'I lost my sight when I was five. By the time I was ten I had only the vaguest memory of what seeing meant. I still dreamed in pictures, for a while, but I couldn't join them up with the things I felt and heard and smelt. They were just images in the head. So you could say that my desire to see was a bit like the desire to fly for people like you, Dan. People who can see. You can dream it but you can't do it… I'm sorry… Does that make sense?'

I said it did, because I knew it would, in time, on reflection. I voiced my sympathy. It was a sincere enough sympathy, too, but perhaps also a little more effusive than it ought to have been, so great was my relief that my unruly behaviour of the previous evening was not, after all, the subject of our conversation. And perhaps it was my sympathy which gave her a new confidence, which allowed her to speak with less hesitation. I flatter myself too much, no doubt, but who can predict what effect we have on others? And how could I know but that Cerys had had no opportunity to share these thoughts, for many months, even years? It was possible. I say no more.

Cerys proceeded to tell me how her memory – that is, her visual memory – had faded, bit by little bit, like footprints in the sand, she said, the tide dissolving each one until nothing remained, as though there had never, ever been a footprint there, or a foot to make it.

'But blindness is a foreign country to you, Dan. As foreign as flying.' She looked at me again and then turned her head away, shielding her eyes with her hand. 'Would you mind moving to another chair, Dan?' she said. 'I'm sorry to be a pain.'

So I moved.

'I can see you better now... You were too big before.'

And then, no doubt sensing my confusion, my discomfort, she explained that it was the shadows' fault.

'Bright lights hurt my eyes... But without them, the shadows take over... I'm not sure which is worse... The shadows look exactly like tables and chairs to me, I can see no difference... Sometimes I find myself putting my papers down on a shadow... And you...'

'Me?'

Cerys went on, in her quiet, undemonstrative way, to explain that she could see branches growing out of my body where I had been sitting before. Branches, twigs and leaves where arms and legs ought to be. At one point my face had become part of the wall. At another, my head divided into two. For a moment, said Cerys, I had two heads.

'The shadow of your head on the wall looked for all the world like another head to me. You don't have two heads, do you, Dan?'

She said this with a lightness and humour, even a certain mischievousness, which I found remarkable at the time. Which, today, on reflection, I find utterly beguiling. There was no bitterness in her voice. No resentment.

'Have you read *The Sphinx*, Dan?'

'*The Sphinx*?'

'By Edgar Allan Poe.'

I told Cerys that I was not much of a literary man, but that Bethan, my elder daughter, had a taste for such things. Just a phase, I said. Although it was Stephen King she liked best. In fact, I doubted whether she had actually read any Edgar Allan Poe. Even doubted whether she'd heard of him. 'And that other one, what's his name?

Dean something or other...' I suggested, beginning to regret my digression.

'It describes how it feels to get your sight back,' she said. 'And how you don't know, at the beginning, what to do with it.'

Because Cerys is only learning to see. That, in a nutshell, is what she wanted to tell me. For the next hour I learned many things about what this meant. I learned about seeing and not seeing, about the different kinds of mis-seeing, about how she had learned to recognise the furniture in her house and her office, and could do so confidently now, provided only that nothing moved, provided that no-one, for example, put a vase of tulips on the table without warning. (At which I wondered whether there was, indeed, someone there, at home, who might inadvertently do such a thing, might move the furniture and the tablecloths and the cups and saucers and confuse her, so that she had to shield her eyes with her hand, just as she had done for me.) Yes, provided that nothing moved. Provided that she herself remained motionless. Because, she said, she could not yet process movement: she could cope only with the *tableaux,* with the still lives.

'And pictures. They don't mean anything to me, either, Dan. Just a mess of colours and shapes. That's all I can see in a picture. The television, too.'

I might have asked, what of words, then? You can read words? But she'd turned the television on by now. For this, it appears, was the true purpose of our meeting. And I saw myself on the screen, my face white with terror, stumbling into Cerys's drama.

'Talk me through it, please, Dan. Be my guide.'

And although the image should have caused me the profoundest humiliation, I felt, instead, a strange elation. I felt that I had, somehow, regained the initiative.

13. Mam's Birthday

'Happy birthday, Mam.'

I give her my present, but not the flowers. Not yet. One thing at a time.

'*Diolch, Daniel.*'

It isn't easy buying presents for my mother. She has always been dismissive of the convention. 'Don't waste your money, *bach,*' she'd say, every Christmas, every birthday, for as long as I can remember. Moving to Cardiff from her house in Pentrepoeth legitimised this inclination. 'No room here, Daniel.' A little stand for her potted plant? A reading lamp, to save the strain on her eyes? 'I can scarcely move as it is, Daniel,' she would say. 'Don't make matters worse. Please, Daniel, don't make matters worse.'

So this time I bought her a CD from that place in the arcade that repackages golden oldies. *Pastimes*. That's it. Or maybe *Past Times*. I chose a miscellany – Doris Day, Ann Shelton, Johnny Mercer, Frankie Lane, Nat King Cole, people of that ilk – judging that, surely, she would find some of them to her taste.

She puts on her glasses and reads the small print.

'Welcome... Home...'

And takes them off again, to have another go, this time holding the CD only an inch or two from her eyes.

'Happy...songs...and...music...'

'Songs from the end of the War, Mam.'

I give her the flowers and put the CD in the portable player. The flat fills with the mellow brass croonings of Glenn Miller: a sound which, even for me, who was born many years later, is wrapped in a glow of vicarious nostalgia.

A son does not choose his mother's present on an idle whim. And purchasing an item 'from the past', as it were, presents particular problems. He must distinguish between that 'past' which, for her, conjures pleasure and contentment and all those other 'pasts' which do not – indeed, which sometimes do the opposite. He must recognise those 'pasts' which, if only by a few years, are too remote and will court her ridicule. He must, equally, be able to identify those more recent 'pasts' which, to her ears, will be mere noise. She spurned a CD of Al Bowlly once, on the grounds that it was much, much too old-fashioned, and what did I think I was playing at? 'You're getting me mixed up with Mam-gu,' she said. 'But it was recorded in 1940, Mam. It says here.' I read out the details to her, the name of the band, the name of the leader, where the recording was made, and so on. 'Before my time, *bach*,' she said. And I thought, well, what *is* your time, then, Mam?

'Songs to welcome the troops home, Mam. You see the picture on the front?' I point to the CD cover, to the black and white picture of families, caught by the photographer in the joy of reunion. But my mother has lost interest. She looks at the flowers.

'Nice flowers, Daniel. But you shouldn't waste your money.'

She gets up from her chair, steadies herself and totters towards the kitchen. There, she takes a jug from the cupboard, unwraps the flowers, cuts their stems, one by one, to the required length and puts them in the vase. All this she does in a no-nonsense, even perfunctory manner: my mother has never been one for flower-arranging or any other domestic indulgences. She fills the vase with water from the tap. It is heavy, then, but I know that this is her ritual and it would be improper for me to intervene. So, as she does these things, I sit back in my armchair and allow the melodies to wash over me. Glenn Miller, Jo Stafford and, by now, Vera Lynn's 'White Cliffs of Dover'. To their accompaniment, my gaze wanders around the room.

And what *is* your time, Mam?

There are relics here from the house in Pentrepoeth. The chair on which I'm sitting. Mam's chair, too. The embroidered antimacassars which adorn them. The maroon woollen cushion covers she knitted, somewhere around the time I started at the big school. I know this because I recall the embarrassment I felt, on bringing friends back to the house, and it was full of such things, home-made things, get-by things. The colour has faded now. And behind me, the sideboard. The blue service, the one she inherited from Mam-gu, is inside, out of sight. Only the old jug, the Gaudy Welsh, is on display. My mother thinks it is valuable, but I doubt it. A fine crack runs down one side, the side that is turned towards the wall. The dresser never came. 'Too big,' Mam said. 'Can't swing a cat in here.'

Gaudy Welsh

On top of the television there are two pictures: one of Nia and Bethan when they were small, the other of John, my brother, and his family. They have lived in Canada for more than ten years and send photographs from time to time, little updates, *in lieu* of the real thing. The pictures are placed at a slant, as though the two groups were happily smiling at each other.

On the wall, above the television, rather obscured by shadow, is the only photograph of my mother: a black and white snap taken when she was still living with Mam-gu, near Llanelli. Her hair is set in bold waves, as was the fashion in those days. She is standing with her father, their arms entwined, their eyes slightly closed, because of the bright sun. Tad-cu. His age then similar to mine now. There is no picture of my father, at least not here. A studio portrait of him used to hang in my mother's bedroom in the old house. My father in his uniform, his head leaning cheekily to one side. And much, much younger than I am now.

There were other photographs, too, in Pentrepoeth. Two or three lived on the mantelpiece, more still in Mam's room – I can't remember them all, and this is really not surprising, given that I knew so few of the subjects. 'Before your time, Daniel *bach*,' Mam would say, without elaboration. But no, Mam, that's not right, they weren't all before my time. I know, for a fact, that I was the baby in some of them. In a pram, in a pushchair, in someone's arms. Surely that gives me rights?

I would enjoy telling my friends stories about these strangers from the past. There is nothing odd about that, of course. But, in my case, these anecdotes had, I think, an additional function. They gave me a means of declaring my rights, of staking my claim to a kind of ownership. I'm not sure now where I got hold of the stories – from my brother, more than likely – but through telling them I felt, in time, that I came somehow to know these people, to rediscover a connection with them.

I remember the picture of Wncwl Alun, a thin sliver of a man with round spectacles. He became a transatlantic pilot in my stories. (Didn't I have the Brooke Bond cards to prove it? To show them, the doubting Thomases, *precisely* what Wncwl Alun's Boeing 720 EI-ALC looked like.) And the picture of Dad, of course. 'Dad was a sea captain in the war and he killed a lot of Germans!' This time I had an abundance of cigarette cards to back up my case. It was, I suppose, all quite diverting, in a silly, boyish way. But my stories also proved useful in deflecting unkind comments from some of the more spiteful among my childhood acquaintances. 'Your Dad's run away 'cos your mam's a slag.' That sort of thing. I'm pretty sure we had a picture of Wncwl Wil, too, but I can't for the life of me remember where.

Anyway, there's no fireplace here, no mantelpiece, and the pictures have all gone. I can't say how many. I can't say how many other things, either. Because everything is somehow out of place now – the furniture, the jug, the clock, Mam herself, moving about in the kitchen – nothing's where my memory says it should be. And it's difficult to fill the gaps, then, when you don't have a pattern to work to. 'A few lost letters may make a sentence unintelligible,' Wallace said. He was talking about animals, of course, not furniture. About animals and the invisible boundaries that kept them in their proper habitats, the kangaroo and cockatoo in Australia, the tapir and the hornbill in Bali. But the same rules apply. A place for everything and everything in its place, as Mam-gu would have said. But not here. I shall never be able to make sense of this place, to see it whole. My mother's flat is a broken, incomplete sentence, scarcely more than a jumble of words, stray syllables. Too many of the native letters have died out. Others have migrated, God knows where.

My mother calls out from the kitchen. 'Home Guard Tad-cu was. Never in the Army. Not Tad-cu.'

'Yes, Mam, I know. The Home Guard.' Of course I know. That wasn't the point I was trying to make.

I am pouring each of us a sherry when the girls ring and let themselves in. Mam smiles for the first time since my arrival. They take a chair each from under the dining table – the room is too small to accommodate more than two armchairs – and place them either side of their grandmother, so that they can help her open the small, neat parcels they have brought with them. I dare say they contain the usual mixture of scent and soap and other toiletries. Each item has been wrapped separately, in shiny paper, and tied with a ribbon. Opening the parcels will take some time, I know, as Mam will want to provide a commentary on each; the girls, too, will want to expound on why they chose this item rather than that, on the virtues of Body Shop over some other outlet. I put my sherry on the table and go to the kitchen.

I look for a suitable knife to cut the cake. It is a creamy chocolate cake more to the girls' taste than my mother's, which is not surprising, given that it is the girls who have chosen it. It will prove something of a challenge, I fear, however keen the blade. And it is now, as I remove the cake from its wrapping, transfer it to the wooden bread board, that I hear Mam stirring into speech. I'm not sure what prompted her. Perhaps it was the music. Al Bowlly is singing now. Al Bowlly, of all people. Or the scent. They say that nothing can beat smell for reviving dormant memories. Or maybe it's just that this is how she is with the girls. How the old are with the young. There's nothing to be lost on either side. And because they are all girls, of course. They are in it together.

She's talking about her childhood. I have heard these stories many times before. I could even tell you in what order she will tell them. It's as though they were all tied to a piece of string, she'd light one end and there'd be nothing for it then but to wait patiently until the flame ran its course and petered out. Not a string. A fuse. A sparking, spluttering fuse, but without the explosives. Bethan has mentioned a school outing. So this is the end at which she lights the fuse.

'We had four free passes a year, see, because Dat worked on the railway. Go anywhere, see. Without paying.'

They could go as far as Scotland.

'We went to Scotland once.'

And turn back after a cup of tea.

'Got off at Gretna Green and came straight back!'

My mother laughs. She takes a sip of sherry, leaving a gap for her audience to respond, for me to carry in the girls' drinks.

'I'll bring the cake now.'

I return to the kitchen, knowing that I must be quick. But the fuse has a life of its own.

'And her hair went yellow then.'

The yellow hair. Because she's catching the early morning train to Bridgend now. And the train is all she needs, to take her from Gretna Green to Bridgend and the yellow hair. Catching the train to the munitions factory.

'The powder, see... The powder in the explosives... Turned your hair...'

At this point she will usually tell the story of the girl who lost her hands: the girl who was working in the detonator section, and the detonators exploded, a whole box of them. And she was just one of many, she'd say, during those years, the years that Mam spent on the Home Front. She will detail this story with the same diligence, the same desire to put on a polished performance, as when she tells the story of the train-going-to-Scotland, or the hair-turning-yellow.

But this time she doesn't. She pauses. 'Yes, turned your hair yellow...' Pauses, and thinks better of it. There can be no other explanation. Instead of telling the girls about the detonators, the mangled hands, she stays with the hair. She describes how they would have to colour their hair every week before they'd go out. 'Patti Pavilion... That's where we'd go dancing in those days... The GIs would be there, see... That's what we called the Americans... GIs...'

I have cut the cake and placed four pieces on separate plates. I bring them into the living room on a tray, singing 'Happy Birthday'.

The girls join in. Mam does her best to look appreciative, although I know that she dislikes fuss.

'Just a small piece for me, Daniel,' she says, as I place the plate on her lap.

'That's as small as they come, Mam.'

She looks anxiously at the icing and chocolate cream. Puts the tiniest morsel on her fork and passes it to her mouth.

'Mm. Nice. Very nice.'

As a rule, following the usual sequence of anecdotes, I should expect my mother to move on then to that other factory, in Cwmfelin, where she made jerrycans: a much more congenial place of work than Bridgend, by all accounts, and less perilous, for obvious reasons. She would describe how she did messages for her dad, when he was on duty. (In fact, I thought she was already warming up for this chapter in her recollections when she mentioned the Home Guard.) And having talked about jerrycans for a while, and her father's errands, she would then, given a fair wind and a receptive listener, describe how she met my own father, when he docked at Swansea after the war. 1947, she'd say. April 1947. And she'd stop, then, for a while. 'Why am I telling you this?' she'd say. 'You don't know who I'm talking about.' She'd turn to me then and say, 'You don't remember him either.' And turn back to the listener. 'Never knew his father, see. Not really.' And stop again although, of course, my father is no more a stranger to me than any of the other characters about whom she's been spinning tales.

So this is what I expect. Given a fair wind, an attentive audience. But, this time, she isn't afforded that indulgence. No, not even on her birthday. Because Nia now has a plastic bag on her lap. She is taking out the contents with great care and placing them on the table. A cardigan. A skirt. A set of pearls. In so doing, she is declaring that the stage is now hers by right, that the pause in my mother's story is an opportunity for her to embark on her own, for which the clothes she is now returning are the props. The story of how she, Nia, made everybody believe that she was an old woman. 'Edith Sorrell, Mam-gu. That was her name.' Not that Edith Sorrell was a real person, of course, she was just a character in a book. And how sad it was that this Edith Sorrell had lost her son, but then she found another boy, Robert was his name, and that made her a little less sad, yes, except that there was another boy again, his name was Niker, and he was nasty. 'Well, perhaps not really nasty, not deep down, you know what I mean, Mam-gu, like perhaps it wasn't his fault?' And one day they had a big falling out, these two boys, but Robert had learned to fly and he climbed up onto a table…'

Despite leaning forward in her chair, despite setting her eyes and ears diligently to the task, I can tell that my mother is overwhelmed by this breathless outpouring. I ask Nia not to tire Mam-gu, I explain that people do not always appreciate being told the story of one's favourite book or film, no, nor even one's favourite play, not even if one had the lead role. I say this cheerily, jokingly, of course, not wishing to hurt feelings. '*Twt-twt*,' my mother says, and tells me not to be so mean. In any case, Nia is a determined creature and has no intention of curtailing her story, not for anyone, particularly as the best is yet to come. 'And he climbed up onto the table…' At this point Nia turns to me, with that look so characteristic of the ten-year-old, made up in equal parts of trepidation and mischief, that says, 'I'm going to tell Mam-gu about how you made a fool of yourself at the drama workshop.' Which implies, also, that the story has already done the rounds at school. That she has, in fact, worked it up into quite a little party piece. So that, you might say, the fuse has a kick in its tale after all.

I have no option but to intervene. And if my mother and daughter will not allow me to extinguish the fuse entirely, then at least I can move it to a safer place, where it can do less harm. So that is what I do. I take hold of Nia's story and make it my own.

'The mother...'

With an inventiveness that surprises even me, I describe how the boy's mother – that is, the real mother of the real boy who was standing on the table – had been frightened nearly out of her wits as she watched the screen in the lobby at Tŷ Dedwydd ('She was there the same time as me, Mam, when I was waiting for Nia') and thought that her son was about to have a nasty fall. Seeing her in such a state – because she was really quite beside herself – I took the bull by the horns, as they say. ('Do you realise, Mam, that I've been doing translation work for them? Yes, for some time, now… And that I'm quite friendly with the teacher? Cerys her name is.') Yes, well, so I took the bull by the horns, I went straight to the room where they were rehearsing, to let Cerys know that the boy's mother was anxious, so that I could come back then and assure her that all was well, that everything was under control, that there was nothing to worry about. Yes. Because there was a rope, you see. Wasn't there, Nia?

It is a credible story. And its credibility is enhanced, I believe, by my somewhat stumbling, unpolished delivery. That, after all, is the nature of this particular story: it is a tale of stumblings. Its delivery, therefore, is at one with its content, which is only right and proper. Moreover, it is a story, to judge by the expressions on Nia's and Bethan's faces, that is believed. This surprises me a little, as I have not said so much as a word to them before about the boy's mother. And I am so delighted with my performance, so surprised at the amount of pleasure it has given me, that I am unable to resist taking the story one step further. You may well ask why. I ask myself why. Such is the power of adrenalin, of an eager audience, of their eyes, yes, even Mam's eyes, craving more.

'And the girls will be seeing a good deal more of me at Tŷ Dedwydd…'

The girls look at me expectantly. I know I am pushing things a bit far now, this is not really part of the script. But there's no going back.

'If I get the job… the job I've applied for.'

The girls look stunned. Of course they do. I must say that I have stunned myself. My mother, for some reason, simply raises her eyes to the ceiling and shakes her head.

'But Daniel *bach,* Daniel *bach*... You've tried for that job before… Haven't you heard from them yet?'

14. Sphinx

Near the close of an exceedingly warm day, I was sitting, book in hand, at an open window, commanding, through a long vista of the river banks, a view of a distant hill, the face of which nearest my position had been denuded by what is termed a land-slide, of the principal portion of its trees. My thoughts had been long wandering from the volume before me to the gloom and desolation of the neighbouring city. Uplifting my eyes from the page, they fell upon the naked face of the hill, and upon an object – upon some living monster of hideous conformation, which very rapidly made its way from the summit to the bottom, disappearing finally in the dense forest below. As this creature first came in sight, I doubted my own sanity – or at least the evidence of my own eyes; and many minutes passed before I succeeded in convincing myself that I was neither mad nor in a dream. Yet when I described the monster (which I distinctly saw, and calmly surveyed through the whole period of its progress), my readers, I fear, will feel more difficulty in being convinced of these points than even I did myself.

The chief peculiarity of this horrible thing was the representation of a Death's Head, which covered nearly the whole surface of its breast, and which was as accurately traced in glaring white, upon the dark ground of the body, as if it had been carefully designed by an artist. While I regarded the terrific animal, and more especially the appearance on its breast, with a feeling or horror and awe – with a sentiment of forthcoming evil, which I found it impossible to quell by any effort of the reason, I perceived the huge jaws at the extremity of the proboscis suddenly expand themselves, and from them there proceeded a sound so loud and so expressive of woe, that it struck upon my nerves like a knell and as the monster disappeared at the foot of the hill, I fell at once, fainting, to the floor.

I bought a copy of Poe's *Tales of Mystery and Imagination* in the second-hand bookshop near the castle. On the cover is a picture of a girl in a white nightdress reading a large heavy tome by candlelight. Her face is suspended between the darkness and the light. 'A present for my daughter,' I told the man behind the counter. He nodded. I kept the book in its paper bag until I reached home.

If you can endure the florid prose, the story is easy enough to follow. The narrator is looking at a small insect climbing the thread of a spider's web on a window a mere inch from his nose. He sees, however, because of the backdrop of hills and trees, not an insect but rather a great monster: a beast as big as a ship with wings a hundred yards long. He believes with such certainty in the verity of this illusion that he even *hears* the beast's dreadful howls and falls into a dead faint. Yes, it is all quite absurd.

You will tell me that I must not be too heavy-handed. That this is, after all, a work of the imagination. Yes, I'll grant you that. And I'll grant you more. A few of the details do actually bear closer scrutiny. The beast itself, for example. This is, without a doubt, according to Poe's detailed description, an authentic creature. Its name is *Acherontia Atropos*, one of the Sphingoidea: more specifically, the Death's-head Hawkmoth. Its name derives from the markings on its thorax which, in part, if you are given to such extravagant comparisons, resemble the silhouette of a human skull. (You can see this feature clearly enough on the Hawkmoth in the National Museum's public gallery, although I'm afraid this specimen's colours have much faded.) And yes, I'll also grant that this Sphinx moth does, indeed, squeak in a manner which, if it were ever amplified through a powerful sound system, might well resemble the 'loud sound' imagined by Mr Poe.

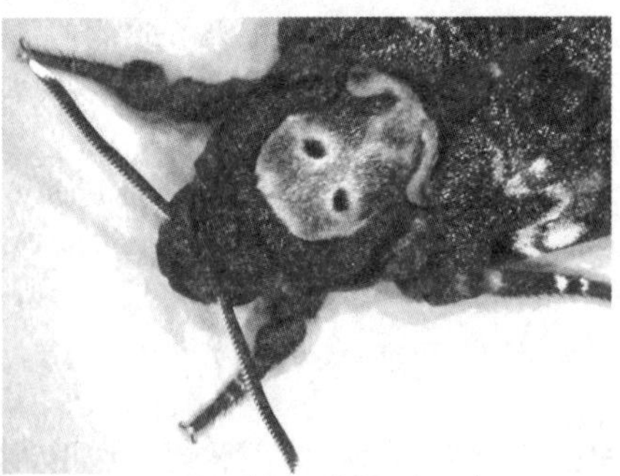

Death's-head Hawkmoth

So far so good. Unfortunately, the author does not maintain these standards of verisimilitude. Take the death's-head, for example. As I said earlier, this is to be found on the creature's thorax. The author quite risibly locates it on its 'breast'. And that squeak. Why, I wonder, is it 'so expressive of woe'? No, I don't wonder. I know very well. It is because Mr Poe, dragged along on the coat-tails of his own whimsy, requires it to be so. We know why the Sphinx moth squeaks. It does so to attract bees and induce in them a somnolence which gives the little thief free rein to steal their honey. An underhand trick, certainly, but not one designed to instill fear: quite the contrary. The author has simply distorted the facts to spice up his tale.

But the story contains an even more serious error of fact. America is not and never has been home to the death's-head Hawkmoth. It has never, as far as I know, spent so much as a summer holiday there. Now, it is possible that the author encountered a specimen during one of his seasonal visits to London or Europe. But Poe himself says, elsewhere, that New York is the location for the 'gloom and desolation' alluded to here. The whole foundation of his narrative, therefore, is a blatant untruth.

So I am forced to ask myself, should I tell Cerys about these flaws? Should I suggest to her, politely, that Poe's hero, far from being blind, was prone to see *too much*? That she should perhaps seek elsewhere if she needs an explanation of her condition. When all is said and done, Edgar Allen Poe was no more blind than his fanciful hero, so what can he know of the matter? Yes, when all is said and done, a moth is a moth. It lays eggs. It steals honey. It, in turn, is eaten by bats and birds. That is its meaning, and it is a meaning we should respect.

I translated the first few lines. If you understand Welsh, you may judge whether I have captured something of the flavour of the original.

Ar derfyn diwetydd cynnes odiaeth, eisteddwn, â llyfr yn fy llaw, yn ymyl ffenest agored. Trwyddi, ceid golygfa helaeth o lannau'r afon, a'r tu hwnt i'r rheiny, yn y pellter, gwelwn fynydd yr oedd ei wyneb wedi'i ddinoethi o'r rhan fwyaf o'i goed gan yr hyn a elwir yn 'dir-lithriad'. Bu fy meddwl yn crwydro ers amser oddi ar y gyfrol yn fy llaw tuag at drallod a digalondid y ddinas gyfagos. O godi fy llygaid, trawodd fy ngolwg ar wyneb moel y mynydd, ac ar wrthrych – ar ryw anghenfil byw, erchyll ei wedd, a symudai'n chwim o'r copa i'r gwaelod gan ddiflannu wedyn i'r goedwig drwchus.

It was an interesting exercise, but I soon tired of it and proceeded no further.

15. A Lie

Yes, of course, I lied when I told my mother and the girls that I'd tried for a job in Tŷ Dedwydd. So I suppose it's hypocritical of me to cast aspersions on others. Except that it was not, in my case, a premeditated act. It was more what I would call a lie of convenience. A little wedge of a fib designed to fill an awkward gap. And, as it happens, it was the only lie I could lay my hands on at the time. Although I had not for a single moment considered a change of career, or even so much as glanced at the *Western Mail*'s situations vacant pages, I knew quite well that such a position was available. I knew more. I knew that *happinesstheexperience.com* had 47 vacant posts. I knew that they were seeking an engineer to maintain the Astrojet Simulators at their American Adventure Park in Derby. I knew that workers were needed at the Fun-with-Clay Experience in Cornwall. And I knew that the new centre at Tŷ Dedwydd in Cardiff required a Project Officer. I knew all of this because it was I who had translated the advertisements, every one.

As I say, I had no interest in being a Project Officer at Tŷ Dedwydd. I am an entomologist and know nothing of the leisure industry. You might well ask why, then, did I not retract my lie, once it had served its purpose? Why did I not say I was merely speaking in jest?

The answer is simple, if not altogether honourable. Because then I should have had to admit to the lie, and the reasons for the lie, and if not the real reasons, then some other, made-up ones. And you can imagine, I'm sure, what contortions would have followed: the further lies and evasions, to hide the shame of the first untruth. Much easier, then, just to follow it through. A lie can, after all, in a sense, be made true if you stick with it, if you refuse to use it as a means of disguise or deceit, if you set it, on the contrary, as a goal, a *desideratum*. Perhaps, indeed, this is the only means of drawing its sting.

16. Interview

Your letter was only the start of it, one letter and now you're a part of it...la la la... Now you've done it, Jim has fixed for it you, and you and you. There must be something... ba ba... Something... ba ba... Something...

What comes next? *Something...ba ba... Something... something that you always want to do, the one thing that you always wanted to... Now you've done it, Jim has fixed it for you, and you and you and you... ba ba ba... Jim has fixed it for you, and you and you and you-ou-ou.*

The words come back to me as I remember the tune. Like a river, carrying its tiny pieces of quartz and flint from source to sea. I watched *Jim'll Fix It* every week – it was on after *Doctor Who* on Saturday and my mother would come in just before the end to catch *The Generation Game* – but I don't think I could ever recite the words separately, independently of the tune. How I have remembered the tune, I cannot say. It is as banal as the words. But that is how it works. The tune plays, the little flints of words begin to flow again. And not only the words, but the whole paraphernalia. Jimmy Saville in his tracksuit, the leather chair, the inane grin, the enormous cigar, the kitsch rings, the way he would strike the arm of the chair with his hand, and bingo! There it is, the big round badge, declaring to the whole world that *Jim Fixed It For Me.*

What did Jim fix? I'm not so sure. In fact I think that most of those little sherds of flint must have sunk into the mud. Children visiting a chocolate factory. And the one where they got to appear in a special episode of *Doctor Who* and no-one knew what to say. I remember that episode as well. I recall the children's embarrassment and my certainty, at ten, perhaps eleven years of age, that I never, ever wanted to be in their shoes. Yes, *Doctor Who*. Jim fixed that. And now, another episode has slipped back into place. Peter Cushing, hero of the old Hammer Horrors. The episode where a rose was named after his late wife. I remember him smelling the flower. And the scent, in turn, stirring the actor's memories. Or so it seemed. He was an actor, after all. This was television.

So, then, it was the cheap jingle that reminded me of these things. And what brought back the cheap jingle? It was the interview at Tŷ Dedwydd.

At a quarter to eleven a young man met me in Reception. Thin and pale-faced, he spoke with the hesitancy of one who has been cloistered in silence for many years. He told me that Dr Someone-or-Other was ready to see me. I said 'Pardon me' twice, but still didn't catch the name. 'I'm the first, I suppose,' I suggested, in an effort to initiate a little conversation, to settle our nerves. He blushed and smiled.

Cerys was waiting for me outside the room. Under other circumstances, a familiar face would no doubt have raised my spirits. On this occasion, however, I felt acutely embarrassed. This was an over-reaction, I know. I am altogether too sensitive in such circumstances, too anxious about the feelings of others. So be it. The truth is that I had not told Cerys about my decision to apply for the job. I had not told her for the simple reason that I had no expectation even of being offered an interview. But then, having been offered that interview, I should indeed have informed her. I offer no defence to such a charge except to say this: perhaps such a move would have been misinterpreted – as an attempt to curry favour, to get her to put in a good word for me, that sort of thing. My situation, you might say, was compromised.

And yet, when Cerys met me at the door, she seemed not at all surprised. As though she already knew. Had perhaps known all along. Did my embarrassment abate? No, it did not.

'Daniel Robson... Dr Bruno...'

Dr Bruno did not at all resemble Jimmy Saville. Whereas the DJ rejoiced in his athletic exploits, his lithe physique, it was clear that Dr Bruno had dedicated himself with equal rigour to cultivating his belly and his jowls. He was wrapped in a red jacket and black shirt, topped by a big white dicky-bow. The jacket was of a more fashionable cut than that of a Butlins Redcoat and less grand than that of a circus ringmaster, yet in the round – and I use the word advisedly – Dr Bruno had about him an air that reminded me of both.

The Doctor rose from his chair and shook my hand. This is when I realized that the Doctor's height was fully equalled, if not exceeded, by his breadth. Indeed, I should say, without a word of exaggeration, that I had never seen a specimen of humanity so closely approximating the spherical as Tŷ Dedwydd's own Dr Bruno. And owing to the striking combination of red and white in his livery, I am quite certain, if I had had a telescope to hand at that moment and had been bold enough to hold the wrong end to my eye and gaze through it at Dr Bruno, yes, I am quite sure that I should have spied a perfect ladybird.

'Ma'n dda 'da fi gwrdd â ti, Dan.'

The Doctor's opening sentence told me three things. Yes, of course, it conveyed the standard pleasantry that he was pleased to see me. But I am referring to deeper meanings. First of all, it told me that he was a native of the west. For do not accent and idiom betray our roots just as clearly as the ladybird's spots betray hers? What is home for the *Coccinella septempunctata* is *terra incognita* for the *Adalia bipunctata.* And vice versa, of course. Although I could not be certain whether it was from the uplands of Llansawel or else the lusher acres of Ciliau Aeron that the specimen in question had flown, I was reasonably confident that these two parishes marked the extreme boundaries of his likely habitat.

The second thing that the greeting told me about Dr Bruno was this. His voice had a more guttural quality than is normal, I believe, in the areas I have mentioned. This may be no more than a slight speech impediment. On the other hand, it might also suggest that there are – how shall I say it? – exogenous elements mixed in with the expected west Walian characteristics. For the uninitiated, how easy it is to confuse one of our rare native species – the five-spot, for example – with some alien coloniser – the Harlequin, say. And I am a dilettante, at best, in matters concerning accents and dialects.

Thirdly, the sentence told me that Dr Bruno was a kindly and self-effacing man, anxious to put me at my ease. Even though the familiar *'ti'* had an effect on me quite opposite to that intended, in fact profoundly disconcerted me, as it did not conform to the usual interview *etiquette* – yes, notwithstanding this, that little word proved to me that he was a man of humility, doing his best to put himself in the shoes of the quivering interviewee before him.

'I am very pleased to welcome you to Tŷ Dedwydd.'

Whilst uttering this greeting, Dr Bruno raised his arms in the air, somewhat after the manner of the Pope speaking *urbi et orbi*. Or perhaps again, as I said before, like a ringmaster. The effect was enhanced by the dramatic backdrop. On the wall behind the Doctor was a huge mural depicting the inside of a theatre so that, as he spoke, as he waved his arms, it seemed for all the world that he was delivering an oration on stage, or conducting a choir, or else warming up the audience for the entry of the lions. I recollect few of the details, save that the theatre had, set about its stage, an abundance of little windows and doors and balconies, and that its illusion of three dimensions made the interview room appear as though it extended a further fifty feet or so behind the Doctor. It was all rather dizzying and I did my best to avert my eyes.

The Doctor then introduced me to two younger men, Hefin and Wilbert, who sat either side of him. They, by contrast, were dressed soberly, in dark suits and ties. Hefin, the Doctor said, represented the organisation's training section. Wilbert was the company's accountant: he wore earphones.

I sat down and we chatted briefly about the unseasonal chill in the air. 'An old fox of a day, isn't it, Dan?' said the Doctor. But I was not at my ease with small talk. The sight of that theatre, so large, so insistent, weighed heavily upon me. And you may judge it rather late in the day to change tack, to lose my nerve, but there are times when it is best to anticipate the inevitable. Forewarned is forearmed, as they say. So I confessed to Dr Bruno my complete lack of competence in the field of drama. 'My children know more than I do, Dr Bruno... The younger one, in particular... Thanks to Cerys, of course...' Yes, there are times when it is best to be candid. Whatever happens, then, whatever mishaps befall you, it is always possible to say, 'Ah! But I did warn you!'

I cast a glance at Cerys, to underline the point. And I would happily have proceeded to confess my lack of qualifications as a translator, too, and to suggest, perhaps, that life as an entomologist was not the best preparation for a career in entertainment. But the Doctor was having none of it. 'You mustn't worry about that, Dan,' he said. 'We'll give you full training.'

'We will.' Yes, that's what he said. 'We will give you training.' As though it were a foregone conclusion. And he went on to describe, without pause, how the company was extending the reach of its work. How the splendid new centre in Cardiff was eloquent testimony to its ambitions. But did I know, he wondered, his voice full of boyish enthusiasm, his hands punctuating every phrase – did I know about the centres opened recently in Moscow and Shanghai, in Milan and Chicago, yes, and in less familiar places, too, in cities such as Yerevan, Cusco and even Meshed? I believe it was a rhetorical question, for he left no pause for reply. 'You will be part of a worldwide movement,' he said. And there was that word 'will' again. But how important it was, he said, how central to the mission of *happinesstheexperience.com*, that each of these centres take its message to the people with due respect and humility. That, although it was a global corporation – indeed, *because* it was a global corporation – *happinesstheexperience.com* had a bounden duty to reflect, indeed to embrace, the cultures of those places in which it set down its roots. It would be the devil of a thing, he said, wrinkling his brow and raising a stern finger of caution, to treat a farmer from Sarawak as though he were a New York banker, or a fisherman from Newfoundland as though he were…'

'As though he ran a chip shop in Brynaman,' I suggested, to prove that I understood the drift of his message.

'Ivy for the sheep,' he said. 'Bread and butter for the pig.'

I nodded enthusiastically. For the Doctor's wisdom had taken a pleasing new direction: a direction which I was more than happy to follow, flattered by my inclusion in the Doctor's sweeping vision.

'Sow barley in the fire,' I said.

'And wheat in the mire,' he chimed, as I knew he would, his eyes sparkling, his jowels rippling with the unexpected pleasure of exchanging rustic proverbs with a stranger such as myself. Yes, quite contrary to my expectations, I found that Doctor Bruno and I spoke the same language. We were, you might say, 'Potatoes from the same furrow.' Although I think some of that saying's honest earthiness falls away in translation. '*Tato o'r un rhych.*' Yes, that's better.

'We have come to plough a new field here in Wales, Dan,' said the Doctor. 'But the soil is heavy and the ploughmen are few…' At this point, his voice suddenly became more earnest. His eyes darkened. His jowels composed themselves. He shepherded his unruly hands and penned them, one inside the other, on the table. Yes, I thought, the small talk has come to an end: the interview has begun.

'Our mission here is simple, Dan. And yet it is the most difficult you could ever imagine. Our mission…' He paused. He pressed his fingertips together. 'Our mission here is to spread happiness.' He paused again. Put his head on one side. 'What do you think of that, Dan?'

What did I think of that? The truth is that I did not, indeed could not, think anything of it, because how could such a question have entered my mind before? But that, of course, was the Doctor's purpose: to test my initiative, my fleetness of foot. So I scrambled around for an answer. And having scrambled for as long as was seemly, I uttered a few incoherent phrases about overwork and stress, about the importance of leisure and creative pursuits, and other clichés of the kind. I am not much given to dealing in abstractions, and happiness is an abstraction in any language. The Doctor smiled at me. A considerate smile. Paternal, almost. Although perhaps also a touch patronising. I cannot say for certain.

'So, then, Dan… You consider happiness to be a form of recreation, do you?'

Yes, a touch patronising, and now a little censorious, too. After the warmth of our earlier exchanges, this rather disdainful response took the wind out of my sails. What were the simulators and the pageants and the party games and the workshops if not recreation? And scarcely that, if truth be told. A good deal less in some cases. And I would, I'm sure, have said something to this effect, but the Doctor slapped his hand on the table.

'Consider the trees,' he said.

'The trees?' I looked through the window, at the *morfa,* at its stunted shrubs and bushes. The Doctor followed my gaze. 'No, no, Dan... Not those…' He laughed dismissively. 'Those aren't trees, Dan, not real trees. You won't find any ambition there.'

'Ambition?'

'Yes, Dan. I want you to consider trees worthy of the name. Trees that will not disappoint.'

So he told me about the Banyan trees on the island of Tanna. I think that was it. It might have been Tenna. But I'm sure it wasn't Tonga. In any case it was there, on that island, that his friend, John Frumm, lived. It was John Frumm, he said, who had taught him about trees. Because you could find no trees nobler, more resplendant than these. Not in Brazil nor Ecuador nor New Caledonia nor Mozambique. In Tanna. In Tanna alone grew the King of Trees.

'Close your eyes, Dan.'

I closed my eyes.

'It is dark, Dan, almost black, under the canopy. And at first you see nothing. There are only the sounds. Of the Rainbow Lorikeet, screeching and chattering high in the branches. Of one of those splendid Jewel Beetles, landing on a leaf, just by your head. And you must have very acute hearing, Dan, to detect such a minute, delicate sound. But then, that is your specialism, isn't it? *Coleoptera.* Is that right, Dan? Is that the right word?

I nodded.

'Good. In time, then, your eyes begin to accustom themselves to the gloom. You can make out only shadows at first. And then, perhaps, a touch of brown here, of green there. But look down now, Dan. Look at your feet. Can you see it? It's very small, so I think you ought to go down on you knees for me. Can you do that, Dan? There you are. That's better. Can you see it now? That green shoot, pushing its way up through the dark earth. Can you make it out?'

'Yes, I can,' I said.

'Now then,' he said. 'It is dark. Nothing green can live in such darkness. Consider, therefore, how that little shoot must fight for light. How it must strive, year after year, to become the tallest tree in this forest of giants. It makes you think, Dan, doesn't it? Makes you wonder why it ever embarks on such a hopeless enterprise. Think about it, Dan... Think about how each tendril must stretch and stretch for every second of every hour of every day of every year. Cell by cell, ring by ring, it must grow taller and taller, fatter and fatter, in order to reach that light. Because without the light there's no life, there's nothing. Just consider those cells for a moment, Dan. Consider their teeming millions, gathering here to make bark, multiplying there to fashion a branch, a fan of leaves, but most of all, Dan, above all else, to forge that hard core, that unbelievably durable heartwood that will sustain the great ascent to the light for the next century and the next, and another after that, too, no doubt... And for what, Dan? Mm? To what end?'

I shook my head.

'And after those long, dark centuries of striving and yearning, when the tree finally achieves its full height – Can you see it now, Dan? Can you see its topmost branches, at last, at long, long last, fingering the petticoat of that unassailable blue sky? – do you think, Dan, do you really think that it is any better off for its endeavours?'

How could I know?

'No indeed, it is not. Not one iota. And do you know why, Dan?' I shook my head. 'No idea?' I shook my head again. 'Dan *bach,*' he said, with a condescension that quite froze all thought, 'Dan *bach*, it's no better off for the simple reason that every other tree in the forest is doing precisely the same thing. That's why. Year after year, century after century, every single tree stretches for all its worth towards the light. And yet none of them sees one more mote of sunshine than if it had remained a tiny sapling on the jungle floor. Why do they do it, Dan? Mm? You can open your eyes now, Dan.'

I opened my eyes. The Doctor lent forward.

'Why do they do it, Dan, these giant Banyans? Is it to lift a great canopy of leaves a hundred feet into the air? Is it to gather a vast heap of darkness below? Because either way, it's all a waste. A waste of time. A waste of energy. That's what your recreation is, too, Dan. A waste. A little twig twitching pointlessly in the air.'

With these words the Doctor sank back into his chair, tired and dispirited by these tropical imaginings. It was not, of course, my place to dispute his view of things. Under other circumstances I might well have argued that the high canopy, far from being worthless, was in fact extremely beneficial, providing, as it did, secure habitats for countless birds and insects, and that one must have an eye to the overall picture, and so on. I might have said, too, that the little saplings never, in fact, get the chance to start afresh. They always have to battle against those who set out before them. But that might have been to treat his little allegory too literally, too pedantically.

'Jim can't fix it, Dan.'

'Jim can't fix it?' I said. And remembered. 'Ah, yes. Jim can't fix it.'

The Doctor turned to his colleague.

'Hefin, please explain to our friend.'

So Hefin explained. And he did so with conviction, indeed, with a zeal which wholly belied his passivity to this point. Because, although Hefin was dressed quite formally, once animated he acquired an animal energy and restlessness. He reminded me of a boxer sitting in the corner of the ring, seconds before the bout is due to begin, his body wound like a spring. In keeping with this image, his hair was shorn almost to the scalp. I half expected a crooked scar above his left eyebrow. And Hefin related, in a muscular, phlegmy idiom, how the company had investigated, 'with the finest of fine tooth combs', the very nature and essence of happiness – its height, weight, colour and every other discernible attribute. It had done so, he said, using the largest ever sample, examining groups of all ages, creeds and ethnic backgrounds, both here in Wales and throughout the world. It had studied the kingdom of Bhutan and its concept of Gross National Happiness. It had considered whether the equation H = P+5E+3H could adequately measure an individual's level of satisfaction. It had analysed the neurological prerequisites of contentment, tracing the passage of the neurotransmitter, dopamine, along the mesolimbic pathway to the brain and assessing its impact on the *nucleus acumbens*. Hefin described, too, how they had looked afresh at Jeremy Bentham's Hedonistic Calculus. He explained how happiness scores had been allocated to every country in the world (with the exception only of those where a significant proportion of the population suffered chronic famine or the ravages of war or some other condition which might distort the results), employing a wide range of objective criteria, and yielding, after two years of intensive labours, the figure of 5.03 out of 10 for Bulgaria, 6.21 for India, 7.24 for Italy, 7.41 for Mexico ('A bit of a surprise, that one,' said Hefin),

8.39 for Switzerland, and so on. And he said a great deal else, besides, which I can no longer remember.

'Amazing,' I said.

'But for what, Dan?' said the Doctor, who had emerged from his slough of despond. 'Of what use is such a steaming heap of statistics?' He looked again at his colleague.

And then, Hefin explained, after the company had concluded the larger part of its survey and swallowed the bitter pill of disappointment, after it had returned to the world of simulators and the need to generate profit, a remarkable thing happened. An accident, in fact. Something no-one would ever have dreamed of including in the official investigation. And perhaps that was just as it should be: that the company found the answer to its profoundest question without even looking for it. 'I'm sure you'll agree,' he said, 'when I tell you what happened.' And this is what he told me.

A questionnaire was sent to all the staff at Tŷ Dedwydd – a dry run, as it were, to see whether it was worth the bother, after the disappointments of recent months. It contained ten questions. 'Only the tenth concerns us today,' said Hefin. The question was this: *How content are you with your life at this moment*? That is all. A woolly jumper of a question. A question which I, an entomologist used to more exacting methods of inquiry, found embarrassingly inadequate. Yes, as deficient as Poe's giant moth. I might have suggested as much, too, because Hefin was beginning to try my patience. But the answers, he said, were astounding. Or, rather, one of the answers was astounding. So astounding that it alone compensated for all of the others, for their bland predictability. Alun, a shy, diffident young man – the same young man, it transpired, who had met me earlier in the lobby – had declared, against all the odds, that he was as happy as Larry, thank you very much: content in his work, fulfilled in his social life, optimistic about his future prospects, yes, he ticked the top box for every question. Because hadn't he just found a pound coin in the photocopier?

Everyone was amazed, said Hefin. Alun had recorded the highest score. Alun, of all people. Some, of course, dismissed the result. He was simply far too easy to please, poor dab. He was an anomaly, an aberration. Others retorted angrily that he was pulling their legs, the bastard. Look at his other answers, they said. He watches videos of *The Thunderbirds*. He eats pot noodle for dinner. He must surely be the saddest, most pathetic, most dejected of all the company's staff.

There was nothing to be done, said Hefin, but to test the validity of this puzzling result in the time-honoured fashion: by repeating it and comparing the findings. That very same questionnaire, therefore, was sent to a representative sample of companies and then, within each of these companies, distributed amongst a cross-section of social, ethnic and other groups, ensuring that each of them contained *one* person (who, in turn, would vary according to class, gender, ethnic background, and so on) who would (by accident, as it were) discover a pound coin in their photocopier a few minutes before completing the questionnaire.

The same remarkable results were obtained.

'Astonishing,' I said.

'Yes, Dan,' said Dr Bruno. 'Astonishing. But why? Why do you think finding a pound coin in the photocopier made such a difference to these people's lives?'

Yes, why, indeed? 'Surely not because they were a pound better off,' I ventured.

'I hardly think anyone is as poor as that,' said the Accountant, dryly.

'You're quite right, Dan,' said the Doctor. 'The pound coin wasn't the reason. No, not in itself. How could a single pound coin lead to such an access of satisfaction and fulfillment? No, the reason was this. Each one had found that coin without seeking it, without asking for it, without having to do anything but be himself, there, in that place, at that time. Do you see what I mean?'

'Like a free gift,' barked Hefin.

'Like a blessing,' intoned the Doctor. 'As though the Universe had come up to him and placed a fatherly hand on his shoulder and said, Don't worry, old chap, we're on your side. You're one of the anointed. Wherever you walk, there, in your footsteps, flowers will bloom.' The Doctor stretched out his hand before him, as though greeting the anointed one himself. 'And here's a golden sovereign, a small token of the many blessings which are to be bestowed upon you.' He paused a while so that I should feel the full import of his words. 'Blessings, Dan,' he said. 'Kindnesses. Favours. Good turns. *Mitzvot. Cymwynasau.* Call them what you will. These are the currency of our mission here.'

The interview came to an end shortly afterwards. I feared that I had failed, and failed miserably. How could I have done otherwise, as I had scarcely uttered a word? And after such a promising start, too. After we had found so much common ground amongst the potatoes and the barley and the pigs. After Dr Bruno had all but offered me the post. I was so sunk in my dejection that I did not, at the time, fully understand what happened next, and a day's reflection has cast no further light on the matter. I was already making my exit when Dr Bruno called me back. 'Before you go, my friend,' he said, 'I have one more question I'd like to ask you.' Now it is possible, of course, that the Doctor had intended asking this question earlier, before his bout of melancholy. Or perhaps, out of a sense of generosity and fair play, he merely wanted to give me a second chance. And there again, who knows, but this is the theory that most appeals to me, perhaps Cerys had motioned to him somehow, made a sign (for I had turned my back by now) – raised an eyebrow, shook her head, even mimed the shape of some word or other with her lips – and in this way beseeched her boss to give me that last chance. That would, indeed, be a fine thing, if it were true.

'Dan,' he said. 'If you had the chance to do someone a favour today – any favour – what would it be?'

Today, the day after the interview, having spoken to Dr Bruno on the telephone, having accepted the appointment (for a trial period of six months in the first instance), I should not be surprised to learn that this was, indeed, the key question. What favour? I had no need to think.

'I'd give my mother better memories.'

17. Concerning Ladybirds

Ladybird, ladybird, fly way home,
Your house is on fire, your children all roam.

We all love the ladybird. It is a colourful adornment to our gardens. But its loveability, I would argue, derives as much from its usefulness as from its attractive livery. Every gardener knows that his roses have no better friend. Many other plants, too, look to her for protection. Long ago, on the Sierra Nevada, the prudent farmer would buy crateloads of the creatures and release them amongst his crops, a bucketful for every five acres, it is said, to prey on the greenfly. (In her short life, a single ladybird can eat more than five thousand of these pests.) I believe it is this self-same utility that has bestowed upon the ladybird an aura of inherent goodness, so that her benefic image is still passed down on mother's knee, as it were, together with Snow White and Cinderella, so that we extend a special welcome to the red jacket with black polka-dots when it returns to our midst every March. It is no exaggeration, perhaps, to say that we have learned to regard the ladybird as synonymous with the spring itself, with its hope for new life, its extravagant fecundity. Certainly, in my experience, the ladybird arouses in children a fondness which they display towards few, if any, other insects. I remember Nia, when she was small, distressing herself awfully in a vain attempt to save hundreds of them on the beach at Llantwit Major, where they had got bogged down in the wet sand. How she cried, poor thing, at the sight of so many drowning.

And it was this affection, in turn, which gave birth to a store of myth and legend quite remarkable for a creature of such modest dimensions. It was not merely a red insect that the faithful saw in their fields and gardens, but the mantle of the Virgin Mary herself. In Sweden, they still speak of 'the Virgin's Butterfly'. Indian folklore describes how one exceptionally bold ladybird flew too close to the sun, singed her wings and fell back to the earth. At the last moment, she was saved by Indra himself, chief among all the gods. Which serves to explain her Sanskrit name, *Indragopa*, meaning 'protected by

Indra'. In Russian, she is *Bozhia korovka*, or God's little cow, and, as far as I can tell, she rejoices in similarly elevated titles in most languages of the world.

The Welsh name for the cocinnilled, I regret to say, is rather prosaic. '*Buwch goch gota*' is merely a little red cow. '*Buwch Goch Duw*', or 'God's Red Cow' features in the oral traditions of Pembrokeshire, but this was surely a relic of Irish settlement, and in any case it has long fallen out of use. Despite the blandness of her name, however, the insect herself shares many of the attributes of her continental cousins. My mother always used to tell me to count the number of spots on the back of a ladybird, if I happened to spy one in the house, because if I counted them correctly I would then, in due course, find precisely that number of pennies. It seems that the creature could also forecast the weather, although it was from a book of children's nursery rhymes, rather than my mother, that I learned the following:

Little red cow,
Will we have rain or shine?
If it be rain, fall from my hand,
If fair weather, fly away.

This jingle – whose jaunty rhythm and rhyme I have not, I'm afraid, been able to retain in my translation – refers to a phenomenon with which any child will be acquainted. Held in the palm, the ladybird feigns death through rolling up into a little ball, deliberately falling from its perch and lying still until the coast is clear.

The ladybird is loved by all

From a human perspective, therefore, you could say that the *coccinellidae* are a family set apart, a privileged species. On the face of things, Nature appears to concur. The ladybird's unpleasant taste keeps most predators at bay. There are exceptions, of course. I have seen swallows at dusk feasting quite heartily amongst their rather hapless swarms. I have seen their remains in spiders' webs, and it seems that the Southern green stinkbug (*Nezara viridula*) and the Masked hunter (*Redivius personatus*) are both now to be counted amongst the ladybird's natural predators. We need to recognize, too, that when food is scarce, this little innocent can turn into quite a rapacious cannibal and will tuck into her own brothers and sisters without a by-your-leave. Despite such behaviour, however, and bearing in mind that 'tooth and claw' hold sway in the garden as much as in the jungle, it is still true to say that the ladybird has few enemies when compared with other insects of similar size. And it is curious to note, in passing, that the yellow liquid exuded from the ladybird's leg joints when she is under threat – the liquid that is responsible for the insect's unpleasant taste – was once considered a capital remedy for toothache. Even her 'badness' was, at its core, a force for good.

Alas, this is not the end of the story. If Nature has drawn something of a charmed circle around God's little cow, protecting her from many a would-be predator, she has done so, it seems, because she has a much more gruesome fate in store for her. We shouldn't be surprised. Nature does not, ultimately, acknowledge favourites amongst her children. For every peace-loving Abel there is sure to be a Cain at hand, to keep him company. And in the case of the ladybird, Nature has ordained that this companion be none other than the parasitic wasp, *Dinocampus coccinellae.*

To all outward appearances, there is nothing remarkable about this parasite. It is not its looks, however, that set *Dinocampus coccinellae* apart, but rather its manner of procreation. Whereas most parasites lay their eggs in the soft larvae of other insects, the wasp has mastered a much more exacting skill. *Dinocampus coccinellae* prefers to lay her eggs in the insect itself. And, as the name suggests, the *coccinellida* is her favourite host.

It is, indeed, an astonishing feat. Unlike a passive, helpless grub, the ladybird is a serious adversary: a wriggling, sharp-toothed, armour-plated beast not much smaller than the wasp itself. I have never witnessed the event, but those who have say it is all over in a matter of seconds. For that is the time it takes for the wasp to pierce the ladybird's body and deposit its eggs deep inside her bowels. It is not, of course, a 'feat' in the strict sense of the word, as though *Dinocampus coccinellae* had any choice in the matter, as though she had to attend special workshops to perfect the technique. No, this is how it must be. The parasite exists solely for the purpose of colonising the bowels of the ladybird. It can do no other. That is its function, its *raison d'être*. Everything else is mere anthropomorphic sentimentality. But the event is none the less remarkable for all that.

The eggs laid and securely implanted, it is then that the true marvels begin. By dint of some astonishing intuition, the wasp larva knows precisely which parts of the ladybird's internal anatomy he may eat without causing his host fatal injury, and which parts, on the other hand, he must pass up, however tasty they might be. Recent research shows that the ladybird's testicles – or her ovaries, if she is indeed a lady – are a particular favourite of the *Dinocampus coccinellae,* and he can munch away at these quite happily without causing their owner any harm – or, at least, any serious harm, for of what use are the ladybird's sexual organs now?

The larva continues to nibble and gnaw in this way for a month or so, by which time he is happily plump – by which time, you might say, he is ready to be born. But if the larva, to this way of thinking, is the baby, he is also the surgeon. For this particular baby can only be brought into the world by Caesarian section. And what a skilled surgeon he is! Whilst still in the womb – please forgive these fanciful epithets, but you would, I assure you, find the proper terminology much more difficult to follow – yes, whilst still in the womb, he sets about severing the nerves that control his 'mother's' legs. (He knows exactly which nerves to target and does not interfere with any of the others.) Why sever the nerves? We shall see in a moment. Once he has done this, he applies himself immediately to chewing his way out through the ladybird's flank: the cuticle is tough, but the larva's teeth are correspondingly sharp – of course they are, for Nature leaves nothing to chance. So far so good. The surgery is complete. He has delivered himself. His next task is to build a crib, as befits the newly born. (This particular bed is, in fact, more like a hammock than a crib. It is so easy to slip back into the argot of the folk-tales.) He accomplishes this task with the utmost dexterity, using his teeth to tie together the ladybird's legs. Why, you ask, doesn't the ladybird resist these tortures, these mutilations? Why does she not fight back? Yes, you have guessed it. Because her legs are now utterly paralysed. Quite useless. That is why the wasp-larva severed her leg nerves: so that he would have a comfortable bed tonight. There's nothing like booking well in advance to secure the best accommodation. And in this salubrious retreat, still defended from the dangers of the outside world by the ladybird's prodigious deterrents, the chrysalis grows to maturity.

Thus begins the life of *Dinocampus coccinellae*. There is nothing that God or the Virgin Mary or Indra can do about it. That is how things are. An insect is an insect, whatever the stories may say.

BOOK TWO

THE BENEFACTOR

18. The Apprenticeship of a Trainee Benefactor

October 2000

I leave my potted cyclamen on the table – I thought it best to buy some little decoy in order to demonstrate that I am a *bona fide* customer – and walk over to where the fat woman is standing, gathering her bags together. I stop at a respectful distance and greet her with a courteous, unthreatening smile.

'Can I help you?' I say

She looks at me. Her little girl looks at me, takes hold of her mother's hand.

'Can I help you with your bags?' I say. 'Take them to the lift, perhaps?'

They continue to look at me, their mouths tightly closed.

'I'm going that way, you see, it's no trouble.'

The woman looks around her. Does she think I am part of some larger performance? Does she expect someone else, the store manager perhaps, to come to her aid? Or is she just trying to ignore me? It is impossible to tell. I have rehearsed these gambits carefully, in order to erase all traces of fluster, of menace. But this is the acid test.

Yes, the woman is large, and perhaps this makes her look a good deal older than she really is. And the tiredness, of course, the dark rings around the eyes. She could be in her twenties. She could be forty. One thing is certain: she needs help. Her bags, all three of them, are full to bursting. The little girl has been whingeing for some time about going to see Santa Claus and refuses to accept that he hasn't reached Howells yet: the shop is full of baubles and trite jingles are already sugaring the air, so where, oh where is Santa? Not only does her mother need help, therefore: she is also desperate to escape this premature jamboree. And that is the point, of course. That is my reason for choosing here. 'Select your subject carefully,' Hefin said. 'You might only get one chance.'

'Thank you.'

My gambits work. She relents. But her wan smile shows that it was touch and go, and that her need outstripped her suspicion by perhaps no more than a Christmas cracker or two. On our way to the lift, near the café exit, we pass an old man. He has been sniffing and coughing there since I arrived two hours ago. He winks at the girl and then at myself. To acknowledge my good deed, perhaps? It is possible: stranger things have happened. But there is a mischievousness in that wink, in the tilt of his head, which I find disconcerting. Although he is quite bald, he has bushy eyebrows, as though his hair had fled south while he was asleep and set up shop in milder latitudes.

My little good turn turns out to be a protracted affair. The large woman, no doubt emboldened by having accepted my offer and suffering no mishap, now requires me to take her bags down in the lift. This done, she then asks me to carry them out into the Hayes, where there is a taxi rank. 'If you don't mind.' As we put the bags in the cab, the little girl asks her mother whether I am going home with them, and I have to be quite nimble in my explanation, that that would be very nice, thank you, but alas I have my own shopping to do, my own little girls. I say my farewells, perhaps a little hastily, and return to my seat in Howells' café to record the Contract in my Tŷ Dedwydd log book.

I am relieved to find that the cyclamen is still on the table, where I left it. All in all, I am quite content. After a shaky start, I won the subject's confidence. What was the turning point? I cannot say, although Hefin is sure to quiz me on the matter. Anyway, it strikes me that this is no mean feat for one such as myself, a newcomer to the business of doing favours. And I feel confident that, when time and obligation permit, the large woman will look back on our encounter and draw from it some comfort, some consolation for her weary soul. The little girl, in years to come, might even remember this as the day that one of Santa's little helpers came to her mother's aid, to compensate for his master's absence.

Today, I began my apprenticeship as a Trainee Benefactor on the very lowest rung of that profession's lofty ladder. According to Hefin, who is supervising my progress, Tŷ Dedwydd acknowledges five classes of favour. The favour which I have just performed belongs to Class One. This class comprises those little courtesies which we take for granted in a civilized society such as ours but which are, nevertheless, indispensable if we are to oil the wheels of our daily commerce. Carrying a mother's shopping, helping an old lady across the road, buying a pint for some lonely stranger, supplying a few minutes of diverting conversation. Only fifty pounds a go, plus costs, and plenty of demand at Christmas time, says Hefin, so get your orders in quick. Far-off relatives, it appears, doing the best they can. It is a strange idea, to my mind, and somewhat flawed, because the subject receiving the favour will never know by whom it was given. But Hefin says that is the reason for their success. 'Remember Alun and the photocopier,' he says. Perhaps he is right.

I fetch another cup of coffee. The café is quiet now, much too quiet. I can only hope that things pick up by mid-morning, as the early shoppers begin to flag. I can hear the old man by the entrance sipping his tea, sniffing. 'Choose your subject carefully,' said Hefin. 'Read his face. Read the way he speaks to the waitress, the way he counts his change, the way he stuffs his handkerchief back into his pocket. Is he bold? Is he hesitant? Is he excessively polite? Because every movement, every gesture, will tell you something about those things you *cannot* see. Will tell you how you must approach him. How you will clinch the Contract.'

In this, at least, I knew that Hefin could not be faulted. For had not Wallace himself mastered precisely this ability to 'see' that which cannot be seen. Without it, he could never have made some of his most extraordinary discoveries. Take, for example, the celebrated case of the Amazonian moth. Having found, in the depths of the jungle, the longest 'honey tube' ever seen in a flower, Wallace knew for certain that there would be a moth to hand endowed with a proboscis of precisely the same length, a length utterly improbable for even the very largest of the *lepidoptera*. Because how else would the flower be pollinated? He had never seen such a moth. He simply deduced, from the evidence available to him, that it must exist. And for that reason I was not too disheartened by my first Contract. I was sure that my path would become smoother and clearer, as I learned its twists and turns, as I transferred my skills of close observation from insect to human subjects. As I developed a keener eye for their idiosyncracies – their needs, their weaknesses, their foibles and above all, of course, their desires.

The café at Howells is an impersonal place, and I should have much preferred spending these hours in one of the friendly little coffee shops of Pontcanna. But I am not here for my own pleasure and, in any case, anonymity is a prerequisite for effective training in my new profession. At Café Brava or Cibo's or the Cameo my face would have been too familiar. At the same time, sitting here, in Howells' café with the express purpose of duping people – call it what you will, Hefin, but that is the nub of the matter – makes me feel queasy. I fear taking one of my Contracts just that little bit too far, through being too generous, too insistent. It is a sad comment on modern society when doing someone a good turn can be regarded as eccentric, even threatening. For all I know, it might already a breach of the peace. 'Daniel Robson: you stand accused, under the Statute of Deceptions and Impostures, that you did commit a criminal act, in so much as you did willfully carry the bags of the plaintiff' – the bags stand drunkenly on the table in front of the judge, tipping their goods, a trio of silent witnesses – 'and did so in the egregious pursuit of your own aggrandizement'. Are such things possible?

Observe the subject.

I suspect that the waitress with the red hair, the one who comes by every once in a while to clear the tables, can read my face. I have a tendency to bite my lower lip when stressed, to furrow my brow. Such things betray one. I decide to hide my face behind a book: a sad figure, perhaps, but a less dubious one. There's nothing like a book, held six inches from the nose, for conferring an aura of studious respectability. I take *Two in a Boat* out of my shopping bag and push the cyclamen to one side. This is one of two titles we shall be discussing tomorrow night. Despite the fact that we're meeting in my flat (which implies, I feel, an extra obligation on my part) I have so far read only five chapters. It is an engaging book – about a Cardiff couple who set sail through storms and high seas, and have to endure endless problems with the boat and illness and so on, and the whole experience puts a dreadful strain on their relationship. It contains perhaps a few too many knots and spinnakers. Sailing is a somewhat specialist pursuit, after all, with its own argot, its recondite ways, and these are not easily understood by landlubbers such as myself. Although I must admit that terms like *topgallant futtock* do have a certain charm. Yes, and the little diagrams, too. How to fill your Royal Navy Kit Bag: that's a good one. They hold up a small but beautifully detailed mirror to the rigours of life on board ship. I should not be surprised if it appealed to Ahmed, because I believe he has a seafaring background.

Observe the subject.

The sailing couple in *Two in a Boat* are leaving Belém when I see the old man preparing to hoist his own anchor. Despite my earlier misgivings, further scrutiny has led me to believe that he might, after all, prove a suitable subject. He is clearly alone, and almost certainly lonely. A widower, perhaps. (He wears a ring on his fourth finger.) He is also short of money: two cups of tea have lasted him all morning. His jacket is well tailored but several sizes too big for him: a charity shop purchase, no doubt. Which, I've no doubt, is also true of the trousers and shoes. The whole ensemble tells me that here is a man doing his best to maintain the standards of yesteryear, the habits of a more comfortable and genteel lifestyle, but achieving, alas, only a parody, a fancy-dress version, of that blessed and lamented condition. Most importantly, he is clearly amenable to human intercourse.

This was evident from those winks, earlier this morning; or, at least, the first of them. So perhaps he will welcome a further advance. These are the things one must attend to. The details. The signs.

After sitting still for so long in the same place, the old man has difficulty getting to his feet. He leans on the corner of the table with one hand and the back of his chair with the other and tries to pull himself up, coughing and grunting all the while. He succeeds at the third attempt. He stands for a few seconds, still leaning on the table, steadying himself for his first step. Having got his breath back, he shuffles a few paces and picks up the raincoat and shopping bag which he has left on the seat opposite his own. I seize my opportunity.

'Excuse me.'

The old man starts.

'You what?'

He stares at me with bloodshot eyes.

'I think you dropped this…'

I pick up a ten pound note from the floor and offer it to him. He looks at the money and recoils as though it were a gun or a dagger. Perhaps, I think, he is hard of hearing. I repeat myself, in a louder voice. 'You dropped this.' He throws my words back at me.

'Dropped it?'

I tell him I saw the note fall from his coat pocket as he lifted it from the seat.

'My coat?'

'Yes... It fell out of your coat...'

He stares at the money again. Sniffs. And then, with what I take, erroneously, to be a first glimmer of understanding, he looks me in the eye.

'What's your game then?'

I explain, a little less coherently than I would wish – I was unprepared for such a churlish response – that I have been sitting in the far corner of the café. (I turn and point at the cyclamen in its pot.) I explain how I happened to see him get up from his seat and take his coat and then, just as he turned to go… But he is uninterested in my explanation.

'You're with *them*, are you?'

Without moving his head, the old man turns his gaze in the direction of an Indian family that has just sat down on the other side of the café. I say Indian only because the woman in the group wears a *sari* – a red one with black and gold edging – but I am not well-informed on such matters.

'Take it,' I say. 'It's yours.'

But my words are in vain.

'You're not taking any of *my* money... None of you.'

*

'You see now, Dan?' said Hefin after my morning at Howells. 'Not such a doddle after all, is it?' He chuckled, hands on hips, feet spread apart. (I am beginning to think that the boxing mannerisms are something of an affectation.) And that was only a Class One favour.' He chuckled again, smugly and, if I'm not mistaken, with more than a little amusement at my account of the day's embarrassments. 'You'll get there,' he said. 'Eventually.' Did I tell you that he has a Blaenau accent? I mean Blaenau Ffestiniog, of course, not Blaenau Gwent. There is a great deal more slate and rain in Hefin's humour than I had first realised.

Between my challenging encounters with the Howells clientele and the intense concentration required to observe and interpret their every gesture – I am, as you know, more used to passive specimens – the first morning of my apprenticeship proved quite exhausting. But there was to be no respite. 'We don't pay you to drink tea all day, Dan,' said Hefin. I truly expected him to bring out the skipping rope next, or perhaps a punch-bag.

So, that afternoon, after a hurried lunch, Hefin took me to meet one Francis Bates, who lives in a pretty little village not far from Cowbridge in the Vale. Mr Bates wished us to organize a visit for his wife.

On the whole, Hefin said, unexpected visits were held to be Class 2 favours. They required more advance preparation and consultation than Class 1. By the same token they are a good deal more expensive. It takes more than a couple of Green Shield stamps, said Hefin, to get Robbie Williams or Cliff Richard to knock on 11

Balaclava Terrace, Aberafan, and ask Mrs Parry Jones Buttersnap if he can please see his grandpa's bedroom. He spoke figuratively, of course. Favours in this category are strictly confidential.

For the first time, as we walked to Hefin's car, I noticed his limp. That he could not fully bend his left leg. Or perhaps that it was a little shorter than the other leg. And I wondered whether his eagerness always to lead the way, to guide his new charge, and his assertive demeanour generally, were not devices for disguising this disability. I mention this only to remind myself how fickle, how unreliable are our perceptions of people, how they constantly surprise us.

Mr and Mrs Bates's home was comfortable, in a florid, old-fashioned kind of way, with shag-pile carpets, velvet curtains and plumped cushions as far as the eye could see. The walls carried pictures of tranquil rural scenes. I recognised a reproduction of one of Thomas Jones's landscapes from the Museum. To the innocent eye, Mr Bates was at one with it all: a stout, rubicund, well turned-out gentleman in his seventies, a man of means and content with his lot. He was, you might say, as plumped as his cushions. Except that today a dark shadow had been cast over that contentment. And it was for this reason, I think, that Mr Bates had dressed rather formally. Although in his own house, he wore a jacket and tie, and black shoes. 'The wife's dying,' he said, stoically. 'Cancer. Three months, the doctors say.' And that is why he wanted us to arrange a visit from her son. 'I want you to get the lad to come and see her.,' he said. 'Before it's too late.' He sank into a mournful silence. I dare say he was fighting back the tears.

'So this is your son here, Mr Bates?' I asked, to break the ice. I had already observed the framed photograph on the coffee table. It showed a young Mr Bates in military uniform. He carried less weight in those days, of course, and his hair was darker and thicker, but he was still instantly recognisable. Mrs Bates sat at his side. In her arms she held a baby, wrapped in a loose white shawl. In front of them stood a boy of around four years of age dressed in a sailor's suit.

'Yes, that's *our* son, right enough.' He stressed the 'our'. Paused. 'But that's not the lad I'm talking about.'

And although it was, I must emphasise, Mr Bates who had instigated this meeting, he appeared strangely reluctant to confide in us. He stumbled over his words, as though he hadn't spoken to a living soul for many months, or as though, perhaps, he dared not speak the words that needed to be spoken. Only quite determined and pointed questioning from Hefin – there are, I suppose, times when the no-nonsense Blaenau approach pays dividends – gleaned from our client what we needed to know. The person in question – the 'lad' Mr Bates wished to visit his wife – was, indeed, Mrs Bates's son, but had been born several years before she met her husband-to-be. There was no mention of the father. As was common in those days, the mother was whisked off to some remote, hush-hush sort of place to give birth.

'They took the lad away before he was a week old,' said Mr Bates. 'Her mother told her she'd never find anyone else, not if she kept the baby.' And now Mrs Bates felt guilty, not for having the baby, but for losing it, for rejecting it. I asked Mr Bates where the son might be found.

'But... You don't... You haven't understood, have you?'

Mr Bates lent forward in his chair, placed his hands on his knees, shook his head. 'The lad doesn't want to see his mother. That's the point, you see... If the lad were willing to see his mother, then...' He looked imploringly at Hefin. 'If he *wanted* to see his mam then I wouldn't have come to you, would I?'

Yes, as I mentioned earlier, visits generally belong to Class 2. What raised Mr Bates's Contract to Class 3 was the extraordinary nature of the visitor, and the unusual steps we should have to take to facilitate a reunion. As we drove back to Cardiff, Hefin and I discussed the cruel ramifications of these circumstances. I had been not a little touched by the Bates's plight and it was clear to me, at least, that there was nothing to be done but appeal to the better nature of the reluctant son. 'It is a poor show, and no mistake,' I told Hefin, 'when a son refuses to see his dying mother. A poor show.' Hefin could only agree with my sentiments. But, to my surprise, he had no time for my strategy. Indeed, he made it quite clear that he would not be contacting the son again. 'That would be playing with fire, Dan,' he said. 'What if he turned on his mother? Remonstrated with her for rejecting him when he was a mere babe in arms? What if the visit, for him, were nothing but a means of exacting revenge? Mm? What would we do then?'

And I had to agree. How could we change history? What had been done had been done: it could not be undone. But not to lose heart, he said. Because once we reconciled ourselves to these few, irresistible facts, only one course of action remained. There was nothing for it, said Hefin, but to hire an actor and train him up to impersonate the rejected son. As Mrs Bates had not seen her first-born since he was a week old, this would not, in many ways, be too daunting a task. We would have to find someone with at least a passing resemblance to Mrs Bates, of course – the same chin, perhaps, or the same nose – if only because the father was unknown to us. One or two features of that kind, Hefin was sure, would suffice: Mrs Bates's desire to believe, her need to believe, would fill in the gaps. We should also have to provide a biography for him – an outline sketch, together with a few illustrative details from his school days, his career, his family life and so on. ('These are your grandchildren, Mam… Do you see the resemblance?') And yes, of course, he would have to mention that awful, yet wonderful, day when he was told about his natural mother. A little summary, then, the potted highlights, of his long search, its tortuous twists and turns (perhaps he had emigrated to Australia or America), the fruitless letter-writing to faceless bureaucracies, the bizarre characters encountered on the way. (A pinch of humour was essential, said Hefin, to make the dish more appealing. After all, the aim was to raise Mrs Bates's spirits, not depress them further.) Until, at the eleventh hour, he finally tracked down the object of his quest. Yes, at the eleventh hour, but better late than later, as we say in Welsh, because it was still not too late, he hoped, to heal the wounds of the past.

'But Mother, dearest Mother... Of course I forgive you.'

19. Books and Caterpillars

If I had only observed more diligently, had listened more attentively, I would surely have realised that something was afoot. If I had noticed that Cerys, in her yellow beret and lilac coat, had dressed more garishly than usual. That Ahmed had become abnormally engrossed in the contents of a brown envelope which Cerys had given him, so that he made little contribution to the discussion. But these things have become significant only in retrospect. Welcoming the reading group to my flat – a modest enough obligation, I grant you – somehow dulled my senses. I saw only the externals, I heard only the words. Perhaps, without realising it, I was ashamed of my flat. When compared with the homes of the others it is, indeed, a sad little dwelling, full of tide-me-over things that I gathered together in haste on first moving in. Flotsam. That's what such things are. In and out with the tide, not real possessions, not really possessed.

Be that as it may, my sole desire last night was to put my friends at their ease. To prove that my hospitality, although modest, was every bit as genuine, as valid, as anything they could offer. I was pleased, therefore, that Cerys and Ahmed were conversing so warmly before our discussion began. This gave the occasion a homely, friendly aura; and it made me, the host, feel that I was making a tolerable fist of things, that my role had been accepted, even embraced. And it is a difficult calculation, because the host – like the entomologist and, as I have said before, the translator – is, I think, at his best when not drawing attention to himself. Don't try too hard is the best advice. Yes. Although that itself can be hard work, of course. But then, as each of us in turn caught wind of what Cerys and Ahmed were discussing – the new developments in the Bay, as it happened – we were all soon gathered in a warm embrace and I believe no-one was in the least put out by the shoddiness of my furnishings.

So if it was at first my discomfort that blunted my senses, it was then, perhaps, my increasing comfort, my relief that things were going so smoothly after a hesitant start, that made me reluctant to acknowledge anything that might disturb our equilibrium. I began to talk more animatedly than usual, partly because of this sense of relief but also because Cardiff Bay was a subject I knew something about. I held forth, then, about the insects that had begun to colonise the still waters separating the city from the barrage; and, in particular, about the astonishing increase in numbers of sludge worm, which thrive there in the deep accumulations of mud and waste. The others, I believe, found my little discourse quite droll. I was glad, too, that Ahmed seemed much less down-hearted than at our previous meeting.

Our *esprit de corps* lasted for an hour or more. We agreed that *Hi yw fy Ffrind* by Bethan Gwanas was an amusing read which could also strike a more serious note at times, yes, and what a pity it was, said Ozi, that there weren't more novels like that in his language, meaning the Welsh of south Wales or, perhaps more particularly, the Welsh of the upper Gwendraeth Fach, I'm not sure which. 'His' language: that's all he said. And Haf told us how her Dolgellau childhood came alive again as she read the book, which prompted me to ask whether we were to expect some colourful revelations – for, if you have not read it, you should know that *Hi yw fy Ffrind* is quite a racy novel, even *risqué* by Haf's standards – and I pulled her leg rather when she blushed and refused to tell more. Yes, I was quite the life and soul.

And so we chuckled and reminisced together, in pleasing harmony, until we came to *Two in a Boat.* Our unravelling was slow, so slow that, if you did not know us, you would scarcely have noticed. If you did not realise, for example, that Ozi had begun to speak with a kind of sighing gravity that was not his custom. Saying that he wanted to hear the husband's side of the story. That the husband always got a raw deal in stories like this. If you didn't know that Ahmed was, as a rule, reluctant to cross swords with anyone but, on this occasion, found us all at fault (and therefore, perhaps, especially myself) for selecting a book so intent on baring the souls of its characters, who were, of course, not really characters at all, not as you'd find in a novel, but people of flesh and blood, 'people like you and me'. If you didn't know that Sonia was the most tolerant of souls, that she would never, ever lose her temper. Yet this is what she did. She lost her temper with Phil for protesting at the crude way, in his opinion, the author had turned the sea voyage into a metaphor for her marriage. She laughed at him. A short, bitter laugh. 'You don't know the half of it, Phil, do you?' she said. Because, if I paraphrase correctly, there are storms at sea of which those on shore can know nothing. Something to that effect. And left it at that. Afraid to say more, no doubt. Probably regretting that she'd said as much. And no-one bold enough to ask, but each of us, no doubt, interpreting her cryptic words as we saw fit. I, too, refrained from comment, although it occurs to me now that I might have said something at this juncture about my father, who was killed at sea. But I didn't. I refrained. I smiled. I tried, as you might say, not to rock the boat. I tried, as was my obligation, to hold our little family together.

*

No two families are identical, of course. Not all of us pull together as harmoniously as the ants or the bees. Not all put on such a show of synchronised living as the Monarchs, draping their coats of many colours over the trees and shrubs. Few, very few families, can emulate the terrible musterings of the locust. And if the less well favoured – be they insects or people – sometimes aspire to such standards of collective achievement, we cannot blame them, but their efforts will always end in tears. They do their best, poor things, and they never give up failing.

Consider the Tent Caterpillar. You will find no family more sociable, more agreeable than a nest-full of these moth larvae. And at the outset, at least, they thrive. Once hatched, hundreds of them set out together, a single wriggly mass, to scout for a suitable home. Their choice is always unanimous: dissent, breaking ranks, insubordination are unheard of. A V-shaped fork between tree and branch is the preferred site: it offers the best foraging and also ensures a reasonable consistency of temperature.

Unfortunately, when it comes to supplying heat, the sun is a fickle friend. Don't we all have to take measures to compensate for its serial failings? As its name suggests, the Tent Caterpillar does this by weaving itself a tent of pure silk. Nothing better manifests the self-help virtues of this family than its unfussy, uncomplaining dedication to this end. The caterpillar spins its tent, remarkably, from glands in its head and the result is highly effective at controlling the community's temperature. It may be brass monkey weather outside, but the heart of the nest, in its silken bower, is as warm and cosy as Mamgu's kitchen. A home in every sense of the word.

It is at this point, when everything seems to be going so well, that the Tent Caterpillars' intricate elysium begins to fray at the edges. As it grows, each caterpillar must venture further and further away from its refuge in search of food. This inevitably brings it face-to-face, jaw-to-jaw, with an increasing number of predators. (The Tent Caterpillar is prey to some 170 insects, many of them parasites of the fiercest stamp.) It is, of course, alive to this fact: millenia of evolution have not gone to waste. It knows, also, that most parasites, if they get their way, choose the caterpillar's head as the preferred location for laying their eggs. Yes, its head. With the benefit of this knowledge, the Tent Caterpillar has devised an extraordinary method of defending itself.

Now I have no doubt that this little creature would be much happier if it could discharge a poison or brandish a sting or bare its teeth. But it is none the better for harbouring such fanciful dreams. The Tent Caterpillar has one weapon, and one weapon only, in its armoury: it can shake its backside. And shake it again. And again. So this is what it does. And it does so with every fibre of its being. As soon as a caterpillar hears the rustle of a beetle's wings or the *dump-dump-dump* of an ant's approaching feet, it calls its brothers and sisters into action. And they come, as one, so that the whole tribe may shake its collective posterior. As though to say, *Do what you will with my arse, you dirty parasite, but you're not going to lay your eggs on my head!'*

I admire these plucky creatures. They keep the faith, whatever the odds. And I'm certain that they do, genuinely, feel safer gathering together in this way, turning their backs on the world. I admire them, and I pity them. Because feeling cosy was never much of a defence strategy. Personally, when it comes to the crunch, I have a higher regard for those of a more down-to-earth, pragmatic disposition. Consider the *Malos gregaris*, for example. These spiders have the best of both worlds. Their communities are every bit as tightly knit as the Tent Caterpillars'. Their home – a super-web that would, if relocated to Pontcanna, extend easily from my bedroom window to the eaves of Mrs Kropowski's house on the other side of the street – is both an invincible fortress and a vast trap for the capture of prey. However – and this is a very big 'however' – *Malos gregaris* are no anonymous mass, blindly following the party line. For within the miracle of collective endeavour that is the super-web, each spider is permitted his own autonomous space, where he can come and go without let or hindrance. Because, in truth, the spiders' home is not a single web at all, but rather a vast network of webs, each one slightly different from the next, individual, bespoke. For these, you might say, are the terraced houses of the arachnids, together and yet apart. Except that there are no busybodies. In fact, no-one is expected to sacrifice the least morsel of his independence. If an enemy threatens, no-one will be conscripted, because there is no need for an army: each citizen has his own weapon, his M2 Browning, mounted ready on his window-sill. *Malos gregaris* are the snipers of the spider world. If they are not, to the human mind, a particularly affectionate family, who can say that this is not part of their success? They tie their little webs together, not out of sentimental attachment, not because it is a good or pretty thing to do, but in order to achieve a mutual benefit. And if I had the opportunity to adopt the form of some creature other than myself, it is this family, the *Malos gregaris*, to which I should apply for membership. For they, I think, would offer me that balance of security and autonomy which I most prize.

*

'Thanks, Dan... If you're sure... I wouldn't say no.'

After the meeting, after the desultory chatter that followed, the ritual mending of bridges, the farewells, I plucked up courage to ask Cerys whether, if she had the time, she might help me finish the half bottle of wine that remained.

'I'd prefer coffee, Dan, if you don't mind... I'm a bit tired.'

Which was fine. Which was more than fine.

'Well, it all got a little heated, towards the end,' I said, to show that I understood how a sensitive person like herself might feel the strain of such acrimonious debate. 'A little prickly. A little too personal.'

'Did it? I didn't notice.'

Well, well, I thought. There's a thing. And perhaps, of course, she *hadn't* noticed. Or perhaps she was just being polite. It is true that she'd had little to say about either book. But I'd been too preoccupied with other things to ascribe any import to this reticence. With the state of the flat. With looking out for that tell-tale wince of offended good taste which, I was certain, Haf and Sonia would sooner or later exchange with each other.

'A cuppa, then.'

And over our coffees – a mistake, I know, at such a late hour – we spent a pleasant half hour discussing a variety of topics: my apprenticeship at Tŷ Dedwydd, the enigmatic ways of the Chief Benefactor and then Cerys herself. She told me about the lack of opportunities for actors with impaired vision, about her hope that regaining her sight would open new doors in this respect. She described, very sweetly, the miracle of seeing her family, her mother and father, her brother and his children, children who had become so close that she was all but a second mother to them. The miracle of seeing them laughing, playing, opening presents. Even of seeing them cry, she said. That, too, was a miracle.

'But sometimes I think that I don't really know them as well as I used to. I think I know them better – this is going to sound awful, Dan, but it's true – I think I know them better when I just hear them, when I touch them. You could even say, in a way, that seeing them has turned them into strangers.'

And Cerys described how her brother and her father would get cross when she cupped the cheeks of her little nephew in her hands, and scolded her for squandering the money they'd spent on her treatment, for raising everyone's hopes only to dash them with her stubborn ways. She described how they would always relent, then, and assure her that it would all come good in the end, but that she must, she really must, make more of an effort.

'But things haven't come good yet, Dan, and I'm not sure how long I can go on like this.'

I saw, in my mind's eye, an image of the unfeeling, uncomprehending father, scolding his daughter in front of the children, while they, in turn, wept in confusion, because what did it matter to them? This was the Cerys they had always known, the Cerys who saw them with her hands, her gentle fingers. And this image prompted in me a desire – a naïve, sentimental desire, I have no doubt – to right her wrong. More than that, it aroused in me a curiosity about that different kind of knowing that Cerys had described, a quieter sort of familiarity, I thought, but also, surely, more intimate.

'I'd best go home now, Dan, if you don't mind.'

I offered her a lift. And there is, of course, a pleasure in giving a favour as well as receiving one, even when that favour is as small, as insignificant as offering someone a lift. There is pleasure in the thanks that follow, in the sweet little moment of closeness.

'That's kind of you, Dan... I'm so tired... And I can't face taking a taxi... It's too late to see.'

'Too late to see?'

'Just too much work, Dan. Too much concentration. By ten o'clock the colours all break loose, I can't hold them together any more.'

She rested her head on the back of the chair and closed her eyes. 'That's better.' And breathed deeply. We continued to sit there, silently, Cerys and I. Every now and then I heard a car, hissing through the rain. Leaving a greater silence in its wake. We sat for two minutes. Three. Perhaps more. And the silence led me to a place of great tranquillity, a place I recognised but had not visited for some time. Perhaps I did not realise it then, but today I truly believe that this tranquillity was made possible, at least in part, because Cerys could not see me. I enjoyed, for a short while, the rare pleasure of being invisible.

'Please forgive me, Dan.'

I said there was nothing to forgive. But her apology was like a kiss. I told her to keep her eyes closed. We went out into the night, arm-in-arm.

Yes, if I had only observed more closely, more diligently.

20. Tracking Cerys and Ahmed

It is five o'clock on Thursday afternoon and already dark. I am sitting at the Hayes Island Snack Bar, waiting for Bethan and Nia, so that we can begin our Christmas shopping. This is no common-or-garden shopping, mind you. We have, over the last two or three years, developed a ritual of our own to lend a little frisson to what otherwise might become a somewhat routine, mechanical activity. We go to our favourite shops – Virgin, Accessorize, Howells, Waterstones, Monsoon, and so on – and say out loud, as we pass by, 'Oh! That's a nice scarf!' Or 'I'd like to read one of *her* novels!' Or 'Listen to this, Dad!' While everyone makes a discrete note of the others' wishes; while I, at least, try to place these wishes in some order of priority (since they are numerous and often extravagant) according to the fervour of the ejaculation. And while all, of course, pretend that they know nothing of what is going on. It is less impersonal than exchanging lists and then waging a lonely battle through the crowds in order to fulfil the order. It also ensures that each present is to the recipient's satisfaction. And it is a merry little game. Bethan, it must be said, is a more reluctant participant these days. I believe she thinks we're being childish. She has become a touch supercilious of late.

I wrap my hands around the mug of tea. This is not the best place to sit late on a cold November afternoon, the wind whipping the city's detritus about my ankles. I am, nevertheless, fond of the old snack bar. The steaming tea, the clinking china, the genial banter – all give it an unpretentious, welcoming air. It is a place where everyone can feel at home, whatever their cast or creed. A good spot for watching the world go by, for gathering one's thoughts. Except not today. Today, there is too much to do. And the girls are late.

Cerys didn't come in to work this morning. She wasn't answering her mobile either. According to the appointments diary which Tŷ Dedwydd requires all of its officers to complete on its internal information system, she was undertaking fieldwork in Cardiff. The meaning of this term was obscure to me, but I assumed that she must be preparing or directing or otherwise participating in some open-air activity – an over-literal understanding of the word 'field', perhaps, at which you may well laugh, but this is what I thought. And it made me anxious on her behalf, particularly in light of her condition after the reading group. I have thought of nothing else all day. I admit, too, that I have come to feel a little responsible for Cerys. Why? I have been asking myself the same question ever since I said goodbye to her outside her house in Riverside. You will think it presumptuous of me, I know. And I certainly wouldn't admit as much to Cerys. But the question has a clear and unambiguous answer. I am responsible for her because she has *asked* me to be responsible for her. She has entrusted a portion of her welfare to me. And she has done so not *in extremis,* not merely to sustain her through the sort of debilitating frailty in which I found her last night, but in a more general way. For this, I am sure, is what she meant when she asked me to be her guide. She did not merely want a labrador with good road sense.

I have almost drunk the last of my tea when I see Nia approaching from behind the old library. Bethan follows, some ten yards to the rear, talking into her mobile. Despite the cold, she is wearing a short-sleeved top in order, no doubt, to show off the little rose tattoo on her arm. Nia apologises for being late and casts an accusatory glance over her shoulder at her sister, who is now remonstrating with her friend, and doing so with a vigour, with an extreme of adolescent exasperation for which a diminutive mobile phone seems a poor vehicle. A megaphone would be better. Perhaps with semaphore. As to the subject of her vituperation, I have not the slightest idea

Our perambulations come to an end on the first floor of Pier, amongst the cushions and rugs and glasses. To appease Bethan, we have spent most of our time in Zara and Top Shop. Nia's feeling aggrieved. That, I've no doubt, is why she's taking the lids off the cocktail shakers, one after the other, row upon row. 'Nia, do you have to do that?' And that is when I see them. Ahmed, to begin with, his foot on the first step of the open staircase below me. I am about to call out, indeed my lips have already parted, my tongue has readied itself to sound the 'A...', when I see him turn and stretch out a hand. It is met by another. Cerys's hand.

Cerys? What's your game, then?

I hurry back to the cocktail shakers and tell Bethan and Nia that we must leave at once. 'Why are you whispering, Dad?' says Nia, and protests that she hasn't pointed out half enough things. 'We'll come again next week,' I tell her, intending to sound cheery, but cheer and panic are not good bedfellows. I hear Cerys and Ahmed coming up the stairs, the light flutter of their conversation. I can delay no longer. By a stroke of luck, it is possible to walk straight to the upper level of Queen's Arcade without returning to the ground floor. So this is what I do. I aim for the open door. I turn left. I stand in front of Potters for Children. I immerse myself in the window display. Finger paints, only £4.99. Emu, £9.99. My brow, my neck are beaded with sweat. I wait.

A minute later, the girls appear, asking why I am in such a hurry. On regarding me more closely, Nia asks why I look so awful. 'So awful?' At first I am aghast that my inner turmoil should be so obvious for all to see. I panic at my panic, you might say. But then I think, no. Because what a perfect little stratagem this is for calling an early halt to our shopping expedition. 'Yes,' I say. 'I do feel rather weak...' I raise my palm to my brow. 'Starting a fever, I think.' Although the girls offer to stay with me, bless them, I assure them that I'll be fine and dandy once I take the weight off my feet, have something to drink, get a couple of paracetamols down me. 'I have some in my pocket,' I tell them. 'Always do. Just in case.' This does the trick. Which is a little surprising, but who can tell the workings of the adolescent mind? Perhaps my display of bluff stoicism is more accomplished than I had thought. I squeeze a ten pound note into Bethan's hand and send them off to find a taxi. A quick peck on the cheek. An already-feeling-better sort of wave. And off they go, through the big glass doors, back into the November night.

I dare not return to the shop. But I dare not wait here, in the café, either, with nowhere to hide, like a mouse in a cage. Now I do not deny that Ahmed and Cerys might well decide to leave the shop by an exit other than that I used myself and, having done so, might then not come this way at all. They have other options. But that is surely wishful thinking. Both reason and instinct tell me that, whatever the hypothetical alternatives, they will in fact dog my footsteps with a resolute, if wholly unconscious, determination. They will need to do a little more shopping, perhaps, in Gap or Mirage – yes, of course, to look for a present for Cerys. They may even choose to have a cup of tea and a sandwich in this very café where I am sitting and then, sooner or later, will go out to the Hayes, where they, too, will need a taxi to take them home, with all their bags. Which home? Well, Cerys's home, of course. She will open the door, invite Ahmed in, smile and say, 'Milk, no sugar? A little something to eat, perhaps? Sit down here, Ahmed. That's right, on the sofa. I'll be with you now.' And who knows what else? Because that is as far as I got, last night. The front door.

I leave the shopping centre as the children did, descending the stone steps and emerging opposite the old cemetery. I turn left then and stride forth towards St David's Hall. I do not look back. I cannot, I must not, look back. I pull up the collar of my coat and stare at walls, windows, advertisements, at anything which means that my face is not exposed to the world.

It is almost half past seven and the foyer of St David's Hall is heaving with concert-goers. This is a blessing, as the crowd affords me a degree of camouflage. Unfortunately, it also means that my view through the window is repeatedly obscured and it would be very, very easy, in such circumstances, to miss even the most familiar of faces, be they inside or out.

But I do see them, the familiar faces, or at least a few of them. I scan the passing crowds of shoppers, methodically, impersonally, shutting out all other thoughts and concerns, and there they are. Simon, our *diptera* expert from the Museum. Mrs Kropowski, my neighbour, with her daughter. And others. For we are all about the same business, are we not, at this season? I dare not greet them, of course, because my eyes are on duty and to speak, to yield to such distraction for even a second, might mean missing Cerys and Ahmed for ever. And that, in turn, means that I must not be seen, either, I must not give anyone the opportunity of drawing me into conversation. I turn up my collar again, but somewhat higher this time, higher than is usual, indeed higher than is fitting in a place such as this.

I sustain this posture for precisely five minutes, in the midst of the hurly burly. At the end of those five minutes the bell rings, the crowd disperses and I am left alone in the foyer. A member of staff walks over to warn me that I shall miss the first item on the programme if I don't get a move on. And, if I'm not mistaken, looks at me rather dubiously. I palm him off with a plausible enough excuse about having arranged to meet friends here, and indeed I start cursing them – *Some friends*! – to lend verisimilitude to my story. I turn back to my window, shaking my head, tutting. And that is when I see her. Cerys. Yes, I am about to give up the ghost when I spot a yellow beret. The same beret that she wore last night. And Ahmed by her side. Arm-in-arm. As I predicted, they are making for the taxi rank. They are talking animatedly, Cerys shaking her head, Ahmed nodding his. Suddenly, and for no discernible reason, Cerys looks in my direction and I could swear, for a moment, that she stares me in the eye. I stare back at her. But there's no recognition. Nothing. She continues to walk, arm-in-arm with Ahmed, as though I weren't here. And for her, no doubt, that is the case. The lights behind me have dazzled her. Or perhaps I have been swallowed up by the shadows in front, so that I am a mere patch of grey and white on the retina.

I wait until the yellow beret has all but disappeared from view and then join the crowd. I was mistaken. They're not looking for a taxi. They do not give the taxi rank so much as a glance. Having crossed the road, they walk past David Morgan's, past the Duke of Wellington, past the entrance to Wyndham Arcade. I follow, circumspectly, keeping my distance, hugging the shop fronts, ready to duck inside should the need arise. Another few yards and they turn into Mill Street. I steal a cautious peek around the corner before doing the same. The Mill Lane restaurants pulse with the rhythms of the *samba* and the *mariachi*. Despite the wintry gusts, young men and women sit outside, drinking their lagers and tequilas and alcopops. And there, between Las Iguanas and Juboraj, Cerys and Ahmed stop and wait. I also stop. I scrutinise the menu in the window of the Ranch Grill, looking over my collar every now and again to check their progress and thinking, this is no place for you, Cerys. And you, Ahmed? Surely not. But they aren't interested in the cafés. They stand where they stopped. Ahmed points towards the Marriott. But perhaps not the hotel itself but rather at something beyond it. Soon the whole hand becomes animated, as he tries to explain to Cerys what it is he can see. And what can he see? I have no idea. I stand still, staring at their staring. I look for clues. In the way her eyes follow his. (But how much of this do you really see, Cerys?) In the way his fingers touch her arm. And I understand nothing.

They carry on walking. They enter St Mary Street and are swallowed up again by crowds of shoppers. They cross the road at Gamlin's. I cross a little lower down, concealing myself behind a group of young office workers, laughing raucously at some ribald remark. It is not the best camouflage, but needs must. They turn for the station, and I think, yes, a train – or a bus, maybe – even, by now, a taxi. But the station is not their destination. They walk on, they cross the bridge by the Millenium Stadium. And I suddenly feel exposed. The crowds of shoppers have disappeared. The road is straight. The bridge offers no escape route, except for the river below. If Ahmed turned now, this very second, in order to cross the road, for example, or because he has dropped something on the pavement, or because he senses, as we all do sometimes, that someone is following him, he would see me instantly. Yes, and recognise me, too. Even with my collar raised, I know he would recognise me. I lean on the parapet of the bridge and look down at the river. At two seagulls landing on the water. At a Tesco trolley, stranded far from home.

When I raise my eyes again, Cerys and Ahmed are already in the middle of China Town and approaching the crossroads. But that's fine. I know that I can't lose them now. I know exactly where they're going. I know that, after another few yards, they will take a right turn, and then a left, and within a few seconds, certainly no more than half a minute, they will be in De Burgh Street. Cerys will open her front door, invite her visitor to come in out of the cold and it will all unfold as I had foreseen. *Milk, no sugar? A little something to eat?* I am so sure of this outcome, and so downhearted by its inevitability, that I very nearly abandon my mission there and then and take the river path home. I am already preparing a few choice verbal grenades to lob at the treacherous when I next get the chance. *So then,* I shall say, *I see that you and Ahmed are an item. Were you going to mention this to me at some stage, in passing, perhaps, in an email?* Which would be petty and spiteful, of course. So I draft a variant, a more measured, more forensic attack, a ripost worthier of my scientific calling. *So then, Cerys, did you go into town last night? Wasn't it busy? Yes, hellishly busy. How did you cope? Me? Well, I took the girls shopping. I like to have the company, you see, especially at this time of year, at Christmas time.* And pause for a moment. Leave a little gap. Like an honesty box. To receive the tinkling pennies of her confession.

Yes, as I say, I am so certain that Cerys's house is their destination, that I can scarcely believe my eyes when I see them turn, not to the right but to the left. I almost shout out, *Stop, you fools! You've taken the wrong turn!* Because Cerys has lost her way. The lights, the shadows have betrayed her once more. There is no other explanation. At the crossroads, I see them, still arm-in-arm, walking under the railway bridge. But there is not the slightest hint of hesitation or uncertainty in their gait. They do not pause. They do not ponder. Indeed I would say, by now, that it is not Ahmed leading the way but Cerys. Yes, strange as it may seem, it is Cerys who is taking the initiative, pointing, explaining, nodding vigorously. I cross the road and make a bee-line for the little shop on the corner of Court Road. This will be my refuge should the need arise. Two girls in hajibs and denims gawp at me from the pavement opposite, giggling behind their hands. I pretend to study the advertisements in the window. Out of the corner of my eye I see Cerys and Ahmed standing together, waiting. They are in Monmouth Street. Her hand, in its yellow glove, raises the knocker.

21. A Walk in the Park

We enter the park by the gap in the wall and follow the path through the avenue of horse chestnuts. My mother holds on tightly to my arm and insists that I warn her of every hole and twig and slippery leaf on the way. We inch forward, as though our shoes were made of lead. The park is littered with the debris of recent storms and my mother won't budge until she's weighed up each and every obstacle.

'High time they cleared this rubbish, Daniel, don't you think?'

'They will, Mam, they will.'

But it is sunny today, the wind has dropped and it's possible we won't get another chance to go out until the spring. And how slow will our progress be then? Anyway, I've got to keep busy.

The same scene plays over and over in my mind. Cerys (not Ahmed) knocking on the door of the terraced house. Cerys placing a hand, then, on his arm. I freeze the scene there for a moment. What is that hand doing? What is its touch? Is it taking or giving? The door opens and I see a brief shaft of warm yellow light from inside. A young boy appears, shouts 'Dad! Dad!' The father comes to the door, smiling, his hand already extended in welcome, because this is no chance visit, it has been planned, anticipated, and this is the moment of fulfilment. Yes, I can see all this. Even through the corner of my eye, even though the girls in their hajibs are still looking at me, still wondering, it is all abundantly clear. The father is a tall, slim man. He wears a blue shirt with an open collar. And, judging by his facial features, the high forehead, the slender cheeks, the long straight nose, I should hazard a guess that he and Ahmed are of similar origins. But this is a delicate business and I can't be certain. Unfortunately, I am too far away to hear their greetings, to measure their warmth, their true import. Is this the welcome dictated by courtesy alone? Would it be extended to anyone, friend and stranger alike? Or is it the sort of welcome reserved for a close relative? I have no way of knowing.

This, then, is the scene that plays over and over in my mind's eye. I press the replay, the pause, to get a better look. I peer through the zoom lens, but to no avail. Cerys wasn't in work yesterday, so I couldn't ask her. Or, rather, I couldn't sit there, waiting for her to come up to me, at coffee break, at lunch, and say, 'Guess what, Dan..?' Or even, 'Ahmed took me to see his uncle last night.' Something like that. No, because her timetable insisted that she was still immersed in field work. 'So, then, Hefin, what's this field work that Cerys is so busy doing?' He feigned ignorance. 'She's not far,' he said. 'No, no, can't be far. Try her mobile.' He said it in that bluff, slate-quarry way of his. It was a parrying move, an Ali shuffle, designed to wrong-foot his adversary. But I knew he was fibbing. In any case, I'd already tried her mobile. And what do words like 'near' and 'far' mean when you don't get an answer? She could be around the corner, on the Morfa somewhere. She could be on the other side of the world. I'd be none the wiser.

Cerys said that distance meant nothing to her when she was blind. 'Is it far, where you live?' I asked, after offering her a lift. I don't mean she didn't know her own address. No, she could tell me where she lived, of course she could. And a good deal else, besides, I'm sure, about the streets and houses of her locality. No, what I mean is this. She had regained her sight, after a fashion, but her grasp of space – of the length and breadth and depth of things – was still very shaky. 'I'd have to take lots of steps if I walked there,' she said. 'I'd be ten minutes in a taxi.' But what this meant in terms of distance was obscure to her. Or in Howells, say, when she wanted to go to the children's toy department, she'd have no problem finding the lift and could use the words 'up' and 'down' quite accurately, like anyone else. But she couldn't understand them. No, not really. Going in a lift meant standing in a box, hearing a whirring sound above her and feeling a little disturbance in the stomach. It was the duration of the whirr, the intensity of the disturbance, that told her for which floor she was bound. She heard the explanations of the sighted, accepted them, even used them when necessary, but she could not *feel* them. For Cerys, space was an elusive dimension.

But space does exist. And you, Cerys , must be in it somewhere. Today, at this precise moment, you must be somewhere.

'I don't want to go too far, Daniel. It's a biting wind.'

To my mother, space is everything. Time, however, has dissolved into an eternal yesterday: an endless sequence of mirrors stretching before and behind, so that she can never be sure which is the real thing and which the mere copy. She is her own mirror. And although she might, in all innocence and eager anticipation, look forward to a bright and shiny tomorrow, it arrives only to be consumed by its rapacious past. My mother's time is a snake, swallowing its own tail. That is what I mean when I say that, for her, only space is real. And for that reason, every disturbed divot, every stray pebble, every bump and deviation and crack in the pavement must be studied and assessed.

I do not complain. No, I must emphasise this. I know that these intensive, time-consuming scrutinies are much more troubling to my mother than they are to me. In fact, you might say that they are almost second nature to me, given the rigours of my former occupation. I feel, indeed, that I have spent half my life walking in precisely this manner, stopping every few paces, bending down to examine the little universes at my feet, waiting, staring, and sometimes seeing nothing for hours on end. For such is the privilege, and the plight, of the jobbing entomologist, who must abjure the strictures of time and become instead a part of the great vastness of small things. And this, of necessity, has become my mother's condition, too. The slower she moves, the greater the space through which she must pass. Today, the park is a jungle and a desert in one. A sea and an armada of little icebergs. It's touch and go whether she'll make it to the other side.

We pause for a while. My mother says, 'It's too far to walk to the gate today, Daniel,' although we have less than fifty yards left to go. She tells me to watch out for the young scallywags on their bikes because she almost got knocked over yesterday. She tells me to give the dogs a wide berth, too. One came up to her yesterday and barked at her. Bared its teeth and barked. She tells me not to follow this path, not to sit on that bench, not to stray onto the grass verge, because that is what she did yesterday, and 'Never again, Daniel, never again!' But it's the scallywags who bother her the most. 'I'm sure they'll keep their distance, Mam,' I say. 'No need to worry.' My mother hasn't been in the park for weeks.

What is odd is that she has begun, inadvertently, to mimic precisely those youths against whom she rails so vehemently. To protect her eyes from the glare of the sun – particularly the low winter sun – my mother now wears a hat. No, not the sober piece of sculpted millinery you would normally associate with an elderly lady of taste and discretion. 'It needs a wider brim, Daniel,' she said, when I showed her some samples in a catalogue. So I suggested other models. 'I'm not wearing that,' she said. 'That's for weddings. There's daft people would think I am, going to the shops in a wedding hat!'

Nor did she want something floppy. 'You think I want to look like Bill 'n' Ben?' No, what she wanted was a peaked hat. And although I searched high and low, I could find nothing suitable, nothing at all, and had to make do with a baseball cap from JJB Sports, a red one bearing the St Louis logo: the simplest, plainest model in the shop. She now looks like a clown, little sprigs of hair sticking out in all directions. Not a clown. A scarecrow. But she is none the wiser, and it does the job well enough.

Mam's Cap

'The trees are still fine, aren't they Mam?'

The horse chestnuts, although now quite old, have kept much of their foliage and the low November sun draws out the rich yellows, browns and reds.

'You remember us bringing Nia here to gather conkers?'

We chat quite sensibly then about how Nia is coming along with her acting. We chuckle and tut-tut, in turns, at Bethan's shopping antics, at the dreadful busyness of town, at how much people spend on presents these days. She begins to reel in some of her old memories about childhood Christmasses, about how everyone knew the value of money in those days, yes, how tough things were, even for a family like her own, her father working right through the worst of it on the railways. Because, she says, you'd no choice, see. You had to help your sisters and brothers. Your neighbours, too. Your friends. Anyone. Because people pulled together in those days. Oh, yes. And one present you'd get at Christmas, *just the one*, and you'd be grateful for it. You'd be grateful for what you got.

An old couple walk past from the direction of the bowling green. They, too, are walking arm-in-arm. We exchange smiles.

'A fine day...'

'... to be out...'

'... make the most of it...'

I imagine Mam and Dad walking together in this way, in the old age they might have had together. Dad, of course, is little more than a silhouette. He links arms with my mother – with his wife, I should say, for that is what she was to him – and they swap anecdotes about the old days. What, I wonder, would such days have been like? Would she be any the happier now, for having had them?

'Have you thought of asking the others whether they'd like to come out for a walk?'

She looks at me, suddenly alert, on her guard.

'What do you mean, "the others"?'

'At Conway Court... The ones you get on with...'

'And why would I want to do that?'

'So you can get out... You, know, when I'm at work...'

She looks away, says something which I don't catch, so that I must ask her to say it again.

'I said, you didn't have to come out with me today, Daniel,' she says. 'Not if you didn't want to. Not if it was inconvenient. Not if you had something else to do.'

She makes these utterances with a surprising assurance, pausing after each for greater effect. In fact, so assured is her little homily that I play with the idea of telling her the truth. Of explaining that I should, indeed, prefer to be elsewhere. That I have matters to attend to, quite pressing matters. That there is one matter in particular that I have neglected in order to be here, amongst the leaves and the dogs and the scallywags and the empty words.

'But this is what I want to do, Mam.'

So we walk a little further. Only the rotting cases of the conkers remain, the same colour as the earth and mixed in with the shrivelled leaves. I bend down and pick up one of the leaves. Its colour and condition tell me that it has been on the ground for some time. I examine it more closely. I hold it up to the light so that I can make out its internal structure, its veins and capillaries. There are traces of mould, probably *Guignardia aesculi*, which is particularly fond of the horse chestnut. Is that all? I'm not sure. By late autumn, the signs are ambiguous. I study the premature wrinkling, the rust-coloured blotching, the ragged perforations. Yes, mould, but perhaps not only mould. At the edge, the *dermis* and the *epidermis* have separated and darkened. I am sure, as sure as the evidence permits me to be, that a moth has laid its eggs here. But I cannot see the grubs themselves, or their pupae. It is too late in the season to be certain. But I should like to know.

'I'm just going to phone somebody, Mam.'

I dial Cerys's number, hear her recorded voice, her public voice, holding me at arm's length. I do not leave a message. What message could I possibly leave?

I should like to know about the chestnuts, in particular, because this was one of the concluding tasks of my employment at the Museum. In August, we received word from naturalists in Newport. Chestnut trees in that city, they said, were already shedding their leaves. The leaves themselves were prematurely wrinkled and discoloured. They mentioned that infamous Leaf Miner, *Camerariae ohridellae*, and asked, could it be here already? Because the Leaf Miner had recently become the subject of some wonder, not to say terror, amongst naturalists, who had observed its steady migration across Europe. Twelve miles separate the centres of Newport and Cardiff: a short enough outing for such a determined traveller. But I cannot say whether or not they are upon us. My researches were cut short.

I dial Cerys's number once more. And hear the same message.

'Phoning Sue?'

I remind my mother that Sue and I are no longer seeing each other. She says, yes, she knows that, of course she does, she isn't senile yet. But, she says, it's such a pity, yes, and it makes her feel sad, that we have split up, what with Sue being so nice, a real lady, what with me being on my own again. She says that people have become very… they've become very… But can't find the right word. And she says that she's sorry she's got to say this again, she knows she said it yesterday, but it's just like I wasn't listening to her then.

I release my mother's arm. I look into her pale eyes and say, clearly and slowly, leaning heavily on each syllable, 'Mam, I'm not seeing Sue any more. Do you understand that? Do you hear what I'm saying? I'm not seeing her any more and I don't want to see her ever again. I don't like Sue, Mam. I doubt whether I ever liked her. And I don't want to hear any more on the subject. Do you understand?'

I remain standing under the chestnut tree, looking at her, doing my best to reinforce these words with my eyes. With my lips, now tightly shut. With my head, which I lower to her level, as though I were scolding a child. And I wait. I wait for some sign that she has understood. That she accepts what I have said and will remember. A nod, that's all, no more. Indeed, that would be best. A silent nod. To show that she has seen sense, that she will remember these words, this silence, this fact that she cannot change. She looks back at me. It is as if she were seeking something in my face. As though she knew that something important was afoot and that she was expected to respond in kind, with gravity, but just can't grasp what that response might be. So her eyes burrow in my face for an answer, but I have already given her the only answer I have to offer, and that is beyond her reach. However hard she may try, it is forever beyond her reach. And I know that it is my fault.

'Sorry, Mam.'

I take her arm.

'Go back then now, Mam, is it?'

And I tell her about the leaves and the moths and the trees. I explain to her that the trees themselves, the beautiful old chestnuts, were newcomers once, many centuries ago, and she didn't know that, she thought that there'd always been conkers here, that it was odd, very odd, to think there was a time when there was nothing here for the children to come out and collect. And with the help of the trees and the moths and the leaves we reach dry land once more, a quiet plateau of repose, way, way beyond the sea and the icebergs.

I do not, of course, tell my mother about the tests I was required to carry out on both pupa and moth in order to establish that they were indeed of the *Camerariae* family. Nor do I mention the artificial pheromones we were about to use (and which my successor no doubt did use) in order to lure the male moths to their death; or, as some experimenters on the Continent have done, to provoke them to bugger each other, with similar results. Despite her wartime troubles, she has always been a little squeamish about such matters.

23. Fire and Water

The story didn't make the front pages, not even in the *Argus*. Barely half a column on the second page. But it will suffice. I take my scissors and cut out the report, together with a picture of the happy mother and her proud rescuer, and transfer them to the file. I take a bite from my mid-morning sandwich, glance at the framed Monarch which I received as a farewell present from my colleagues at the Museum, and lean back in my chair.

Monarch in a frame:

The last fortnight has been busy, and I've been glad of it. It's the Christmas rush, of course: visits from Santa Claus for the children, surprise parties for the adults, that sort of thing. I am now permitted to process orders for Grade 1 and Grade 2 favours. By and large, customers ring first and then call by. This makes for a very crowded schedule but is no doubt for the best, because there are always senior officers on hand to offer further advice, should the need arise, and it often does. I have not yet made what you might call a creative contribution, let alone a strategic input, to the organisation's programme of work. I must be patient.

I have said already that I harboured a number of misgivings

about Tŷ Dedwydd. You are perhaps surprised that, despite these feelings, I decided to embark on a career in the organisation. And I have to confess that it took some time before my doubts were dispelled. I had serious reservations, for example, about the 'invisibility' of the favours. No, I didn't doubt that anonymity was a precondition of the service's success: you cannot. after all, advertise such things in the papers or on the Web. But how, then, *do* you advertise them? And in so doing, how do you safeguard confidentiality? I asked Hefin. He was unmoved. 'Everyone who commissions a favour,' he said, with a knowing wink, 'has a good reason for keeping his head down.'

But then I imagined some time in the distant future when our service had penetrated every walk of life, every demographic, every suburb and parish and ghetto, a time when we would all be deceiving each other without stint and no-one would have a clue which were the real favours and which the concoctions. A long-lost relative arrives, unannounced, full of wonders and revelations. The phone rings: you've got that part – a bit-part, yes, just a walk-on, really, but nevertheless a part – in that new soap on S4C. And who can tell? 'The recipient,' said Hefin, 'wants his favour too much to disbelieve it. Some think they *deserve* it, they think it's only natural it should come to them. Others – the meek, the mild, the humble – they think it's the last thing they deserve. They're the best. They'll swallow anything.' I said I could not square this with my unsettling experiences in Howell's. 'You'll see, Dan,' said Hefin. 'In time, you'll see.' I am grateful for his faith in me. Fair play, Hefin, I thought. Thank you for believing in me. I shall try not to disappoint you.

Quite unexpectedly, I did, indeed, come to see the things which Hefin said I would see. Because, as well as fulfilling my rather undemanding Grade 1 and 2 duties, I have now been given the green light to observe some of the more elevated Contracts. So far, I have witnessed only one of these in its full execution, that is, from first enquiry right through to customer debrief. But it was an eye-opener. The Contract was classified as Grade 4+ because it was demanding both in its execution and in the delicate profiling work that had to be done in advance. Unlike the lower grade favours, which could be purchased 'off the peg', like a shirt or a pair of jeans, the favour in question had been tailor-made for its recipient. The subject, Mr R., had sunk into a slough of despond following the death of his wife in a motor accident some two years previously. In addition, he felt guilty because he himself had emerged unscathed. He had saved himself: he had failed to save his wife. That failure bred further failure. He lost his job. He neglected his health. He turned his back on his friends and family. On top of which, and despite consulting a number of doctors, therapists and quacks, he could find no treatment, no medication, to relieve his condition. And thus it was, on the basis of a detailed profile supplied by the commissioning party (whoever that might have been), that the decision was made to pursue a rather unconventional and, to use Hefin's word, 'bold' strategy.

It was this strategy that brought me, last Friday afternoon, to the banks of the River Wye, not far from the castle at Chepstow, where Mr R. lives. Here, according to the profile, our subject takes his dog for a walk every afternoon at four, following the little incline down to Welsh Street and then turning for the river. It was drizzling and few pedestrians had ventured out other than those who, like Mr R., needed to exercise their dogs. (We, too – Hefin and I – took a dog, a friendly old Border Collie by the name of Spike, who acted as our decoy.) Three or four such pedestrians passed by before Hefin received a message on his mobile to say that Mr R. was on his way. A second or two later I noticed a young woman in a bright yellow tracksuit jogging towards us along the river bank. I shall call her Ms T., to avoid awkward circumlocutions: you will understand, I'm sure, why I cannot reveal her true identity. Anyway, Ms T. stumbled, slipped and fell into the river. (The bank is steep at this point and the water deep.) She screamed. Heads turned. Dogs barked. (Yes, our own Spike barked, too.) But only one person moved. Mr R. took off his shoes and jacket and jumper and waded into the river, where Ms T. was now kicking and shrieking in the most distressing manner: whatever her talents as a jogger, she was clearly unaccustomed to water. Mr R. swam like a seal. In no time at all, he had the victim under his control, her head couched safely in the crook of his arm, her kicking and screaming quelled. By a stroke of luck, the bank is a great deal less steep only a few yards from where the accident had taken place, and it was at this point that the two figures, dripping, gasping but mightily relieved, reached the security of dry land. By further good fortune, an ambulance arrived less than a minute later, so that they were not long exposed to the cold.

Ms T., it transpired, was a single mother with two little children. She coughed and spluttered her gratitude on behalf of them all. Mr R., although dreadfully bedraggled, seemed pleased with how things had turned out and kept saying, over and over: 'If I hadn't come by at that minute, no, that very second... If you'd fallen in a little earlier... If... If...' And, of course, had I not known better – had I been a wholly innocent witness to the event, like one of the other dog-walkers – I should have been quite certain that it was Ms T. who had been the beneficiary, that Mr. R. had bestowed upon her the greatest of all favours, the gift of life itself. Not so. Indeed, according to the tenets of Tŷ Dedwydd, it is quite the reverse. To be saved is, indeed, a blessing, but to save is better. And Mr R. had been privileged with the opportunity to save the life of a mother. Surely there could be no favour greater than this?

As I say, the story of Mr R. and Ms T did not make the front page even of *The Argus.* It is difficult to understand journalists' priorities these days. But the episode gave my spirits a little boost, which was no bad thing, under the circumstances. On Sunday morning, the day after our fraught walk in the park, my mother telephoned. 'Don't put the phone down,' she said, brusquely, before I'd had a chance even to say hello. 'You're trying to kill me, Daniel. I know you are, so don't deny it.' And this in a more hesitant voice, as though she found it difficult to believe her own words. I was taken aback, as I'm sure you'll understand. It was my silence, I presume, that set her off again. 'Don't put the phone down now, Daniel, don't put...' 'I won't, Mam, I won't,' I said, and scrambled around for some way of placating her. I suggested that perhaps she'd had a nasty dream. 'Did it start during the night?' I asked. 'Perhaps you've not quite woken up yet, Mam.' I even tried to strike a slightly lighter note. Why should I kill her? I said, Surely I wasn't in line for some big inheritance, was I? Apart from the Gaudy Welsh, of course, and I could pinch that any time, if

I wanted to. Ha! *If I wanted to*! Which I said in a mock-sarcastic voice, backed up by a little chuckle, so that I was immediately anxious that I'd pushed things a tadge too far, that Mam might think I was making light of her anxieties. But no, she took the joke in good part. At least, I think she did. A little leg-pulling has always gone a long way between me and my mother, especially when we haven't seen eye-to-eye. 'It's not like you, Daniel, I know…' I walked over at lunch-time to make her something to eat.

And that is another reason why the last fortnight has been more busy than usual. Instead of visiting my mother twice or three times a week, as was my custom, I now call around almost every evening. I also make a special effort to hold myself in check when she becomes irritable, as she does, without fail, before the end of each visit. And it might be reasonable to ask, I know, in these circumstances, whether she does in fact desire my company at all. But how else can I be of help? Sue would know what to do. Of course she would.

Just as I am chewing the last crust of my sandwich and preparing to get to grips with the latest batch of contracts – Christmas items, in the main, as I believe I have already mentioned – the fire alarm goes off. This is a weekly ritual, an exercise only, so I take no notice. I carry on with the orders, categorising them according to grade and date, trying to ignore the din. It is only after a minute or two that I become aware of a commotion in the corridor outside my room. The sound of doors being opened and closed. Someone shouting, 'Don't use the lift!' Some blather, then, about leaving keys in a bag and another voice – Hefin's, I think – saying not to be so silly, there were much more important things to worry about than keys and bags. Yes, Hefin, because that's who I see, now, sticking his head around my door and yelling in his most phlegmy quarryman's voice to get the hell out. Then the sound of feet, scuttling towards the stairs.

Although I can neither see fire nor smell smoke, I begin to suspect that this may not, after all, be a mere ritual. So I deem it prudent to follow Hefin's instructions. I get up and make for the door. My hand is on the handle. My mind is already speeding down the corridor, and I would follow it eagerly, I assure you, except for one awful, palpitating thought. Cerys is on the fourth floor. Have I heard her voice, as she made her escape? No, I haven't. And then the other questions which derive from it. Could the fire have started there, on the fourth floor? Perhaps in Cerys's own room? I see, in my mind's eye, Cerys facing the flames, her hand raised in front of her, dazzled, trapped, unable to move. Because I know about these things, I know about her difficulties. But the others? How much do they know? So I run back to my desk and ring her extension. There is no answer. No answer can mean one of two things. She is safe. Or else she cannot reach the phone.

I can hear nothing but the alarm now. I run to the end of the corridor. I open the fire doors and listen. Nothing. I run up one flight of stairs and listen. Nothing. I continue until I reach the third floor, where I look through the window. My colleagues have already gathered in the car park. I scan the faces, once, twice, three times. She is not there. Cerys is not there. So I climb again, two steps at a time now, until I am on the fourth floor. I push open the fire doors and stumble forward, as fast as I dare, my arms stretched out in front of me. (The lights have been extinguished and there are no windows here.) I throw myself recklessly into Cerys's room. She is not there. There is nothing there except the evidence of her hasty departure. Her panic, perhaps. A spectacle case on the floor. A handbag, open, on the desk.

I return to the corridor and shout, 'Cerys! Cerys!' Only the alarm answers. I open each door in turn. The door to the Accounts Department. 'Anyone there?' The Personnel Director's door. 'Anyone there?' Even the Chief Benefactor's door. And then, somewhere in the distance, almost but not quite drowned out by the alarm, I hear a voice.

At the far end of the room where I now stand, Dr Bruno's own room, the room where I was interviewed, there is a door. I did not notice this door on my previous visit. At least, I did not recognise it as a real door, as it had been so ingeniously and thoroughly camouflaged within the extravagant painting that covers the wall. Today it is open, only a few inches, but sufficient for me to be sure that this is no mere image or *trompe l'oeil*. Through these few inches I can see that there is another room beyond. I can see, on moving closer, that it is bigger even than that of the Chief Benefactor. And I can hear quite distinctly, from within, a familiar voice.

'That's us... in Barry.'

A voice that cannot, surely, be there.

'Ahmed?'

I walk through the door.

'A...'

I see a video machine, playing in front of empty chairs. And there he is, on the screen. Ahmed. He holds a book in his hands. A big, red book with hard covers. 'That's the back garden in Paget Street,' he says, turning the pages. I see pictures, only pictures. 'There's my mother...' he says. Pictures that bring a smile to his face. A woman walks into the frame. She is dressed in black. Is it Cerys? I see only her shoulders, the back of her head. She leaves again, but the camera does not follow her. It is, it must be, a static camera, just like the one in the Tŷ Dedwydd studio, giving only one angle, one view. But Ahmed is not in a studio, he's in a sitting room, an ordinary sitting room in an ordinary house. I can see the curtains now, the flowery wallpaper, the armchairs. I can hear the tinkling of china from somewhere off camera. A man comes into view. Only the face, slender, dark. He has short hair. Now I see his shirt, blue, open at the collar. I remember this face.

I draw up a chair and sit down. In so doing, I catch sight, through the corner of my eye, on the table, to the left of the television, a red book. I get up again and am about to take a closer look when the alarm stops ringing. The sudden silence is more unnerving even than the alarm. I feel naked, exposed. I hear a voice. 'Dan!' I hear steps. 'Are you there, Dan?' Cerys's voice. I go out into the corridor. 'I heard a voice,' I say. 'I had to… I had to…'

'I was worried about you, Dan.'

24. Dr Bruno Goes Home

Having reached the half-way point in my probationary period, I was confident I had acquitted myself quite adequately. Nevertheless, as I reached the top of the stairs once more and turned for Dr Bruno's room, my mouth was dry, the palms of my hands unpleasantly damp. And although dryness and dampness are contraries, they derived, in this case, from the same source. The Chief Benefactor knew. What did he know? Ha! That is the question. Well, he knew about me. Which was only to be expected: he was my employer, after all. He had received progress reports from Hefin, of that I had no doubt. From Cerys too, perhaps. But what else did he know? He knew about Ahmed. He knew more about Ahmed than I did myself. And if he knew this, then how would he not know that I had been here, in this very room, his own room, prying, trespassing?

'Bachan, bachan... You've got a look on you like a broody hen.'

I was tempted to confess all, there and then, and put myself at his mercy. 'The alarm... The voice... The video...' What I said, however, was that I had a nasty cold coming on and proffered a dry little cough as evidence. The Doctor went to fetch me a glass of water and there we were, for the next hour or so, talking about this and that, chewing the cud, as they say. To my surprise, I had quite a jolly time relating some of the more colourful amongst my Grade 3 outings. Dr Bruno seemed amused, even impressed. He asked me, did I find my current duties enough of a challenge? Would I perhaps like to branch out, to 'stretch my beak', as we say. Yes, for a full hour or more, and not once did he refer to fire drills or videos or photograph albums or anything else of the sort. Bit by bit, as I came to realise that my employment was not under threat, that my behaviour was not being held up to scrutiny, as I saw that Dr Bruno was as genial, as affable as ever, my anxiety receded. My palms dried, my mouth regained its natural lubrication, my voice steadied. I announced, with much zeal – which, of course, was merely the mask of relief – that I would gladly embrace every opportunity, thank you very much, indeed that I had already been introduced to Grade 4 – and what an introduction! – yes, and was there, I asked, any special training which I might undertake in order to advance, in the fulness of time, to Grade 5? I asked this, not because I needed an answer – Hefin had explained Tŷ Dedwydd's procedures quite fully – but because I wanted to show willing, because I wanted to seem ambitious and dedicated in the eyes of my superior. A vanity, no doubt, but not, I think, a great fault. Yes, and also because I was now sailing, you might say, on a fair wind, on the steady westerlies of my new confidence. And not for the first time, as I believe I have already mentioned, I sailed further and more boldly than was perhaps wise for a sailor of such limited experience on the high seas.

'Special training?' he asked, with a chuckle.

'Yes,' I said.

'Coleg cyrn yr arad, Dan,' he said, tapping the side of his nose. *'Coleg cyrn yr arad.'* I confess that I am at a loss as to how I might translate this idiom. 'The college of plough handles,' he said. 'That's where you'll learn your trade.' And that is how I must leave it. I am sure you get the drift.

'I'm glad to hear it,' I chirped

'I'm glad you're glad, Dan,' he chirped back and smiled at me with something I can only describe, in my innocence of such things, as paternal affection. '*Ody'r fuwch yn gistwn*?' he asked, then. I had not heard this idiom before and had little idea of its meaning, other than that its provenance, like the others, was agricultural and that it concerned the condition of a cow.

'Ody ddi ar ben ei hâl?'

This idiom, too, was obscure to me. Was the cow *ar ben ei hâl* or was she not? How was I to know? But I nodded for all I was worth, smiled and told the Doctor that I was prepared to do anything I could to further my career and the interests of Tŷ Dedwydd alike, begging him as I did so to forgive the excessive zeal of a newcomer like myself.

Was it this, I wonder – my jejeune ways, my bubbling enthusiasm – that won him over? Or did I, perhaps, touch upon something deeper, something for which the word 'paternal' – a word I used rather flippantly a moment ago – is in fact a not inaccurate epithet? I cannot say. But it was at this point, as I smiled and bubbled, that Dr

Bruno rose from his chair and pointed an index finger at me. It was not an accusatory finger, still less a scolding finger, but rather a finger that said, 'Stay there, my boy, I'll be back in a trice!'

Dr Bruno made for the door, the same door through which I had gone the previous day in search of Ahmed. In my foolishness, I half expected him to take hold of the doorknob and turn it. But this, of course, was a doorknob of paint only, a vivid illusion. Instead, he placed his left hand on the doorframe, a small section of which then opened, like the cover of a book, to reveal a finger pad. The Doctor pushed four buttons and entered the room. At this point I felt a sudden stab of panic as I re-lived the events of my previous visit, as I tried to remember whether, horror of horrors, I might have left incriminating evidence. Had I dropped a handkerchief, perhaps? And if I had, did it matter? Did I still possess a handkerchief with my initials on it? And if not a handkerchief, what else? Had I knocked a picture onto the floor? Had I even scattered a whole pile of them when I heard Cerys's voice and rushed back into the corridor? Did the Doctor know about these things? Each question pierced me with its cruel stiletto.

Two minutes later, Dr Bruno returned, as benignly as he had left, carrying a tray. On the tray were a number of objects. He placed them on the table in front of me.

'Here you are, Dan... Choose two.'

I examined each object in turn. A medicine botel, empty, with no label. A map, the name **GORS FAWR** on its cover. A glass of red wine. A mobile phone. An accounts book, black, with the word *Accounts* in gold italic on the front cover. And a pretty blue flower – a Christmas rose, I believe – in a small vial. I looked again, seeking some connection, with Tŷ Dedwydd, between the objects themselves. Finding none.

'Just two?'

At this point you are, no doubt, wondering why I did not ask the Doctor for some explanation. All I can say is that questions of this kind did not seem to be on the agenda today. There you have it. I can say no more. So I chose two objects: the glass of wine (because I thought it might settle my nerves) and the map (because it stirred my curiosity).

'An interesting choice, Dan. The map.' He moved the tray to one side, unfolded the map and laid it out across the table. 'And the Cariad Dry White.' He placed the glass upon the map. 'Yes, a very good choice. The map and one of our very best Welsh wines.'

'Ah,' I said, with rather heavy-handed sarcasm. 'Is there such a thing?' I know nothing about wines, Welsh or otherwise. Indeed, beyond the sarcasm, you might say that this was the thrust of my question. I was resolved to pursue a policy of absolute truthfulness with regard both to my abilities and my deficiencies. If necessary, I should even make a display of my ignorance. And yes, you might also say, is not such exaggerated self-deprecation not the clearest sign of a guilty conscience? Indeed. But then you were not there, locking horns with one such as Dr Bruno.

'Yes, there is, Dan. And a fine wine it is, too. Except, of course, that it is Welsh only in respect of its *terroir.* The grapes – the Bacchus and the Kernling – are of German origin.'

'I see,' I said. 'Welsh, and yet German, too.'

'Quite.'

The Doctor looked at the glass and raised a cautionary finger. 'And yet, having said as much, you might then conclude that, in taste, it more closely resembles a Sauvignon Blanc. Which, of course, is a wine of the Bordeaux region. In fact, if you were not a connoisseur, you might well think this fine little German-Welsh creation as quintessentially French as the Eiffel Tower, as Edith Piaf, as... You get my meaning, Dan?'

'Yes, I do,' I said. He offered me the glass.

'So, then, Dan, are you a connoisseur?'

'Of wine?'

'Yes, Dan, of wine.'

I explained to Dr Bruno that my preference was for beer, but that I possessed little expertise even in that department. No, as I say, I was not to be caught out making any false claims. I would keep to the plain, unvarnished, unflattering truth. He nodded.

'*Iechyd da,* Dan'.

'Iechyd da,' I replied. 'And yourself?'

But it was too early for the Doctor to imbibe, he said. Too early and, in any case, his preferences, like my own, lay elsewhere. He proceeded, then, while I sipped at my dry white Cariad, to outline what those preferences were. They were all wines, but few, as far as I could tell, were Welsh. He extolled the full body of Marcel Guigal's Côtes du Rhône, the crisp tanginess of the Petaluma Riesling from Australia, the honey nose of a South African Grenache Blanc, the spicy, blackcurrant flavours of the Gran Feudo Vinas Viejas Reserva from Navarra. And he named many, many more, both red and white, giving each its provenance, its optimum year of production, its particularities of palate and nose, and then writing each down on a piece of paper. 'In case you wish to give them a try,' he said. Two of them he underlined as meriting particular comment. Martinborough Vineyard's Pinot Noir, from New Zealand, was one because it rivalled 'any Burgundy you care to name'. And likewise the Argentinian Bonarda Mendoza. 'The Bonarda is an Italian grape,' said the Doctor. 'A migrant that has made its home quite happily on the other side of the world.' I have these details here in the Doctor's own hand. 'Like a Burgundy.' 'Italian grapes.' And so on.

The Doctor went on to explain some of the remarkable things that can be done these days to mimic the most distinctive wines. Through using different kinds of oak in making the barrels, for example. Through the addition of some over-ripened fruit and perhaps a little cultured yeast. Through micro-oxygenation, too, and a dozen other new-fangled ruses. With due care and attention, he said, you can mask the influence of *terroir* entirely. Or, rather, you can take the *terroir* with you, wherever you go. Because no-one will know the difference. Not if you get it right.

'So, Dan, are you enjoying your dry Cariad, your Welsh German Sauvignon Blanc?'

I said I was.

'Good. Because now we must look at the map. For the map is our main course today. That is where the meat is. The wine is there merely to whet the appetite. Now then, it is a six-inch map, as you can see.'

A map so detailed that I could discern hardly any of those features which, as a rule, make it possible to recognise, as a bird might do, or a helicopter pilot, the world that the map represented: the blue ribbon of a river here, the crescent of a bay there, the rust-coloured smudge of mountain in between, that quite specific combination of signs and symbols that denote 'Pembrokeshire' or 'Eifionydd' or 'The Gower'. Nothing. Not a single clue.

'My home turf. My square mile.'

The map was also illegible in a more literal sense, because it was upside down. On looking more closely, I could certainly make out hedges and streams and chapels and houses and hillforts and so on. I could see clusters of houses, which no doubt merited the status of hamlet or even village. But I could read none of their names.

Dr Bruno placed the tip of his index finger at the bottom right-hand corner of the map and closed his eyes. 'We're going home,' he said. 'We're going home by Lôn Cwm Bach.' And the Doctor moved his finger, ever so slowly, across the map. Slowly, but with the confidence of a man who need see nothing, so certain and complete and unerring is his knowledge of this, his own habitat.

'Down by the bridge. That's where we'll start,' he said. 'That's where the bus puts us down, you see, Dan, the school bus, over on the far side of the bridge, by the grit box. Every afternoon at a quarter past four. Walk up past Ca' Dafi James then, just a few yards, and bear left at Blaenhirbant. That's the whitewashed cottage on the corner. Do you see it, Dan? It's the one with the little iron gate. Where Wncwl Jacob used to live, long ago. Yes, old Wncwl Jacob, by himself all those years, poor dab, and kept the fire in day and night they say, summer and winter. So that's what we'll do, Dan, when we come to the iron gate. We shan't turn the corner, not just yet, we'll go inside and sit with Wncwl Jacob for a little while, sit by the fire and keep him company, have a cup of tea. And after we've drunk our tea perhaps we'll get up and have a look around. Because such cottages are few and far between these days. Yes, I reckon you'd have to go to a museum to find another cottage like Blaenhirbant. There now, Dan, can you see the little *lowset?* Over there, between the kitchen and the byre? And the *côr.* And the *eirw.* And the *cratsh*, too, yes, although there's no calf there now, of course. No, no calf been raised there in many a long year. There are so many things to see, Dan, if only we had the time.

'But we can't be all day. No. Otherwise Mam will get worried. She'll think we're lost. She'll think the *bwci bo* has come and snatched us away. So wave goodbye to Wncwl Jacob, Dan, and let's be on our way. Through the iron gate, bear left, and carry on a while, down the hill. We've got a spring in our step now, haven't we, after our little refreshment? Down hill, just a hundred yards or so, until we come to Capel Waun Fach. The name's up there on the wall, see. On its plaque. Yes, and the round window below. And if we wanted to, Dan, if we had the time, we could have a little break here, too. We could stop by and look at some of the gravestones, especially the old ones, the ones with the pediment, because that's a feature of the gravestones in these parts. The pediment. But best come back later, isn't it? Yes, there'll be plenty of time later. We've still got a fair way to walk before we get home. And Mam will be worrying.

'The road levels out here,' said the Doctor. 'Just by Danrhelyg barn, yes, and there's the signpost, at the turn of the wall, the ivy growing up it, almost to the top, so if it grew any more you wouldn't see a thing. The signpost, pointing the way to Penlangarreg, not that the name is there, no, just the sign, to say that there's a path, and the path much, much shorter than the road, just half a mile across the fields, barely that. So that's the way we go, Dan, we follow the path, minding our step now, because it can be muddy here after rain, yes, the path curving around the edge of the *gwndwn*, holding tight to the hedge until we come to the old stone stile, up and over, Dan, up and over and we're into Cae Canol and it's not far now, no, not far at all. Do you see the two holly trees at the top of the field? One each side of the gate? That's the way we go now, Dan. They're the only sign we need now. Just a few yards, we can't get lost now. Through the gate and into Cae Banc... And there it is, Dan! There it is! Just the chimney to begin with, till you come over the brow of the field, and then you can see it all, the *clôs* and the stables and the byre. Yes, and the hayloft above, where I would hide my little treasures, the treasures Mam wouldn't let me bring into the house, the ram's skull, the buzzard feather, the little blue eggs I found behind the water trough. And there she is, Dan. There's Mam. Standing on the doorstep, calling us in to tea, because the broth has stars on it. So put your boots under the *ffwrwm*, Dan, because they've got half of Cae Banc on them, Mam says, and hang your coat on one of the wooden pegs by the side of the door. My brother's jacket is there already, on its own peg. But the fourth, the fourth peg, is empty for the moment, because Dad hasn't come back from town. He won't be long, says Mam. But we can't wait for ever, can we?'

Dr Bruno opened his eyes and tapped his index finger on the map.

'Such a pity,' he said. 'Such a pity that Penlangarreg is just a little grey square. That our map is too small to show the real Penlangarreg. The rooms, and within those rooms, the cupboards and chests and coffers, the tables and chairs. Too small even to show the great oak dresser, with its cups and saucers and plates and jugs. Much, much too small to show, inside the wooden box in the parlour, Mam's sewing things, the bobbins of thread, white, red, blue and grey, the needles, big and small, the scissors, the thimble, the darning egg, the box of spare buttons. But I have another map,' said Dr Bruno. 'No, not a paper one. I have a much better map than that. A map that has a place for everything, and everything is in its place. Here, Dan… Here is my map.'

The Doctor touched his temple with the tips of his fingers, then fell into silence, his eyes lowered, his hands now folded together. He leaned back in his chair and took a deep breath. So I thanked him. I made to leave the room. That is what I thought was expected, because the journey, as far as I could tell, had come to an end. The story, too. Yes, and a happy enough ending it was, to my mind. He had a map. Everything was in its place, where it ought to be. What else was there to say? It sounded like an ending, too. Rounded. Complete. The Doctor's voice settling into a quiet repose, content, resigned, so that I, too, felt something of that same resignation. And if I was none the wiser about the nature of Grade 5 favours, well, it scarcely seemed to matter any more, because my curiosity had dissipated. Yes, at that moment I can honestly say that I wouldn't have given a fig even to know about Ahmed and the secrets of the rear room and the photo album and Cerys and all the other tribulations of the last few days.

'Thank you very much, Doctor.'

But no. I had clearly misunderstood, because the Doctor raised a hand and indicated that I should resume my seat.

'What's the rush, Dan?' he said. 'Have you forgotten the cemetery?'

And I had, I had forgotten it utterly.

'Don't you want to go back to the cemetery, Dan?'

No, I cannot say that I did wish to go back to Dr Bruno's cemetery, for why would anyone wish to visit the graves of strangers? I had prepared myself to leave. I was ready to leave.

But the Doctor had already closed his eyes again.

'So then, Dan,' he said, and paused. 'The first grave.' And paused again. 'Hannah Rebecca Thomas, Bryn Bedw.' He pronounced the name with great deliberation and solemnity, as though he were tracing the letters with the tips of his fingers. 'There she is. Under the first stone. See how it's tilted forward slightly, the lead letters beginning to peel.' And having pronounced the first name, the others came as though of their own accord, with an unfailing fluency. 'Hannah Thomas and her husband, John, and their two children, Mary and David. Yes. Died in infancy, you see. And next to them, but set back a little, there's William Evans, my old Wncwl Wil – Wil Beili Glas to his neighbours – and his wife, Gwendoline, daughter of Dole Gwyrddon in the south of the county. "Beloved wife," it says here. Not so sure about that. Their sons are over by the water tap. Huw and Robert Evans. And Robert's wife, too. Huw didn't marry. Killed in the first war, you see. But it's too wet, too muddy to go over there today.

'So on we go. Eben the cobbler next. Then Lewis Jenkins, my grand-dad on my mother's side. A collier down Tŷ Cro's way, all his life, just about, but came back home to be buried. Catherine Boswell, then, "formerly of this parish", it says. Drowned whilst sailing to the East Indies in 1868. The ship's name is on the stone. They always do that, Dan, don't they? Put the ship's name. Why do they do that, do you think? Anyway, I doubt whether her body's here. How could it be? Perhaps that's why they put the name of the ship, to fill the stone up with facts and figures, to make up for the fact they've got no body to offer you. Poor Kate.

'But you must be getting tired now, Dan, listening to me whittering on about people you've never heard of. And there are fifty-seven others that I haven't mentioned yet. Some in tidy rows, others all higgledy piggledy, filling the space between the chapel and the wall, the low wall with the barbed wire on top that borders Dôl y Dderi. Do you want me to tell you about them, Dan? No, I shouldn't think so. Enough is enough, eh? And in any case, they are all yesterday's people.'

Which was clear enough, I thought. Aunties and uncles and grandfathers and the like. Cold in their graves for many a long year. I nodded. Yesterday's people indeed.

'But today's different, Dan.'

Which was not clear at all. Because aren't graves, by their very nature, unchanging? I mean in their essence, of course: they peel, they weather, of course they do, but they remain what they say they are. They can be nothing else. The Doctor read the confusion on my face.

'The names, Dan. Today is different because all the names have changed. Where Hannah and John Thomas lay, today I have interred a crate each of Marcel Guigal's Côtes du Rhône and the Argentinian Bonarda Mendoza. Where Wncwl Tom and Anti Gwen thought they were bound together for all eternity – pity for her, I say! – there I have buried the Grenache Blanc and the Pinot Noir. For how else would you expect me to remember all those names, all those years, all those vineyards? And it is not, I hope, too disrespectful an act, given the quality of the wines in question. No, and not wholly inappropriate, either, because a grave would make quite a tolerable wine cellar, I should think.'

'But if today's different…'

'Yes, Dan. Then tomorrow will be different again. Quite right. Because God only knows who will lay claim to this little patch of earth in years to come. Have you any idea, Dan? Mm? Have you any idea what *you* would like to bury there, if you had the chance?'

No, I had not the slightest idea.

'Because that's your Grade 5 for you, Dan. You've got to learn the art of burial if you want to attain Grade 5. Are you ready to learn how to bury, Dan?'

No, Dr Bruno. I no longer have the appetite to learn. Not now.

'Of course,' I said, 'I want to learn as much as I can.'

'Splendid. Then I shall set you a task. We'll call it homework. A little exercise to put you on the right path. What shall we say, Dan? Any ideas? Any suggestions? What can you offer in place of my crates of wine?'

What, indeed, could I offer? I could think of nothing.

'I know, Dan. Start at your feet, as they say. With something familiar. Something like my Pinot Noir, my Côtes du Rhône. Something not too challenging, so you can ease your way in gradually, a step at a time. Because we're not as young as we once were, Dan, are we? Not so good at learning tricks. But I think I've got it. Yes, yes. That's it. We'll start with your insects, Dan. A splendid idea, don't you think? Can't be too many surprises there, surely. Now, then, I want you to imagine that you've got to talk about your insects, nothing too ambitious, just a brief introduction.'

But there are so many insects.

'Yes, a short lecture, over in the meeting room, one lunchtime, and we'd ask everyone to come along and listen, ask questions... You'd be paid, of course, oh yes, we couldn't expect a professional entomologist like yourself to deliver a lecture for nothing... And because it's lunchtime, we'd need to lay something on to eat, too... Ah, but I can see from your face, Dan – you have such an expressive face, an open book, as they say – yes, I can see that this might be a bit too much of an undertaking for one lunchtime...'

Yes, Dr Bruno, of course it would be.

'And how many insects are there, Dan? How many in Wales? I'll warrant you there are more insects than there are wines. How many, Dan? How many, just on this bleak stretch of *morfa*? Are there hundreds?'

Thousands.

'And their characteristics, Dan. You would need to describe their distinguishing characteristics. Their size and colour, the shape of their heads and bodies, how they rear their young, what they eat, how they hunt, all that sort of thing. And the males and females quite different from one another, I gather. Yes, quite strikingly different. You can tell us something about that, too. A few choice details, anecdotes even, to leaven the mixture. Yes. A great deal to do. Too much, I'm sure. How would you cope, Dan?'

I would not cope.

'Not to mention the larvae, of course. Because I believe the larvae, too, are different. And the pupae. Is that the correct term, Dan? The pupae? Well, my word, I dare say you'd have to repopulate every cemetery in the county to remember them all. Ha! Every cottage and farm, too, I've no doubt. Yes. And perhaps more than that. Perhaps you'd have to borrow the cupboards and chests and dressers in those farms and cottages, as well. And the plates, the teapots, the knives and forks inside those cupboards. And those balls of wool that Mam-gu keeps in the bottom drawer, still, after all these years, for the baby shawl that she couldn't knit now even if there was a baby to knit for. Just think, Dan! All those little bobbins of thread. The needles she holds tight between her lips. No, it would all be too much.'

It would be far too much.

'So that is why I want to make a suggestion. To get things moving. Why don't you choose just a few to begin with? Mm? A few beetles, perhaps. How many do you think? Fifty? Twenty? Right you are, then, twenty it is. Splendid. You can tell us about twenty beetles of your own choosing, Dan. That will be your homework. The most common ones, perhaps. The ones we might see any day in our gardens, or out on the *morfa*, if we had the time, if we had the patience to look for them. Just enough to fill a small cemetery.'

Twenty beetles. Yes, I could manage that. The black beetle. The ground beetle. The rove beetle. The reed beetle. The hairy click beetle. And not forgetting the sexton beetle itself. How could I leave him out? That's six. So only fourteen more. But enough. Quite enough. And only three minutes for each, allowing for questions. Yes, I could manage that. That is well within my compass.

'Because a cemetery is a convenience, Dan. A facility. Just like a house. Just like a map.'

25. An Unexpected Invitation

'I'll see you tomorrow night, then.'

Today, I agreed to go out with Cerys and her friends. Why? Because when Cerys walked in to the staff room and asked me to I couldn't think of an excuse. I have a thorough, methodical kind of mind, but I am less adept at thinking on my feet. Indeed, method and thoroughness are not, in my experience, on intimate terms with speed. But there was something else which made the invitation difficult to refuse, and this lay, not in the words themselves, but rather in the tone of voice with which they were delivered. When she said, 'Why don't you come out with us tonight?' she placed unusual stress on the word 'Why?'. '*Why* don't you come out with us tonight?' Just like that. It was not a whining sort of 'Why?' One that might imply I was at heart an antisocial sort of creature and needed to be taught a lesson. Nor was it an inquiring 'Why?' She wasn't, after all, seeking an explanation, a recital of extenuating circumstances. But not pitying, either, at least I don't think so, not that I could tell. No, it was – how shall I say it – more of a pleading sort of question As though I should be doing Cerys a favour by accepting her invitation. Yes, and accompanied by a certain knitting of the eyebrows, a slight tilt of the head to one side. But I must not exaggerate these effects. There was nothing whatsoever coquettish about her manner. Indeed, I believe that such strategems must be quite foreign to Cerys. No, I sincerely believe it was an innocent plea from the heart. And it touched me. Yes, I freely admit it, in the part of the brain that governs such matters, I found that gentle innocence, that disingenuousness, sweetly attractive. So that even though, in a quite different part of my brain, I believed her to be a scheming little vixen, it was the benign Cerys who prevailed. I do not defend these feelings, either morally or otherwise, I merely describe them as they welled up in me at the time. In any case, one says things in the heat of the moment sometimes, and having said them, they cannot then be unsaid. What friends? I had no idea.

'Yes, tomorrow night. Thanks, Cerys. It's nice of you to ask.'

26. A Long Night at Ty Dedwydd

It is half past six and I have almost finished processing today's Contracts. Everyone else on my corridor has already gone home, throwing me their farewell quips as they did so, pitying or ribald or mocking, according to their natures. *Don't work too hard, Dan. There'll be nothing left for Santa to do.* That sort of thing. And it is true: today has been very busy. But it is not only the work that keeps me here. It is Monday, so there are no workshops in Tŷ Dedwydd. I look through the window and see Wilbert's red Volvo pulling out of the car park. Only the cleaners are left in the building. Once they have gone, I shall be alone. This is the real reason I am still here.

Fatemeh comes in to my room to empty the bin and hoover the floor. I rest my feet on the corner of the desk, to keep them out of the way, and we chat about the weather, about work, about our children. As she finishes, I gather together my things, just as I would do on an ordinary evening, if I were preparing to go home. I tidy the papers on my desk. I turn off the computer. I put on my coat. 'You want me open the front door?' No, thank you, Fatemeh, I'll open the door myself and pop the key back through the door afterwards. (When the cleaners are at work, the key is always left on the counter in reception.) If that's alright by you, Fatemeh? Excellent.

Fatameh is cleaning the toilets now. I hear the *clunk* of the bucket, the *sloosh sloosh* of the mop from the far end of the corridor. Presently she will go up to the third floor. I wait, ears cocked. *Clunk. Woosh.* Doors open and close. *Clunk.* Then, after a short pause, I hear the whine of the lift descending. The door opens. Another *clunk*. The whining resumes. I put on my fleece, grab my rucksack and turn off the light. Fatemeh and her two colleagues will see, through the window at the top of the stairs, that my room is dark and will assume that I have gone home. They will hear the lift, too. There's the last of them gone, they'll say. Time for a cuppa.

I take the key from the counter and make my way to the front door. I place it on the mat under the letter box so that the cleaners, later on, will have proof positive that I have indeed left, that I have done as I promised. I stand back and consider the tableau of door, mat and key. It is not satisfactory. A key, dropped through the letter box from such a height – what height? three feet, perhaps – would not, I suspect, land so neatly and precisely in the middle of the mat. I pick it up and release it from a position as near as I can get to the letter box, applying a certain amount of forward propulsion, as would be necessary if one were, in fact, to be posting a key through the letter box. It hits the floor and bounces some four inches to one side. Which is much better. I sign the logbook and note my time of departure. I wait a moment to collect my thoughts, to make sure I have forgotten nothing. I shall not be able to return to the reception area tonight nor, therefore, to the front door, because I should then be caught by the CCTV cameras and the alarm scanners. Fortunately, these have been installed only on the ground floor and the first floor, on the premiss that not even the boldest and most inventive burglar could effect an entry to the upper reaches of Tŷ Dedwydd.

I move to the next stage of my plan: to seek a temporary hiding place until the cleaners have left. This cannot, I'm afraid, be found in my own room. The cleaners will return to the first floor before they go home – there is no other way – and they may see me through the window in my door. I could, of course, hide behind my filing cabinet, but that would be a risky strategy: an elbow might protrude, or the toe of a shoe. And who knows what shadows I might cast, what embarrassment might ensue? I have decided, therefore, that my only safe refuge is the gents' toilet which has, I know, already been cleaned. Yes, it is on the same floor as my office but there is no window there – of course there is no window – and even if there were a window, the cleaners would have no reason to pass it, let alone to look through it. But, as I say, there is no such window.

So this is where I go. I open the door of one of the three cubicles, take the sack from my shoulders and stand on the toilet seat. Why stand on the seat? It is not possible, I believe, to explain away every fear or anxiety, nor to rationalise our responses to such feelings. I wish to be as invisible as possible. That is my explanation. I hear water dripping in a tank above my head. It is suddenly very cold. There is a small hole in the window near my right ear. A chill wind blows through it from the *morfa*. I stand. I wait.

Through the same hole, half an hour later, by standing on tiptoe, I see the cleaners disappear into the night. They share a car, whose I cannot say. There is now no-one left but me and the wind. I'm not sure whether it is because I no longer fear detection or because of the unaccustomed silence, but quite unexpectedly, and despite the draught, a great peace descends upon me, a cosy, comforting blanket of peace. And I realise that, for the first time in many months, and certainly the first time under the auspices, you might say, of *happinesstheexperience.com*, I feel some measure of contentment.

I get down from my perch, heave the sack back on to my shoulders, take the tiny pencil torch from my pocket and set forth. On reaching the corridor, I direct its narrow beam at the carpeted floor so that no-one outside can see the spot of light. (I know, through collecting Nia from her workshops, that security staff patrol the site at night.) I climb the stairs, stooping all the while, indeed walking almost on my hunkers, for fear of displaying my silhouette through the windows or casting my shadow on the wall. The weight on my back makes this an awkward and, after a few seconds, quite painful posture. I think, enviously, of the ant's prodigious abilities in this regard.

After what seems an eternity of puffing and panting, and frequent stops to get my breath back, I reach the Chief Benefactor's office. The door is open. I'm surprised at this, but perhaps the cleaners have left it so, to provide some ventilation. I enter. I put my sack on the floor and myself on Dr Bruno's capacious chair. Not that I harbour any ambitions in that direction, you understand: it is merely the nearest chair I can find and I must, I absolutely must, allow my limbs some respite before moving on to the next task. And yet, with that task in mind, it strikes me that this is no bad emplacement. I think, indeed, that it is perhaps best to do just as the Doctor himself did, the other day. To mimic him, as it were. For then, surely, there is much less chance of mishap.

So that is what I do. I start from the Doctor's chair. I get up, turn and make for the door that has been so artfully concealed in the mural. I run my fingers over the surface of the wall until I feel a small recess. In the light of my pencil torch, I see that this recess is masquerading as a gap, a shadow, a strip of mortar between two stones. I tuck a finger under its edge and pull. The cover lifts, revealing the pad beneath. My fingers know what must be done next, although I must confess that my brain is not quite so sure. They do not remember the numbers, of course, not as such, but they do recall the pattern. And they recall it with remarkable clarity. How can this be? you ask. What is it that can turn an image on the retina into a memory in the fingers? Well, I shall tell you. It is the telephone. Two telephones, to be precise. The mobile phone on Dr Bruno's tray, for one, because this provided the necessary association, the stimulus, if you like. But also, and more particularly, the telephone in the fingers. The instinct – because that is what it is by now – that compels my fingers to dial 1571 every evening when I return home from work in order to hear my messages. And it is precisely that instinct, that code, that is awakened in me now as I recall Dr Bruno's fingers, tapping out the same pattern.

Slowly and with great deliberation – I may get only the one chance – I press the buttons. One... Five... Seven... One... I turn the handle. The door opens. And I am compelled to smile, somewhat smugly, at my success, as though I have already completed my mission. This is silly, I know, but I can't help it. It is as though the door itself, in agreeing to be opened, has offered me some kind of immunity, a guarantee of safe passage. As I say, silly, but that is how it is, and I proceed with somewhat more of a spring in my step.

I return to the Doctor's desk to collect my rucksack and then make for the anteroom, or the secret room, as I have come to think of it. I enter, close the door behind me and start emptying my sack. The first item I take out is the largest and heaviest, but it is also the most delicate. I am relieved to see that it has suffered no damage in being hauled around the corridors of Tŷ Dedwydd. Its name is the Monk's Wood Light Trap and it will be my main source of illumination tonight. I have gone to the trouble of bringing this cumbersome article for two reasons. First, my pencil torch is inadequate for the task I have in mind. Secondly, a more conventional light would be detected through the external windows: these are small and narrow, and set high in the walls, but light is a slippery customer and can wheedle its way through the tiniest of cracks. The Monk's Wood Light Trap, however, has a little hood on it so that it shines only downwards. As its name suggests, this contraption is designed principally to be used out of doors, for the purpose of catching insects. Under its light, there is a small motor which draws the captured specimens down into a bag. Yes, an insect trap. But I must say, it is just the ticket for tonight's operations, although these have nothing whatsoever to do with insects. I have not, of course, turned on the motor, nor attached the collection bag. Tonight, the Light Trap has to do only two things: provide adequate illumination and refrain from drawing attention to itself.

I put the lamp down next to the metal cupboards that fill one side of the room and start emptying my sack of its remaining contents: pyjamas, clean clothes for tomorrow, sleeping bag, toilet bag, electric razor, spare batteries for the lamp and the pencil torch, a writing pad and pens, and sufficient food and drink for supper and breakfast. I sit down at the table and collect my thoughts. I have until dawn to complete my work. A full ten hours. Everything is in place. I have been discrete. As far as the world knows, I am not here at all.

I open my sandwich box and start to eat my cheese and beetroot sandwiches. (I do so over the sandwich box in order not to scatter crumbs on the floor but I shall need to check again in the morning.) I am pleased to say that, despite my circumstances, I have quite an appetite. I pour myself a cup of tea from the flask, and I allow my gaze to wander, with an idle, unhurried sort of curiosity, around the room.

I notice the things I didn't notice on my first visit. There is a large white freezer by the door, and next to it a wine-rack, half-full. On a bench, which runs the length of the far wall, stand six computers, each with its chair. And then there are the cabinets, four of them, in grey metal. I put down my sandwich and amble over to the first of these. It is full of files, suspended in a concertina of compartments. I pull one out at random and turn on my pencil torch. It contains press cuttings. I see *The Western Mail, The Daily Post, Die Welt, The Observer, The Vale of Glamorgan Gem, The Sidney Morning Post, The Washington Post* and other newspapers. I read a few headlines. About cats and budgies and little puppy dogs being rescued from improbable dangers. About an old German soldier – one of the guards at Biberach, it says here – who arranged to meet one of his former prisoners to beg forgiveness. About a child who saw a ghost in some mansion or other and broke his neck as a result. Are these Tŷ Dedwydd contracts? I have no way of telling.

The files are in alphabetical order. I take out the letter *R*. And there he is. Mr R from Chepstow, the story that I myself cut out from the *Argus*. And a slightly later report, too, which I have not seen before, stating that Mr R and Ms T are to be married. Well, well, I think. Her acting was perhaps more credible than had at first appeared. I wonder, will she tell all one day, on the marital pillow? I move to the letter *S*. There is little of note here so I return to *A*, a much more weighty file. To a story, about one Armin Meiwes, that quite turns my stomach. But Ahmed is absent. So I conclude that my friend has not reached the papers under either of his names, Ahmed or Senini, and I am much relieved.

I return the file to its compartment and move to the next cabinet, the smallest of them all. Arrayed on its rows of grey metal shelves are a variety of packets, tubes and bottles. I examine the first. Its label says Ampalex. I replace it, taking care not to disturb the precise regularity of the display. Then another. Gilatide. Another. H3-blocker. Another. Sodium thiopental. The names mean nothing to me, but I jot them down in my notebook, just in case. My eyes have already wandered in the direction of a third cabinet, which has an altogether more promising aspect. It contains boxes. Boxes have always appealed to me. Except that crates is probably a better word for these particular items, which resemble the deep plastic containers used to carry children's toys and books. They fill the five long shelves from top to bottom, from end to end. Blue at the top, red in the middle, bright yellow on the lowest shelf.

I climb the small wooden stepladder which has been placed here for the purpose and peer into the first crate. It contains a dozen or so diaries. I know they are diaries because each has the year emblazoned in gold letters on its cover. On each spine is the name 'Anselm'. The most recent is some fifteen years old. I open it, but the writing inside is illegible, so I replace it and move on to the next crate. There is only one item here. A hat. A straw hat. The label selotaped to the end of the crate says 'Anthropos'. What this could mean I have not the slightest idea. I do know, however, that I cannot afford to waste any more time with such idle fiddling.

I move down to the second shelf and there, to my relief, amongst the *Bs*, I see a familiar name. Bates. His is one of four items in the crate, and it is the flimsiest of them. Letters, in the main. Letters, according to the Melbourne address at the top of each, written over a number of years by the long-lost son – that is, the son devised by Tŷ Dedwydd, not the real long-lost son – but never posted, because the son didn't know his mother's address, did he? Indeed, he didn't even know who she was. Not real letters, of course, but quite touching for all that, if you don't know what lies behind them. Little acts of piety, of hope that one day they might find their intended recipient. Little testimonies to the son's relationship, if not with a real mother, then at least with the idea of a mother, with the *need* for a mother, throughout the decades of their separation. I'm sure they left a deep impression on Mrs Bates when he came to see her in hospital, when he left them for her to read and re-read, at her leisure, after he had gone. To shed a tear over. And yet, if that is the case, if Mrs Bates was indeed given these letters, I don't understand why they have ended up here, in the archives. Why she isn't at this very moment poring over them, as she sips her bedtime Horlicks.

Yes, I do understand. Of course I understand. Poor Mrs Bates.

I go to the fourth and last of the cabinets. There are two blue crates on the middle row, each marked S. I take down the first. *Salway, Ferdinand. Selkirk, Alexis. Senini, Ahmed.*

Ahmed Senini. Yes, Ahmed Senini. And although I have now been here, in the Chief Benefactor's secret room, for over an hour, I feel it is somehow too early for such a discovery, such a confirmation of my suspicions. That for all my meticulous preparations, I am not yet quite ready *enough*. That my fingers, my eyes are moving too fast, I cannot keep up with them. So I take the crate over to the lamp and sit down on the floor. My hand shakes as I pour myself another cup of tea, as I raise the cup to my lips.

I spend ten minutes like this. Sipping slowly. Contemplating the crate by my side. Reminding myself that it is no more than that: a plastic crate. That it can do me no harm. Almost glad of the growing discomfort in my back, its distraction.

And then I am ready.

There are three items in Ahmed's file. The red photograph album, as I had expected. Also, an A4 envelope, bearing his name. This, too, contains photographs. A swift glance suggests that they are identical to the photographs I saw on the table last week. I have a good memory for details of this kind. The third item is a compact disk in a transparent envelope, bearing two names, *Senini, Ahmed and Senini, Yassuf*, and the dates 1965-1978.

I start with the photograph album. Attached to the first page is a label.

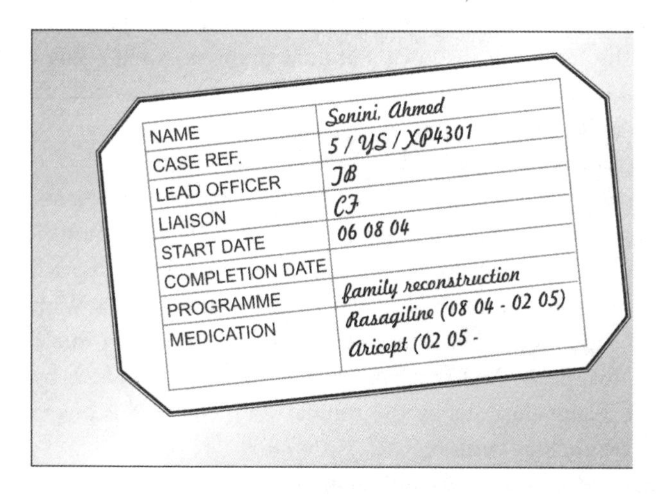

NAME	Senini, Ahmed
CASE REF.	5 / YS / XP4301
LEAD OFFICER	JB
LIAISON	CJ
START DATE	06 08 04
COMPLETION DATE	
PROGRAMME	family reconstruction
MEDICATION	Rasagiline (08 04 - 02 05) Aricept (02 05 -

On the page itself, however, the very first page of the album, is a name that is quite new to me. *This book belongs to Thomas Greenslade*. And under this name, the dates 1965-90. And under these, again, in a more rough-and-ready hand, the quip, NO LOOKING WITHOUT PERMISSION. I turn to the last page of the album, to what I assume will be the more recent items, in search of something familiar. But I find nothing but holiday snaps, the random highlights of strangers' lives. *Naxos 1989. Berchtesgaden 1988.* I turn the pages, working my way backwards in time. A wedding, equally anonymous. Degree day, the suited graduand standing here between his mother and father, there amongst his smiling friends. Where? I have no idea. July 1987. I study the faces more closely. The smart clothes. The big hair. They have that clone-like, inchoate uniformity that the middle-aged always see in the young. An alien species. And this will not do. This is not what I have been trained for. I must try harder.

So I look again. I try to see beyond the sameness. There is a figure at the end of the front row of graduands. He has darker skin than the rest. Is tall and thin. Is he familiar? Or is it merely that I am so eager to find the familiar that I imagine it to be there, wish it into existence? I bring the page closer to the light. I scan the faces a dozen times. And just when I'm about to give up the ghost and turn the page, she suddenly emerges from the crowd. Something transcends the waxen uniformity – the little crescent smile, perhaps, the slight tilt of the head, the shadowing around the eyes – and I know it is Cerys. Her hair is longer, her face fuller, but there is no doubt about it. The smile, the gown, the mortar board, the unseeing eyes, they all belong to Cerys.

I turn the pages and travel back through the years. The same faces smile at me, the one who will soon graduate – who must, I have decided, be Thomas Greenslade himself – his parents, the tall thin man, and sundry aunts and uncles and cousins and friends. With each turned page they regain hair, lose jowels, win back their innocence. Cerys disappears. And the family, the Greenslade family, is back in Cardiff. There they are, by the Animal Wall. The hair is bigger still. Flares are back in fashion.

Ahmed makes his first appearance in 1976. I don't recognise him immediately. He's small for his age and more delicate than the Ahmed of later years, but the caption confirms the identities: *Ahmed, Amat, Helen, Brian and me Barry Summer 1976.* Thomas Greenslade is the 'me', I'm sure, as this is his album. There are several snaps of the same group, sometimes with other children, including one of a picnic in the garden in 1973. I should hazard a guess that Thomas and Helen are brother and sister. Perhaps Ahmed and Amat, too, as they fall out of the record at precisely the same time. For a year. Two years. Three.

And I am beginning to think that perhaps it is at this time, around 1973, that the Senini family moved to the area, that this, therefore, is the end of their story as far as the photograph album is concerned. But no, after turning just another two or three pages, here they are again. It is the summer of 1970. Ahmed is now a small boy in short pants. We are back on Barry beach – I can see the holiday chalets in the background. The parents are in their deckchairs. The children are busy with their buckets and spades. The caption says *Helen, Yassuf, me, Ahmed, Mam, Dad, Amat*. Yassuf, whom I have not seen before, is digging a hole in the sand. Thomas Greenslade watches him. Their faces are turned away from the camera. A picture of the same group appears on the next page, with one addition: a woman, perhaps Ahmed's mother, has joined the children on the sand. The children are licking their ice-creams and making faces at the camera. I can see them all this time. Yassuf, the new child, is on the left, if the order of names on the caption is to be believed. Yassuf. Who is Yassuf? And perhaps it would not matter who he was if Ahmed was not also in the picture. As I say, from the perspective of middle age, the young are of a single mould. But Ahmed *is* in the picture. So there must be some error. Because Yassuf is surely Ahmed. And Ahmed is surely Yassuf. Or, rather, there are two Ahmeds. He is on the left, standing by himself, looking down at the others. But he is in the middle, too, between Thomas and his sister, kneeling on the sand, licking his ice-cream. I turn the page. There they are again, standing in front of a terraced house this time, the two Ahmeds and their friends. Number 11, I can see it plainly. And again. They are younger now, young enough to sit in their mother's lap, while Thomas's mother sits next to them, mug of tea in one hand, cigarette in the other. Quite carefree. And her big hair, her short skirt, her thick make-up declaring to the world that this is no lie, this is history, and who am I to doubt the evidence of my own eyes?

So why do I doubt?

I move the album closer to the light. I look at the two Ahmeds, quite willing, indeed quite keen, to be persuaded that it is I who am at fault, that my doubts are not only impossibly vague but also specious. There are differences. Here, one Ahmed parts his hair on the left, the other on the right. There, one Ahmed wears sandals, the other shoes. The shirt of one has short sleeves, the other long. In every corporeal respect, however, even in the way the smile of each lists slightly to the left, they are as identical as it is possible for them to be.

So then, why do I still doubt?

On the second page of the album there is a gap. The caption is there, but no photograph.

Senini twins birthday 1971 (?)

Common sense says, if there's a caption surely there must also be a photograph, somewhere. Who would go to the trouble of writing out a caption unless there was already a picture to which it belonged? So where has that picture gone?

I put the album to one side and open the A4 envelope. It contains the same photographs as the album, no more, no less. It contains the same gap. I say 'contains' as though the gap were something visible, palpable. I do so deliberately: it sums up how I have come to regard this lacuna in the collection. In fact, I would go so far as to say that the gap has by now acquired a more pressing reality than the photographs themselves. I am not surprised that the gap is here, and yet I feel betrayed and not a little desperate. I have been given three chances and the first two – the album and the envelope – have conspired to disappoint.

The disk is my last hope. It teases me with its opaque promise of something more authoritative, more truthful. I take it out of its plastic sleeve and go to the nearest computer. I turn it on, wait for it to come to life. I key in my password. It is rejected. I try 'Benefactor', 'Tŷ Dedwydd', '*cymwynas*' and 'favour'. They are all rejected. Of course they are. I curse the machine. I curse Ahmed and Cerys. I curse my own fatuous curiosity.

With a groan, I take out my pencil torch, extinguish the Monk's Wood Light Trap and set out for my own room, my own computer. After two short steps, however, I turn off even this meagre source of illumination, for I am in mortal fear that my luck has run out. That a security guard, even a member of the public will, sooner or later, see a spot of light on door-frame, on window, on wall, its halo around my hand, and think, 'A-ha! I've got you now, you little tyke!' And ring the police. And what should I say then? Explanations that hold water at seven leak like sieves at half past eleven.

I leave the Doctor's door ajar, just as I found it, and walk back into the dark. I feel my way along the corridor, counting the rooms, naming them out loud, in a bold whisper, in an effort to raise my spirits. 'Hefin's room... Wilbert's room... Cerys's room...'. I then turn around and, as a precaution against falling (because bad luck rarely strikes with a single blow), descend the stairs backwards, crouching, one hand grasping the bannister, the other planted firmly on the step I have just vacated, like a third leg. I pause a while by the window and take comfort from its little cube of distant city light. And regret doing so, then, as the darkness inside is thereby made only darker. Reaching my own corridor, I stand up straight again, but even here is unfamiliar, has lost its usual shape and size. A wall that was once smooth is now, to my fingertips, quite rough. Because feeling is different to seeing. Yes, a different matter altogether.

I reach my room, relieved and grateful as a shipwrecked sailor fetching up on dry land. It is now numbingly cold. I blow on my fingers and load the disk into my computer. It opens without protest. I see the same photographs. The photographs in the red album, in the A4 envelope. Of course I do. The same photographs exactly. And I see the gap, filled.

Senini twins birthday 1971 (?)

There it is. The tea party. The two twins – for that is what the caption insists they are – both smiling cheekily at the camera. I can almost hear their giggles. And another boy whom I have not seen before, leaning over the table, sticking out his tongue.

But this is what is most remarkable. As I scroll down, I notice a number of other photographs. I take these, at first, simply to be copies of those I have already seen in the album. But no. In these pictures, there is only one Ahmed. Or one Yassuf, of course. It is impossible to distinguish between them. Only Ahmed, or Yassuf, is playing with Thomas on the beach. Ahmed alone stands outside the terraced house. Number 11. And here is another snap of the tea party, the birthday celebration. The same naughty child bends over the table, showing me his tongue. Ahmed smiles mischievously. The same smile. Only Ahmed. Or Yassuf. Only one boy is celebrating his birthday here. There are no twins here. Nor are there twins in the other pictures, scores of them, as I scroll down further. Only one boy, Ahmed or Yassuf, digs a hole in the sand, runs after pigeons in the park, sits on his mother's knee, opens his Christmas presents. There is no brother.

So I return to the picture of the tea party – that is, the twins' tea party, not the lonely little boy's tea party. I notice now that it is not quite as clear as the others. But there is something else about it, something that does not seem right, that does not belong. The twins are separated by a curious white strip, quite narrow, quite unobtrusive. And perhaps you would not look twice, not unless you already had your suspicions. But, then, I do have my suspicions, and looking twice is my business. So what is it? What *is* this white strip? Part of a chair, perhaps? No, that cannot be, it is too high, and in any case no other part of the chair is visible. An effect of the flash, perhaps, casting shadows in one place, bright reflections in another? I think not. Whatever it is, the white strip is too solid, too material simply to be a trick of the light. All I can say with certainty is that it resembles an arm. And that is a patent absurdity, for there is no hand or shoulder attached to it. The picture is a lie.

It was Ahmed himself who taught me how to use Photoshop. As Publications Officer at the Museum, it had always been a key part of his duties to devise new, more engaging ways of presenting our collections, especially to children. Unfortunately, the raw materials for this labour were, for the large part, inert and rather dull: stones, bones, stuffed birds, mounted insects and the like. A museum is not, after all, a zoo or an adventure playground. Nevertheless, through devious use of Photoshop, Ahmed did his level best to bring these exhibits to some semblance of life in the publicity leaflets and the educational packs. It was, to be truthful, something of a cheap trick – a few fronds here, a delving peasant or two there – but at least it reminded us that our ancient arrow-heads, carved stones, iron-age bowls and the like had not always been hidden away in some antiseptic gallery, like abandoned refugees. He did the same for our insects and spiders: he put them back in their original habitats. He would take a picture of a specimen in one of the display cases – the Monarch itself, perhaps, or a particularly photogenic beetle, like the Goliath. He would then scan this image into his computer, removing any extraneous elements such as pins and labels and background reflections, and then superimpose it onto another image: a jungle in South America or a Carmarthenshire hillside or an African desert, as appropriate. The dead were raised into new life, you could say, with a little poetic licence. That is the achievement of Photoshop. It can bring together two disparate worlds and make them one.

Photoshop Twins

Ahmed's knowledge of insect habitats is not, of course, extensive and at the outset, in his first fit of technological zeal, he would often make the most egregious howlers. I remember him taking a splendid shot of a giant woodlouse. (This is one of those fortunate creatures that can reproduce itself without having recourse to a mate.) In his eager naivety, Ahmed placed the woodlouse on the banks of the Amazon, imagining, no doubt, that any old jungle would suffice and quite ignoring the fact that his subject was a native, not of Brazil, but of Malaysia, and Malaysia alone. 'No-one will know the difference!' he said. '*I* will, Ahmed!' I replied. '*I'll* know the difference!' And he had to change it. Since that episode I have insisted that we confer with one another whenever a leaflet or booklet might trespasses upon my discipline. He was not put out. Indeed, we quickly came to respect our different areas of expertise.

The picture of the twins' tea-party is a creation of Photoshop. Opening up the layer pallette, I can disaggregate its elements. I can return to the original photographs, as they were, pristine and innocent. The boy with the tongue is the first to be released. Examining his face more closely, using the zoom function, comparing this image with the others, I can see clearly that this is Thomas Greenslade himself. Yes, Thomas Greenslade has been added. He is an extraneous layer. He was never even on the invitation list. So I think to myself, Out you go, my little dissembler! Ahmed is the next to be expelled. Yes, Ahmed, the birthday boy himself. Only one Ahmed, mind you. The other will have to stay, to entertain his chums: it would be rude to do otherwise. I pluck this stray Ahmed from the group and return him to his mother's knee, because it is this picture, the mother-and-Ahmed picture, that has been cannibalised in order to procure two Ahmeds for the party. Yes, I can see this clearly now. Ahmed on his mother's knee, smiling in that slightly lop-sided way. But through negligence or lack of skill, I cannot say which, the author of this particular piece of fiction, in transferring the son from one image to the other, has failed to expunge the whole of the mother's arm. The job has been left unfinished. Someone has let the side down. Some junior member of staff, no doubt, cutting his teeth, making his first cock-up. And this, of course, is why the tea-party does not appear in the photograph album, in the elaborate tapestry of fabrications that is the Greenslade family, in the secret and mysterious life of Ahmed Senini. This is why there is only a gap, an unfulfilled caption.

And what about you, Cerys? Are you part of the real history? Or are you merely fiction, too, a child of Photoshop? How can I tell? I turn to the other pictures, the grown-up ones, half fearing, half wishing that they, too, will unravel and expose some further deceit. I scrutinise them. I will them to tell me their secrets. Because I am on my mettle now. Nothing will escape the sweep of my net. But they remain dumb. They are complete little worlds, without joins or layers. If they are telling lies, the lies are too devious for me to detect, let alone unpick.

And what is a lie if it can never be detected?

27. In the Cave

I awake at five. It is still dark, and colder than ever. But it is not the cold that wakes me: my sleeping bag is a four season model. It is my own voice. Whether my real voice or else a voice in my head, I cannot tell, but I know what the voice is saying, is shouting. My brother's name, John.

I was eleven at the time; my brother almost sixteen. It was the day we buried Wncwl Wil. My mother went to the funeral in Pontardawe. John, however, had already arranged to go camping with a friend in a cave they'd found near Ystradfellte. It was decided that I should go camping, too, although I had little appetite for such things. My mother said that funerals were for old women, not young boys. I told her she wasn't old, not really, and she liked that. But it didn't change her mind.

On the other hand, although I might well have chosen more congenial company or even, had I been given permission, ventured there alone, the trip did give me an opportunity – indeed, my very first opportunity – to visit one of Alfred Wallace's more remote haunts in south Wales. It was here, in the upper reaches of the Neath valley, that he discovered the bee-beetle, *Trichius fasciatus.* It was here, too, in Porth-yr-Ogof cave, that he spent the night, accompanied by his own brother. I knew these things from reading *My Life*. I also knew that Wallace found the cave very unsalubrious. Had I paid heed to these comments, I am sure I would have prevailed more firmly upon my mother to take me to the funeral. Such are the pitfalls of wishful thinking.

I was not required to speak to my brother during this outing, nor he to me: his friend, Jeff, kept him well enough amused; indeed, they spent most of the journey absorbed in a tedious kind of adolescent tussle, each trying to outdo the other in the ribaldry of their jokes, their puerile innuendos. It was all an unseemly display of guffaws and titters, of which I understood not one word in ten. I remember none of it.

Yes, I do. I remember one crude jingle. *My uncle had a three foot willy, He showed it to the girl next door, She thought it was a snake and hit it with a rake, Now it's only two foot four.* I remember this for the simple reason that my brother, for once, was unable to respond in kind.

'Your Uncle Billy got a big willy then?'

I told Jeff that I didn't have an Uncle Billy. And that Wncwl Wil had died. And that he wasn't a real uncle, anyway.

'You 'it 'im with a rake then did you?'

That's when my brother started trading jokes again. And although he said nothing, although he would never acknowledge as much, I knew that he was doing what he could to save my blushes. I felt better then.

Having taken the bus to Pont Nedd Fechan, we followed the waterfall path to Ystradfellte. (My mother had insisted we phone her before seven o'clock and here, as far as we knew, was the only payphone for miles around.) We then climbed the steep, slippery slope up to the cave. The weather had been quite sultry and, just as we were unpacking our rucksacks, the storm broke. A torrent of rain fell over the mouth of the cave, as fierce and impregnable as any waterfall we had seen that day. We found shelter from the spray through sitting on a wide natural shelf, set back to the left of the cave entrance. There was no escaping the damp, however, nor the roar of the nearby stream, which was now in full spate. Nor could we evade the stones that carpeted the floor. We cleared the sharpest and largest of them. None of us expected much sleep that night.

But sleep we did, for a while at least, because I remember waking suddenly, in a blind panic, shouting for my brother, and panicking still more when I didn't get a reply. I was panicking at nothing, of course – nothing except the dark: at the fact that I couldn't see anything and then, even more frighteningly, at the fact that there was nothing to hand that might compensate for this inability to see. Something I could feel, like my bedside table at home, or hear, like the ticking of my alarm clock. Although I reached out as far as I could, to my right and to my left, and crawled on all fours then, in search of my clothes, my shoes, something familiar, and the darkness thick and syrupy around me, I could find nothing. I thought that perhaps it was all a dream, the cave, my brother, his friend, the walk up through Cwm Mellte. That if I just waited a little, the darkness would stop rubbing its dirty fingers against my lips, my cheeks, the back of my neck. And that's when I heard a sound, the sound of shoes on stone, of tripping and slipping, the sound of my own voice, then, shouting, screaming.

'Don't fall! Don't fall!'

That is the sound that woke me this morning, in Tŷ Dedwydd, the sound of my own voice, shouting at my brother, John.

28. Ahmed Remembers

I arranged to meet Cerys at the Turkish restaurant in Cowbridge Road: a simple, unpretentious sort of place, according to Cerys, but convenient. 'Within walking distance of us all,' she said. I did not know to whom the 'all' referred and was not minded to ask. I had already yielded many an inch and I wasn't going to let her take the whole mile. You may think this obdurate, eccentric even, but that is how it was: I didn't, at that moment, want to give her the hostage of my curiosity. You may wonder why I was going out for dinner with Cerys at all, when I had just discovered her apparent – and I emphasise the word *apparent* – implication in the Ahmed photograph album business. But that is the point, you see: in life, things do not happen with the sort of neat, consecutive logic that we would wish. The truth is that I had not yet resolved these things in my own mind. Indeed, you could say, if you wished, that I was using the meal at the Turkish restaurant as a sort of test, where I would try to tease out the recalcitrant facts, just as I had done with the photographs.

You can imagine my surprise, therefore, when the first to arrive was none other than Ahmed himself and his wife, Helen, and then, hard on their heels, the tall, thin man. Yes, the same tall, thin man who had, in a manner of speaking, been shadowing me for many days – in the video, in the photographs, on the doorstep of the terraced house in Grangetown – and now, tonight, once more, in the Salamis restaurant in Canton. He was with his wife.

'Dan... Nizar... Nadia.'

'Pleased to meet you.'

There was to have been another guest, Cerys said, an old college friend, but he was unable to come because of illness in the family. Did I know him? No, Cerys thought it unlikely. Nizar explained that the person in question lived far away, somewhere in the Midlands, and that he rarely came to Cardiff. A pity. Yes, a great pity. Ahmed concurred and said he looked forward very much to meeting Tom one day.

'Tom?' I said.

'Yes, Tom Greenslade,' said Ahmed. 'Don't tell me *you* know him too, Dan. That would be too much of a coincidence.'

Yes, Ahmed, it would. It's a small world, but not that small. And yet, my dear friend, I fear I already know Thomas Greenslade a great deal better than you do yourself. I did not say this, of course. I studied my menu. I observed. I listened.

Although Tom couldn't be present, said Nizar, he had sent something which we might find interesting. At which point Nizar took an envelope from his jacket pocket. It had arrived in the post that morning, he said. And from the envelope he took a photograph: a photograph, according to Tom, which had fallen out of the album and got lost, until he had found it again on his return home, behind the sofa, or the dresser, or some such place. Nizar showed the picture to Ahmed. (At the same time, he placed the empty envelope on the table by my side. And if I were a more suspicious person, I should have sworn that he did so quite deliberately, to ensure that I saw the Nottingham postmark, the little stamp of verisimilitude.)

'There he is,' said Nizar. 'There's Tom. The cheeky lad, the one leaning over the table, sticking his tongue out. Do you remember him, Ahmed?'

Nizar lifted up the photograph for us all to see.

'Ahmed and Yassuf's birthday party,' he said. 'Must be thirty years ago. And that's me on the left. Look, Helen.'

Helen smiled lovingly at the little boy with the delicate face who would become her husband. And realised, then, that she could not be so certain. 'But which one are you, Ahmed?' she asked. Ahmed had no idea. And I thought, well, of course, how could he know?

'It's all very sad,' said Naida. 'So sad.'

But Nizar, the tall, thin man, knew exactly which was Ahmed. 'You see that little toy on the table?' he said. 'It's just been taken out of its box. What did they call them again..? Ahmed, do you remember what they called them? Those little men…'

Ahmed scratched his head.

'Anyway,' said Nizar, 'I remember Yassuf complaining that he hadn't been given as many presents as you, Ahmed… And your mother saying, no, no, you'd just had *different* presents, that's all, that some were bigger and some were smaller and you couldn't expect to have exactly the same number… Something like that… And you, Ahmed… Don't you remember..? You gave your… your…'

'Action Man..?' I suggested.

'That's it, Dan!' said Nizar, 'That's it!' He said this with a sense of discovery, even revelation, as though the mere name somehow clinched the matter. 'That's what it was. Action Man. Ahmed gave his Action Man to Yassuf, so they could be friends again. Yes, I remember it all. Just like yesterday. Like it all happened yesterday. Ahmed's the one in the middle, Helen. A minute later, he gives the Action Man to his brother. Isn't that right, Ahmed?'

'Well, yes, perhaps,' said Ahmed, staring at the photograph, as though trying to get it into better focus, knowing that if the party itself was a blur, it was hardly surprising he had no memory of the presents, of *that* present. 'Yes, it rings a bell… Just a tinkle…'

'And I thought,' said Nizar, 'I thought how fine it would be to have a brother of my own, you know, to share things with.'

Ahmed showed me the picture.

'You see him, Dan? Here… Just by my side.'

I nodded. What else could I do?

'My brother, Dan. I thought he'd died when he was a baby.'

'Yes, Ahmed, I know. Your brother.' Because we all knew about Ahmed's brother, his Yassuf, his lost daemon.

'My twin, Dan. My identical twin. The same spit. Look… Look at the two of us… I bet you can't tell us apart.'

Of course I couldn't tell them apart. I might stare at the picture all evening and I should still not be able to see a single hair of difference between them

'Don't you remember him, Ahmed?'

Ahmed looked at the picture. Scratched his head. Knitted his brow. Nodded. 'I think so,' he said. 'It's all so long ago.'

As I reflect upon my evening in the Turkish restaurant in Cowbridge Road, what is remarkable is how easily I could play the game. Indeed, I almost forgot, at times, that it was a game we were playing. The reason for this, I believe, is that there was something else going on, something I would not demean by calling it a mere game, although there was certainly a spirit of playfulness in the air. If I am embarrassed now to acknowledge this 'thing', it is not because I was solely, or even chiefly to blame. Oh, no. What, then, was this 'thing'? you ask. What was this playfulness that was not a game? Well, how shall I put it? I do not wish to tempt fate. No, and I have resolved to be on my guard, to take nothing for granted. Nevertheless, it was quite clear from the way that Cerys spoke to me, and more especially from the way she spoke *about* me to the others, that she considered me to be something more than a colleague. Please don't expect me to quote chapter and verse: if you'd been there, you'd understand what I mean. Yes, and more than a friend, too, I should say, although I freely admit that I may be being presumptuous here. More than a friend, but less than a… what would one say? Partner? Yes, patently less than that. But if we were not a couple in the sense that Ahmed and Helen, and Nizar and Nadia were couples – how could we be?– we nevertheless partook somewhat of that status for the purpose of the evening in question. Perhaps no more than that. But even if only that, it was a fine feeling, a feeling I was quite content to savour for a while. Where I had expected to be a figure on the margins, I found myself, instead, to be one of a cosy little 'us'. And I do not refer only to the 'us' around the table, but also to a more significant 'us' which Cerys was all too willing to throw into the pot, as it were. Yes, and come to think of it, it was her coinage entirely, this 'us'. Of course it was. It is not in my nature to be so forward. 'We,' she said. 'We' worked together. 'We' frequented the same reading group. 'We' were both very proud of Nia, who was doing so well in the drama workshop. Even when she talked about her operation, and about her progress afterwards, I was folded into that experience, too, as her support and helpmeet. And whilst Cerys sang my praises, I am sure that Ahmed looked at me with that slightly mischievous smile of his. Because he could sense it as well, this 'thing', this 'us'. So by the time we started on the Yaprak Sarma, I had neither the desire nor even the wherewithal to pour cold water on such an unexpected blessing, nor on anything else that came within reach of its warm embrace.

'It's coming back, Dan…' said Ahmed. 'Mam said he died when he was just a baby, you see… But that was to spare my feelings, I can see that now, to lessen the hurt… It must have been such a shock…'

And what exactly came back to him?

'I can remember the party… Not everything, mind you… I don't think I remember Tom very well…'

But, as Nizar was quick to explain, Tom and his family had moved away when he was still only a little *dwt* of a thing. Somewhere near Nottingham, wasn't it?

'Yes… I remember… I remember being there with Yassuf... I remember wanting to share my presents with him… Felt he'd had a bit of a raw deal… And you shouldn't be like that, should you, not on your birthday, all upset?'

29. Closing the Eyes

After we'd bade the others good night, I offered to walk Cerys home. Did I do so with a clear conscience? I believe I did. Or, at least, I knew it was not my place to judge, to make idle accusations, to impugn others without hard evidence. 'Cerys, tell me what you know about the cut-and-paste job on the photographs of Ahmed and…' No, such an insinuation would have been unconscionable. So why, then, did I not quiz someone else? Someone less vulnerable, someone who occupied a more – how can I put it? – a more *neutral* position with respect to myself. Someone like Nizar, for example. Because Nizar seemed to know a thing or two. Yes, I could have pressed him. Tell me more, I could have said… About this photograph, about what you and Cerys did in college… You were in college together, weren't you...? But the opportunity had passed and was unlikely to return. In any case, Nizar seemed to be a man of good will and generous disposition. His wife, too. Yes, and all the others, for that matter. What is more, there was nothing going on between Cerys and Ahmed, nothing whatsoever, or at least nothing more than a good turn, a favour, that would leave Ahmed feeling much more content with his lot than he had before. And to what end would one wish to undermine that new-found contentment? For what purpose would one deliberately sour the Karisik Izgara and the Imam Bayildi and the other mouth-watering dishes we had enjoyed at Salamis? The feast had been eaten. It had not been found wanting. And that was an end to it.

I offered to walk Cerys home and she accepted. On reaching the crossroad I took hold of her arm but she said she did not need my help, thank you very much. By now, she said, she had learned how to cross both of the roads that ran between her house and the centre of Canton. It was from this spot that she caught the bus to work every morning. The green man was a help, she said, but she preferred to close her eyes and wait for the *beep-beep-beep* and the slow purring of the cars as they came to a stop. Her ears never betrayed her. And it was, of course, more difficult to see at night. The street lamps and the lights from the cars, the pubs and restaurants all became a great kaleidoscope, clusters of garish little suns bobbing in the air. It was so easy to become confused, to panic.

'So I close my eyes, Dan. I close my eyes and listen.'

I followed suit, I closed my own eyes so that I might share that sense of estrangement that Cerys felt in our world, the world of the sighted. 'You can be my guide this time, Cerys,' I said. And I was so glad that I could place my trust in her once more that I decided to disregard, as matters of no further note, the business with the pictures, the fabrication of the twins, and the other concerns whose jabbing little fingers had poked at my conscience only hours before. Somehow her sadness, her disappointment, her longing for something forever lost, washed away any blemish that might, for a while, have tarnished her virtue.

I had not been in Cerys's house before.

'You'll have to excuse the state of the place, Dan. It needs a good lick of paint, I know.'

And there was no doubting this. Every wall and ceiling was of a uniform white, or rather half-white, according to the minimalist fashion of the 1980s. Although, in truth, because of the dull and sporadic lighting, the colour I actually saw was somewhat less than half-white but rather an insipid grey. The paint had started peeling at the corners. Patches of mould spread like rashes beneath the windows.

'Looks fine to me, Cerys.'

Nor were there any pictures to relieve the monotony. Nor flowers. I might almost say that the place was suffused with a kind of monastic austerity. But only almost because, despite the apparent bareness of the house, closer inspection revealed no essential lack of *things*. These things, however, obeyed some logic of distribution, of arrangement, which confounded the usual proprieties pertaining to household articles. For example, the end of the sofa was set tightly up against the frame of the kitchen door. The coffee table was in the corner of the lounge, not in the middle. Most disconcerting of all were the ornaments. Instead of being displayed on the mantlepiece, or else scattered around the place in the usual *faux*-random manner, they had all been coralled and regimented according to a strict classification and set out on parade on wall shelves that had clearly been mounted for the purpose. Yes, a strict classification, just as though they were specimens of *coleoptera*, pinned in display cases for our close perusal. Little stones here. Pieces of bright crystal a yard or so to the left. Then the seashells. And finally the porcelain bowls. All in their own segregated townships.

'I'd be glad to paint the place myself, Dan, but I'm not comfortable with colours… I don't know what to do with them.'

'Well,' I said. 'I can help, if you like.' Because it would have been churlish not to.

She went to the kitchen.

'I've done nothing to the place since the operation. Not even these.'

Cerys opened the cupboard doors. All of the items were laid out in straight, neat rows.

'Alphabetical order?'

'Of course.'

The shelves were not labelled in any way, but then this was not surprising. It was sufficient that the items corresponded to the order in the mind. Flour, then oats, then coffee, then nuts, then crisps, then beans and so on… I list them as they were arranged, according to their Welsh names: some things cannot be translated literally.

'To be sure I don't open a tin of pineapple when I want a tin of salmon,' said Cerys. Without looking, she took a jar of coffee from the top shelf.

The fridge was the same. The vegetable racks, too. Even the cleaning fluids under the sink did, I'm sure, follow the same strict rubric, although I was unable to discern how precisely she distinguished one Jif from another. Smell, perhaps.

'I've committed them all to memory, Dan… There's a place for everything here, and everything's in its place.' She shook her head. 'Why should I lose that, Dan? Why should I give up that order? That certainty?'

'You mustn't,' I said. And I meant it, not only for Cerys's sake but for my own. Because this was a way of doing things that greatly appealed to me. I liked its diligent taxonomies. I liked, too, how it had all been accomplished with such discretion, with the minimum of fuss. Behind closed doors, on such undistinguished, anonymous shelves as these, a whole world submitted to the quiet jurisdiction of the memory. As Cerys made my coffee – a very weak coffee, I insisted, given the lateness of the hour – I assured her that she need give up nothing just to please others. I told her to forget about her eyes for a moment and if she did so, I would do the same, I would enter her world for a while rather than presuming on her willingness to struggle with mine. And there, in that place where Cerys need bend the knee to no-one, she could be my guide again.

'It's, true, Dan,' she said. 'Seeing can be a curse.'

We returned to the lounge and sat down. Small square tables stood at either end of the sofa. On each of these a small square coaster had already been placed, to receive its mug of coffee. As the sofa had been positioned next to the kitchen door, we faced, not a fire nor a television (the room contained neither) but a Victorian wall cupboard, fronted with those little glazed doors which once upon a time, when there was a fireplace here, and a fire burning in it, would have kept the crockery free of soot. Now, the cupboard housed black plastic boxes, stacked neatly in piles of a dozen or so. Talking books, Cerys said, and plays. We chatted about these for a while, and about herself, her own acting career, and then about her mother, because it was from her mother that she had inherited the house. I spoke about my own mother then, my grandmother, too, my childhood visits to her house in Llanelli, and as I did so Cerys closed her eyes – the better to visualise the details, I supposed at the time, although I now realise that this was probably a fanciful notion. Anyway, she closed her eyes, so I closed my eyes too.

'I have closed my eyes, Cerys,' I said, so that she would realise I had done so, so that she would not feel at a disadvantage. 'You have the upper hand now, Cerys.' Which, I felt, was only right and proper in her own home. I said that I knew it was a tired old cliché, the idea that blind people recognised each other through touch, through tracing the contours of each other's faces, and yet, I said, despite the triteness of this notion, it somehow appealed to me, and I'd like to give it a go. Something to that effect. She agreed that it was, indeed, a feeble stereotype, ignorant and patronising to boot, and that blind people were capable of saying 'I'm so-and-so, who are you?' with the best of them. Then she had a little chuckle and said that was no reason not to give it a try. But, she added, there was one condition. I said, yes, Cerys, yes, what is that? And she said, the condition, Dan, is that you keep your eyes closed. This is what she said. This is what she insisted upon. So I closed my eyes once more. I held my hands out, spread my fingers, ever so slowly and hesitantly, because I was unfamiliar with this kind of seeing, and Cerys did the same, so that, in a little while, our fingers touched, only the tips to begin with, each one in turn, until they felt comfortable with each other. After this we explored the palms of our hands, and then our wrists, and lingered there a while, because the wrist, I discovered, contains within it expanses of feeling which quite belie its small dimensions. I had to get closer, then, as my arms were beginning to tire. And in moving closer I could now reach Cerys's face, the turn of the jaw under the ears, the soft, smooth cheeks. And how difficult it was to resist the temptation to peep, just once. To get one's bearings back. To be one's own voyeur. And how strange, as I gently moved the tips of my fingers across Cerys's forehead and cheeks and, more gently still, to her eyebrows, to the little creases at the corners of her eyes, and then the eyelashes, just the lightest of all possible touches, how strange to discover the face to be so expansive, to be so much bigger than it had ever appeared to my eyes. And we both laughed when I said as much. I apologised for being so insensitive, but in a jovial, devil-may-care kind of way, and without the least embarrassment, because that is what happens when you cannot see the other, when you cannot feel her gaze. And I said, if we agreed that our fingers were better than our eyes at tracing the curves and contours of the human face, then how much better still, how very much better even than the fingers, was the tongue. Yes, nothing could beat the tongue for getting to the heart of the matter. So we kept our eyes closed. We saw with our tongues, we spoke with our tongues, but without words. And if I stole a little glance, just the merest peep, I did so only to appreciate more fully Cerys's sweet acquiesence.

30. A Request for Forgiveness

I'm sorry, Mam. Things weren't meant to turn out like this. But for the life of me, I can't see any other way of helping you. And it would be cruel to let things go on as they are. I'm sorry I can't explain it to you, sit you down with a glass of sherry and say, this is what we must do, and it's all for your own good, there's no need to worry. I would if I could. But it wouldn't work then, you see. Like dyeing a piece of cloth: cover it in wax and the colour won't take. Knowledge is like wax. Too much knowledge and the favour won't work. In any case, I know that you'd get confused and anxious, you'd start having nightmares. You'd say I'd planned it all, for God knows what reason, but you'd think of something. But it's not true, Mam. There was no plan, no conspiracy. It all happened by accident. I didn't even know what I was looking for that night in Tŷ Dedwydd.

And what good would it do if I told you about these things now? If I started prattling about Ahmed's little outing with Cerys, about the meal I had with Helen and Nizar and Nadia, about Photoshop and layer pallettes and the fate of some tawdry little Action Man over thirty years ago? Because none of it matters now. It all worked out for the best, you see, both for you and for me. Yes, Mam, for me too. Because I have given up doubting. Doubting doesn't make you happy. And that's the point, you see. Everyone *was* happy in the end. I was happy with them. And this is the point, too. I've realised now that if Ahmed can get rid of his sadness, if I can purge myself of my anger and suspicion, why shouldn't *you* do the same? Why shouldn't you, too, cast off your burden of troubles and bitter memories?

That's what I'd tell you, Mam, if I could. I'd tell you that I've found a way of making you better, of washing your memory clean. It's odd that it didn't occur to me sooner, but there we are, my mind was on other things. I forgot all about the Aricept and the Rasagiline: they were nothing but words in my notebook. I forgot about the cupboard, too, with its packets and tubes and bottles and little black boxes. They were cold and impersonal. The photographs were much more interesting.

I have never found it easy to buy you presents, Mam, but this time I've come up with something which I know will not disappoint. And it's a lot better than anything you had from Sue, that's for sure. Sue gave you nothing. At least, nothing but frivolities, memories that were scarcely worth the effort of remembering. Your son can do a lot better than that. You'll never know this, of course, and I'm sorry about that. But you'll just have to have faith. Put your trust in me, Mam, and you'll see, everything will be fine.

31. Some Tentative Experiments

My plan had two parts. First, I had to select and procure the appropriate medication. As I could not recall with sufficient certainty the names I had seen on the packets and bottles in Dr Bruno's secret room (and these are not things about which one can afford to be slapdash), I was compelled to spend a further night there in order to make a full inventory. I found over fifty items. Fortunately, there was plentiful information on the Web about each of these and within only a few days I had whittled down the options to a more manageable eleven. For these, I compiled detailed profiles, so that I could assess their appropriateness, giving due weight to matters such as side-effects and methods of administration: a crucial issue, this, when a degree of concealment is required.

Of all the drugs I considered, Aricept was the most appealing, if only because it had done the business for Ahmed, rendering him as receptive and pliable as a little puppy. Unfortunately, it had two serious deficiencies. It might take two months to achieve its full effect. I could not afford to wait so long. Also, according to the Web, cholinesterase inhibitors could have vagotonic effects on the sinoatrial and atriventricular nodes. I had no idea what these words meant but they sounded grim so I erred on the side of caution and discarded this option.

At first sight, scopolamine also seemed a promising candidate. The CIA had used it in the 1950s as a truth drug. Very quickly, however, it was discovered to be an unreliable quantity. Subjects became prone to wild hallucinations and delusions: reactions which were of little use in the pursuit of truth. For my own purposes, of course, some tendency in this direction – some openness to alternative realities, you might say – might well have proved beneficial, and I hesitated for some time before putting this option, too, to one side. Once again, the unpredictable side-effects were to blame. The drug is extremely poisonous and the slightest overdose can induce 'delirium, delusion, paralysis, stupor and death'. I was not prepared to take the risk.

In the end, and after much humming and hah-ing, I chose

Sodium thiopental: an old favourite, it appears, for missions such as mine. It is true that this drug also has its side-effects: it can cause lethargy, dizziness, nausea and a number of other unpleasant symptoms. According to one unnecessarily graphic website, it is also often used to pacify the condemned before execution: not a very savoury association, I'm sure you'll agree. Nevertheless, once I had weighed up the advantages and disadvantages, I concluded that Sodium thiopental, though far from perfect, was the best candidate available. It could be taken in water, its effects were felt within a few minutes and they continued for up to half an hour: an optimum period, this, for what I had in mind, and one whose loss would not intrude excessively upon the daily routine, the sense of equilibrium, of the subject. A little nap, that's all. So, the choice was made.

Procuring the substance itself, however, proved more difficult. During the following three weeks, the first three weeks of December, I spent five further nights at Tŷ Dedwydd – five nights of unmitigated tedium and misery – in addition to further evenings of study and preparation. This dedication, without which my task could never have been accomplished, put a great strain on my relationship with Cerys: a relationship which, to my delight and surprise, had begun to bloom, or at least to send out promising shoots. 'Family commitments,' I would say, in mitigation. Alas, those very commitments suffered, too, and I saw a great deal less of both my mother and the girls. 'Work commitments,' I said.

But these drawbacks were small beer indeed when compared with the experience itself, the dreadful, paralysing monotony of spending twelve hours at a time in the freezing solitude of Tŷ Dedwydd, following the same tortuous routine as before: hiding in the toilet, hauling the lamp up to the secret room, tossing and turning all night on the hard floor, enduring the cleaners' mockery. 'Anyone think you camp here, Mr Robson!' 'Ha! What a thought, Fatemeh! As if!' But what choice had I? I dared not take more than a few grammes at a time, just in case someone did a stockcheck, which they very likely did, measuring the amounts every week, perhaps even every day. I amused myself by reading snippets from the archives.

I allowed a week to elapse between the first visit and the second.

This was prudent, I thought. It allowed me to test the waters. They remained pleasingly unruffled. Perhaps the managers of Tŷ Dedwydd were not so particular about their security as I had imagined: a possibility which, if borne out, would cause me disquiet under other circumstances. As for putting the drug through its paces, however, there was no time to be wasted, for Christmas was almost upon us. By a stroke of luck, I discovered from one of the more authoritative-looking websites that it was possible to dissolve the Sodium thiopental powder in alcohol. This came as a surprise, I must admit, but a welcome one: not only because my mother rarely drinks water but also because sherry might, I thought, stand a reasonably good chance of disguising both the colour and the taste of the drug. Sodium thiopental is yellow and smells of garlic. Not intensely, but recognisably. A healthy enough smell, too, to a person of my own tastes, redolent as it is of good health, strong constitutions and hearty curries. My mother, however, ever averse to pungent foods, would find it intolerable. Would she detect it, or would she not? That was my abiding concern.

I therefore proceeded with caution. On the first occasion, having prepared a solution of the required strength, I added five drops to her morning tonic. I then sat opposite her, keeping an eye on her every movement, listening for some alteration in her speech, perhaps some slurring, or some unusual train of thought. I waited for a whole hour. I neither heard nor saw a single departure from the norm. (I say 'norm', but the paramnesia remained as fervid as ever.) On my next visit, I trebled the dose. I also gave her a little less sherry: my mother drinks slowly, although quite copiously, and I feared this would reduce the impact of the drug. But I must have overdone it this time. She soon fell into a deep slumber. Her chin dropped onto her chest and she began to snore with a ferocity that I found quite unnerving. That is how she stayed, for two hours and more, before waking up and complaining that she had a terrible, terrible thirst. And such dreams, she said. Such dreadful dreams.

But three tries for a Welshman, they say. Next time, I waited until my mother went to the toilet and then added twelve drops to the half inch of sherry that remained in her glass. She returned and downed it all in one go. She smacked her lips a little, she even smelt the glass, wondering where the slightly odd taste had come from. But it was too late. Presently, she closed her eyes and slipped into a condition somewhere on the borders of sleep yet still within earshot of my gentle promptings. As I talked to her – about the Christmas presents I'd bought the girls, about the snowy Christmases of the past – she mumbled a few fitful responses, the odd 'yes', the occasional 'well, well', an indistinct 'mm' under her breath when something I said excited a little recognition. But no more.

Thus concluded the first part of my plan. The second part was a more thorny undertaking. Procuring the medication had been a mechanical task; so, too, the act of administering it to the patient and assessing its effects. I was, you could say, an old hand at jobs of this sort. They might not be pleasant, they might have their hits and misses, but if you persevered, you got there in the end. But how was I to create a new life for my mother? This was a challenge of quite different magnitude. It was not sufficient simply to construct a new life for her: the luxury of the *tabula rasa* was not mine – was not ours – to enjoy. Instead, I had somehow to reform the memory of a life already lived. It was my task, not to demolish the dark, winding caves of my mother's past, but to illuminate them; not to shoot those big black crows of hers out of the sky, but to turn them into benign doves. A difficult ask. Difficult enough for someone like Sue, trained up for the job; how much more difficult for one such as myself, unaccustomed both to mending minds and to constructing – or should I say editing? – biographies.

I should not have chosen Christmas Eve to conduct my first serious experiment. I had some notion that the girls, through opening their presents, would stir in their grandmother feelings of nostalgia; that these, in turn, would induce a state of receptivity, would prepare the ground for those little seeds I had all ready for planting. My mother was not in a receptive mood. As soon as she entered my flat, she announced that she could smell a woman's perfume. (Cerys had called around the previous evening before going to visit her brother for Christmas.) 'Susan back, then?' she asked.

'Someone from work, Mam,' I said, nonchalantly. 'Called by yesterday.'

But she would have none of it. 'Got a different scent now, then, has she, Susan? You buy it for, Dan? Mm? Little present, was it?'

I waited until the girls arrived before embarking on the thiopental. She drank this readily enough, in its sherry solution, seemingly unperturbed by the unusual taste, to which she had perhaps by now become accustomed. I asked her about her Christmases long ago. The girls, of course, as I should have anticipated, found it odd that I continued trying to engage their grandmother in conversation long after she had closed her eyes and was, to all appearances, in a deep sleep. 'Wait till she wakes up, Dad,' said Bethan, sensibly enough. So we sat in silence, a silence broken only by my mother's chesty breathing, the sound of the girls turning the pages of their magazines, the ticking of the clock.

'She's not really asleep, you know,' I said, after a while, and placed a hand on her arm. 'Just resting, Mam, isn't it?' I told Nia and Bethan how much their grandmother enjoyed reminiscing with her favourite granddaughters. 'You were looking forward, Mam, weren't you..?' I gave her arm an encouraging squeeze. She moved her head. Muttered.

'See?' I said to the girls. 'Just resting.' And turned back to my mother. 'So then, tell us about your Christmases long ago, Mam. The girls have been waiting.'

She muttered again. The odd word. The odd phrase. Another five minutes, I told myself, and she'll be as clear as a bell. So I persevered, speaking slowly, articulating carefully, as though my life depended on it. 'So, then, Mam… I bet you used to get up really early on Christmas morning? Mm..? When you were a little girl..? In Llanelli..? Yes..?'

'Mm... Early...'

It was a bite. Or at least a nibble. And that was a start. I set to my task with renewed application.

'Tell us, Mam... Tell us about the presents you used to get… About when you woke up on Christmas morning and saw them there, at the foot of the bed. Mm…? Do you remember, Mam? Tell us, Mam, tell us, the girls are waiting to hear...'

At this my mother began to stir. She raised a hand and turned her head a little, as though she'd heard someone calling from afar. More words followed... *Dat... Dat... Time to get up now... But Dat...* Not a torrent of words, no, but more than a trickle. A little mountain stream, finding its way through the rocks, setting its course through the peat and clay. *Not today, Dat... I don't want...*

'Mm? What did you say, Mam?'

Yes, as clear as a bell. Unfortunately, seeing their grandmother aroused in this way – aroused and yet, at the same time, as they imagined, still asleep – the girls became uneasy. In retrospect, I must confess that I was a touch too eager that afternoon, too insistent, so great was my desire to have the matter done and dusted, to tie the bow around my mother's belated Christmas present. The girls, in their innocence, knew nothing of my good intentions and I cannot hold them responsible for what followed. Be that as it may, Bethan, who is normally a somewhat insouciant young girl, told me roundly to leave my mother in peace. 'She's getting confused, Dad,' she said. 'You're confusing her.' Her sister agreed and looked at me quite crossly – indeed, with such exaggerated, melodramatic crossness that, when she knelt down by her grandmother and started stroking the back of her hand, I could not help but smile.

And who can deny that there was, indeed, a certain comicality to the scene being played out in my flat that afternoon, the girls upbraiding their father, the father responding with a sweet, unruffled reason, the confused grandmother mumbling her passionate inconsequentialities in the background. Yes, it would be hard not to smile, even to laugh if you were suddenly inserted into such a tableau. But I kept myself in check. I even apologised, and explained that my sole intention was to draw Mam-gu out of herself: to console her, not to harm her. 'Let's give Mam-gu a good Christmas this year,' I said. We were soon reconciled. Children are so ready to forgive.

Ten more hours passed before I realised quite how much of a gaff this had been. Following our little tea party, I took everyone home in a spirit of seasonal bonhomie: the girls primed for their real Christmas the following day, with their mother and her new partner; my mother ready 'to put her feet up', she said, after such a busy afternoon. For ten hours, all was calm. It was five o'clock on Christmas morning when the phone rang. Yes, five o'clock in the morning, and no other sound to be heard, and even the keenest Santa-watchers still in a deep, dream-filled slumber. It was my mother, all of a fluster, jabbering uncontrollably, apologising one minute for being late for tea, telling me off the next for not coming around to her flat early enough, so that she could do her hair, and she just couldn't understand why she was still wearing her nightdress, because she'd only gone for a little nap after dinner, but she was very pleased, yes, and very relieved, that I'd got back now, and I could come and collect her any time I liked, whenever it was convenient, and she knew that I'd lots of things to do, lots of very important things, and that's why I was a bit late, but not to worry, I mustn't think she was complaining, no.

'What important things?' I asked her.

'Well, fetching the girls, of course,' she said. Because the girls had been over in Ebenezer Street since yesterday afternoon, she said, and Dat had been really nasty, no, not to the little one, the other one. 'What's her name, Daniel? The other one?'

'Nia?'

'No, Daniel, not Nia. The other one. The quiet one, you know…'

'I don't, Mam. I don't know who you mean.'

'Mari. That's it. That's the one. With Mari. Said he'd a special present for Mari... A secret, see... Yes, so just to let you know that Mari's ready to come back now… Yes, ready to come back home… But why's everywhere so quiet, Daniel...? Everybody having their Christmas tea, is it, Daniel? Mm?'

32. A New Autobiography for Mam

For my mother, all memories are parasites. They lurk inside her, waiting their opportunity to feed off the fat of her past. I have no choice, therefore, but to seek other, superior parasites, that can overcome and consume the native varieties. This, after all, is how Nature ordains her affairs. But I must be careful. It is not Nature who is to plant these creatures in my mother's memory, but her son, and what, you might ask, does *he* know about such slippery customers? Doesn't he only deal with dead things, safely pinned in their glass cases? Which is true, I cannot deny it. So, then, how can I be sure that my helpful little parasites will devour only their venomous cousins? That they will chomp away only at the rotten bits, that they will leave my mother – that is, the good in my mother, the parts we must preserve – alone and unharmed? The ghosting of another's autobiography is not a duty one should tackle lightly, even when the subject is one's own kith and kin. And until today, I have been something of a dilettante. It is time to embrace a more rigorous regime, to become more disciplined, more discriminating.

This is where I must introduce you to Elizabeth Reid Hope. You won't have heard of her, I'm sure, although she is well enough known in biological circles. Infamous is a better word. I introduce you to her because it is she, above all others – yes, more even than Dr Bruno or Hefin – who has taught me the biographer's art. Elizabeth Reid Hope, or Lady Hope, as she liked to call herself, has only one biography to her name, but its subject could scarcely be more illustrious: it was none other than that great contemporary of Alfred Wallace and equal pioneer in the field of evolution, Charles Darwin. I say 'biography', although this is much too generous a term to describe such an exercise in self-serving mendacity.

The purpose of her biography, the good Lady Hope insisted, was to record Darwin's final days for posterity. Her true intent, however, as a zealous Christian, was to convince the world that the 'Devil's Chaplain', as the great man described himself, being about to meet his maker, had turned his back on his life's work and re-embraced the orthodoxies of his youth. She succeeded magnificently. Barely a week after publishing her account, the great blasphemer had been well enough rehabilitated to enjoy the privilege of interment in Westminster Abbey. 'Welcome back, Darwin the Believer!' screamed the organs of the godly, as they recounted the tearful but ennobling scene of deathbed repentance.

How did she get away with it? How did Lady Hope execute so proficient a deception that there are many who believe it to this day?

The answer is simple. She succeeded because her version of Darwin's departure from this world was more palatable than the truth, was closer to what the multitude *wished* to believe about the dignity of Man. The people, in short, were all too ready to be duped. But that was only the beginning. By itself, the mere *willingness* to believe would not have been enough. The truth might have been unpalatable, but to vanquish it, Lady Hope had to create an alternative truth which was not only more acceptable but also more *credible*, more *probable* than the truth itself. By weaving a story that no-one could reasonably reject, she gave her readers a means of dissociating themselves from any taint of deceit. 'Well, there's a thing,' I can hear them say. 'But the evidence is before us, and we can only offer our thanks to the good Lord for saving the old sinner's soul at the eleventh hour.'

What was the evidence with which Lady Hope seduced her public? No, it wasn't the scraps of conversation she claimed to have had with the old gentleman. Nor his earnest supplications for divine mercy. Nor his heartfelt repentance for following the false gods of evolution and materialism. No, her 'evidence' had nothing whatsoever to do with weighty matters such as these. It lay, rather, in the little things, the incidentals, the details that the reader might easily skim over in passing. These were the secret of her success. She recalled the 'large gate' in front of Darwin's home in the village of Downe. She encouraged you to accompany her along the 'carriage drive' that lead to his front door. She said: look at my watch, it's exactly three o'clock. Once inside, she ushered you into the opulent drawing room with the high ceiling where the old penitent lay and pointed to its 'fine bay window', to the 'far-reaching scene of woods and cornfields'. And, most importantly, she lingered over the 'long bright coloured dressing gown with a reddish brown or purple hint' that Mr Darwin wore to welcome his visitor. Who could possibly doubt the veracity of such a meticulous witness, one so intimately acquainted with the personal effects of the subject? Whatever else she might have been, Lady Hope was without doubt a consummate storyteller.

I have no storytelling skills. I am an entomologist, not a litterateur. I have been trained to deal with facts, not fancies. I can describe for you the striking livery of the Burnet moth. I can detail the mating behaviour of the clubtail dragonfly. I can map the migratory patterns of the brown hairstreak butterfly. I can tell you about a thousand other marvels that may be seen and recorded and analysed, yes, and marvelled at, too, for these are living and breathing facts, the racing pulse of Nature. I have had little need, therefore, for dreamers and speculators. I have, in fact, been quite dismissive of their imaginings. And yet, on considering these matters afresh in the light of changed circumstances, I am obliged to modify my antipathy somewhat. Because what, after all, is the true character and essence of the storyteller's art, what was the secret of Lady Hope's grand deception, but a very particular form of observation? And is not the supreme attainment of storyteller and observer alike that they become one with the world they describe, that their disguise is complete and seamless? For it is the story we wish to contemplate, not the storyteller. The insects, not the entomologist. And is it not the ultimate goal of each true benefactor to shed light only on the blessings he bestows, whilst concealing himself all the while in the shadows, the foliage, the purpose-built hide?

No, I am not a storyteller, still less a story maker. But I have, in the past few weeks, learned to mimic some of the storyteller's techniques, his tricks of the trade. The BBC World Service's short story readings have been very helpful in this endeavour. (At fifteen minutes' duration, they suited my purpose better than the entire volumes that were broadcast, chapter by chapter, on Radio 4.) I also attended some of the storytelling sessions which are held occasionally at Chapter Arts Centre. Cerys accompanied me on more than one occasion and would explain, on the basis of her own experience, some of the finer nuances of presentation. (In her defence, I should stress that she believed me simply to be taking a father's interest in Nia's new enthusiasm for acting. Yes, this is what I told her. What choice did I have?) In this way I learned, for example, the importance of making eye contact, of varying tone and register and, most tellingly, of knowing what *not* to say, knowing what to leave out, so that the story might reveal its secrets by stealth, as though the listener had teased them out all by herself with her own tweezers.

Thus prepared, I then grafted Lady Hope's method onto that of Dr Bruno. Following the Doctor's example, I set as my goal nothing less than the reconstruction of my mother's houses, judging that these, being familiar, would offer the best home for her new memories. I proceeded, then, to tell stories about them. Like Lady Hope, I made sure that each story had some ring of truth – in order to take root, my mother's new memories needed to be planted in familiar soil – but a truth which then took wing and rose above that deficient, discredited thing we call memory.

The easiest of these houses to rebuild was my mother's childhood home in Ebenezer Street, Llanelli. I had a clear recollection of the small rooms there, packed with dingy furniture, the faded flowery wallpaper, the old grey oven in the kitchen, and most vividly of all, most alive to my senses, the smell of carbolic soap in the bathroom, a *cordon sanitaire* against the world's filth. And my grandmother herself, of course. Yes, my head still rang with her stern injunctions and prohibitions.

The Ebenezer Street story was about buying a frock for my mother's first dance. The frock wasn't the starting point, of course. The sherry came first, to calm the nerves, then the *thiopental*. And then, after precisely four minutes, the Gaudy Welsh. 'That used to be on Mam-gu's sideboard, didn't it, Mam?' Which led me to the other items on the sideboard: the clock, the candlesticks, the photograph. 'Wasn't there a picture of you there once, Mam? Mm..? Wearing a new frock, I think…The one with the belt… You know, that dark-coloured frock… What colour was it, Mam, exactly? I couldn't tell because the photograph was black and white…'

I didn't remember any such picture, of course. But it was a credible detail. I even quoted Mam-gu, sitting in her leather armchair, admiring her daughter in her beautiful new outfit. *Oh, there's a pretty young lady you are, Mari fach!* I even tried to mimic her voice, her long-vowelled Carmarthenshire Welsh.

And Mari would be waiting, heart in mouth, for the knock at the door. Mam-gu, too, because her daughter was stepping out for the first time. Yes, and not with any Tom, Dick or Harry, mind you, but with a 1st Engineer from one of the big boats, and a handsome lad, as well. But he was the lucky one, Mam-gu said, oh, yes, because you'd turned the heads of all the lads, hadn't you, Mam? Yes, he was the lucky one, going out with our Mari, in her new frock, the prettiest girl this side of Swansea. And Mam-gu went through to the kitchen, then, to get the best china from the sideboard, the blue plates with the little Chinamen on them. (You've still got them, Mam, haven't you? Safely tucked away?) Into the front room then to set the table. The fire was already lit, I think, yes, and the two big porcelain dogs peeping down from the mantlepiece. That's where you were standing, Mam, wasn't it? By the window in the front room, waiting for your 1st Engineer, drawing back the red curtains so that you could see better. And there he is, Mam, there he is! He's carrying flowers, pink and yellow flowers. What are they, Mam? Can you tell? Carnations, do you think? Yes, he's carrying carnations. His hand is on the gate, now, Mam. He's opening the gate. He catches your eye…

And so on.

No, it wasn't much of a story. But I had only twenty minutes and, in any case, tales of jaw-dropping excitement were not what was required. I sought to capture something of the *texture* of my mother's life, no more. For a first effort I believe it went down quite well. When I mentioned the frock, my mother smiled, in her half sleep, and mumbled something about '*Siop David Evans*'. And it may be, indeed, that the frock in the story, the frock in the imagination, chimed with some real frock from long ago. After all, are not new frocks and nervous vigils the stock-in-trade of every young woman at some time or other?

I related this story to my mother every week for three months, adding embellishments from time to time, so that it would retain its freshness, its ability to stir the imagination. As well as the dances, I described how my mother and her admirer went to the pictures, too. I even did some research into films of the period, to give my mother's memory an extra little stimulus. It was all grist to the mill. But, generally, she preferred to stay at home, with the best china, waiting by the window. I did not give her 1st Engineer a name. Nor did my mother.

The house in North Shields was a harder nut to crack. I could recall my bedroom, where I had to stand on a chair to look out through the window at the garden below and the trees of the cemetery beyond. But I remembered little else. 'Where did you keep the Gaudy Welsh in North Shields, Mam?' I asked her. 'Did you have a sideboard there, too? Did you put it on top of the sideboard? It was a wedding present, wasn't it, Mam, the Gaudy Welsh?' But I was fishing in dark waters, with meagre bait. So I turned to the garden, to the flowers, their bright reds and yellows and blues.

'We had a nice garden in Shields, didn't we, Mam? Yes… I could see the flowers from my bedroom window. The geraniums... the flox... the marigolds... The marigolds were in the narrow border by the hedge, weren't they? You know, Mam, the tall hedge between us and the Wilsons next door. Remember the Wilsons? Mm? Robert Wilson, the little lad?'

'Jib...'

'Mm? What did you say, Mam?'

'Jibbons...'

'Ah! The jibbons! Yes, of course, Mam, the patch of jibbons, over in the far corner. Ha! You've got a good memory, Mam, I'd never have remembered that, no, never, not the jibbons.'

Having retrieved, between us, this little scrap of memory (if such it was, for I had no way of telling) I proceeded to embroider onto it incidental details of how I would play there, by the jibbons, how I would hunt for insects amongst the flowers, under the stones, how I would talk to Robert next door through the hedge, Mam keeping an eye on me all the while through the kitchen window.

'I'll leave this here for you, Mam, so you can look at it after…'

I took from my pocket one of the old picture postcards I had collected as a child and left it on the table next to the empty sherry glass. 'My birthday, Mam. remember? That's when I got the picture. It showed a large ship. No, not much of an exhibit, you might say, certainly nothing to compete with the picture of the two Ahmeds, but there we are, I had to make the best of what I had at my disposal. A ship it was.

'My birthday, Mam… Dad had come home from sea and everyone was in the garden. You, Dad, John, my friends. Which friends..?

Well, Robert next door, he'd have been there for definite. And Pauline? Yes, probably Pauline. And who else? Well, never mind, we'll come back to that. We had a tea-party, that's what's important. Out in the garden, because it was sunny and warm that day, wasn't it, Mam? You had your summer frock on, the one with the blue spots and the wide collar. And you baked a special cake, didn't you, with thick chocolate icing, you brought it out to the garden and there we were, by the table, the table with the red tablecloth, always the red tablecloth, and Robert waving his hands around to keep the wasps away and Pauline saying No, no, that'll just make them cross. And John said, they're not wasps, they're hornets, hornets are different. He got upset then. Can't remember why. Did he drop his piece of cake on the ground, Mam? Can you remember? Yes, that was it. Dropped his cake on the grass and got upset. Not to worry, John, you said, there's plenty of cake to be had. Don't fret, you said. Because no-one was going to spoil that special day. And you told Dad that there were a couple of jobs to do when he had the time, clearing an old nest from the chimney, something of that sort, mending a gutter before the rain came. He was handy like that, wasn't he, Mam? And Dad said, alright, he'd fettle it all in good time, but not just yet, no, because everybody was having such fun and we wouldn't want him clashing about on top of a ladder, would we, not in the middle of my birthday party? So, after the party, that's when he'd do it, there'd be plenty time then, he said. That's when he came and did his tricks, when he found a penny in my ear, when he put the little stone under the cup and everybody guessed and nobody got it right. We sang 'Happy Birthday' and you said that was the nicest day you'd had in ages, yes, you said it'd been nicer even than your own birthday.

And that is where I finished my story, because I had nowhere else to go. It elicited only the most desultory response from my mother. I had another stab a fortnight later, varying the details somewhat and adding a scene where my father helped my mother tend the garden. I repeated it again, after a few days, but pretended on this occasion that the picture of the ship had been given to me by my father. This was, I admit, a purely whimsical touch on my part, but it proved effective, perhaps because it drew together the disparate elements in the story. I believe we all like our stories to hang together, and my mother is no exception. In any case, she became much more curious about the ship. I was making progress.

Strangely enough, the most intractable of all locations, from a storytelling point of view, was our house in Darren Street, Pentrepoeth. It was easy enough to set the scene. I know the house so intimately that I can still trace its every feature as though it were part of my own body. 'Darren Street, Mam. Now then, the Gaudy Welsh was on the dresser there, wasn't it?' It was easy to move, then, to the big wooden chest in the main bedroom, to the piano in the front room, to this table, to that chair. Easy, too, to give each a voice, a life of its own. 'I remember Auntie Beti playing the piano… The old favourites… Smoke Gets in Your Eyes... la... la la la la la... Who wrote that, Mam, do you remember?' Or, 'That's what was nice about Darren Street, you could sit on the window seat and watch…'

But there it came to an abrupt end. What would she look at through that window? And when she came home from work in the evening, tired, and sat there, wondering, 'Well, what shall I do tonight?' – what would happen next? I had no answer to that question. Who would come knocking at the door on a Saturday evening? No admirer, no, not now, the time for admirers had passed. No children, either, not in the end. And I didn't have the imagination to undo these facts, even with the help of thiopental. So, in the absence of a credible story, I had no choice but to abandon the art of the fabulist and revert to my own métier: the close observation of details.

'The swing was a present from Mam-gu, wasn't it, Mam? You know, out the back…'

And for once, instead of the usual mumblings, she answered with confidence and clarity.

'No, *bach*, Wncwl Wil bought you that.'

'Wncwl Wil? Wncwl Wil gave me the swing? Are you sure, Mam?' I had no recollection of the event and could not imagine why he would do such a thing. In other circumstances I might have pressed my case further, to get to the truth of the matter. But that, of course, would have been to miss the point. I'm glad I had the wisdom to realise that I was not here to challenge my mother's sometimes wayward recollections. My job was only to suggest, to nudge, to imply. Ultimately, my mother had to feel, as they say, ownership of her own stories. If she should become, in the process, a more active participant than I had anticipated, there was nothing to be done. Indeed, I should surely embrace such a development.

I must confess that yielding even a little control over my material was a discomfiting experience. But I know now that this strategy was crucial to my success. In no time at all we became joint authors of the Wncwl Wil story. Indeed, as I listened to my mother's now quite fluent narrations, I even came to see Wncwl Wil in my mind's eye, on some birthday or other, carrying the swing through to the back garden, as though it had all really happened. 'Brought it in his Land Rover, did he, Mam?' I said. 'Yes, that's right, Mam. I remember it well.'

Wnwcwl Wil soon donated other items to our Darren Street house. He became, you might say, something of a benefactor. These were small items, of course, but it's the small things that count, as we have discovered. The marble ash tray. The lampshade with the stamps on it. Things of that sort. And when I saw that Wil-the-benefactor was agreeable to my mother, I allowed him to extend his repertoire somewhat. I placed him in the garden shed, where he would help her prepare her bulbs. I put him on top of a ladder, to clean out the guttering. I had him papering the front room and the passage. Once, I even got him to ask my mother out for a meal. She deserved no less. No, there was no end to the blessings bestowed on Number 14 Darren Street through the generosity of good old Wncwl Wil. In the end, I have no doubt that he outshone all my other characters, that my mother embraced no-one so dearly, so eagerly.

33. June 2006. Where Next?

6th of August, lat. 30 - 30′ N., long. 52 - W.

By noon the flames had burst into the cabin and on deck, and we were driven to take refuge in the boats, which, being much shrunk by exposure to the sun, required all our exertions to keep them from filling with water. The flames spread most rapidly; and by night the masts had fallen, and the deck and cargo was one fierce mass of flame. We staid near the vessel all night: the next morning we left the ship still burning down at the water's edge, and steered for Bermuda, the nearest point of land, but still 700 miles distant from us.

The only things which I saved were my watch, my drawings of fishes, and a portion of my notes and journals. Most of my journals, notes on the habit of the animals, and drawings of the transformations of insects, were lost. My collections were mostly from the country about the sources of the Rio Negro and Orinooko, one of the wildest and least known parts of South America, and their loss is therefore the more to be regretted. I had a fine collection of the river tortoises (Chelydidæ) consisting of ten species, many of which I believe were new. Also upwards of a hundred species of the little known fishes of the Rio Negro: of these last, however, and of many additional species, I have saved my drawings and descriptions. My private collection of Lepidoptera contained illustrations of all the species and varieties I had collected at Santarem, Montalegré, Barra, the Upper Amazons, and the Rio Negro: there must have been at least a hundred new and unique species. I had also a number of curious Coleoptera, several species of ants in all their different states, and complete skeletons and skins of an ant-eater and cow-fish, (Manatus); the whole of which, together with a small collection of living monkeys, parrots, macaws, and other birds, are irrecoverably lost.

Wallace was a mere 29 years of age when his collection was burnt to cinders in the hold of the *Helen*. He had another sixty years before him in which to undo the damage. How different life appears once one has crossed its equator. Nevertheless, I find inspiration in the young man's tenacity. He did not despair. He did not walk off in a sulk. No, he set sail without delay for Malaya and accomplished there the most important work of his life. The catastrophe of the *Helen*, which would have crushed the spirit of a lesser mortal, was thus cancelled out at a single stroke.

I have resumed my work on Wallace. A publisher got back to me in April, saying they were interested in bringing out my translation of the biography on condition that I made some cuts. Some cuts? I asked. And discovered that the condition is, in fact, a good deal more stringent than I had imagined. They insist I omit all of the technical and scientific passages – passages that are, of course, crucial to an appreciation of Wallace's significance; passages, moreover, that took me months to translate – and retain only the material relating to Wales (which is, I regret, all too brief), together with 'highlights' of the overseas expeditions. Even the description of the fire, they say, is too 'pedantic' in style, as though a meticulous attention to detail were a trait of which one should be ashamed. But what can I do? Cerys says it is better to realise half a dream than no dream at all. She does, of course, know about such things.

We returned from Northumberland yesterday, where we'd spent the Whitsun holiday. We didn't take the girls: Bethan had gone on a school trip to Germany and Nia was too busy with her acting. (She's been offered a bit-part as a schoolgirl in *Pobl y Cwm* for a few weeks.) We stayed in B&Bs rather than rent a cottage: this gave us more freedom to travel; it also meant that we could, by and large, avoid replicating my sojourn here with Sue the previous year. That would have stirred too many unhappy memories. We did, however, cross over to Lindisfarne, one of my childhood haunts, where we visited the museum and saw Grace Darling's famous lifeboat. Cerys seemed pleased to explore my 'blue remembered hills', as she called them, and this pleased me in turn. It has given us a history we can share. I hope to reciprocate, before too long, through visiting Cerys's parents near Llandeilo, and helping her relive her own childhood adventures. I shall, of course, need to approach the father and brother with caution, with delicacy. Perhaps I can help mend bridges in that department.

If I were writing my autobiography I should probably draw to a close now through reflecting sagely on the lessons life has taught me: through composing a little epilogue, to give the impression that the tortuous paths I have trod do indeed lead, rationally and purposefully, to this moment of fulfilment, when the veil is removed and truth exposed in all its glory. To do as Wallace himself did at the end of *My Life*, when he became immersed in the mysteries of spiritualism and mesmerism. But I shall refrain. I have no revelations to announce about Cerys and me. I am glad to say that I can relax in her company in a way that was impossible when I was with Sue. Perhaps that is enough. Yes, for the time being, that is enough. I shall miss her during her secondment. (She's helping set up Blithe Hoose, the new *happinesstheexperience.com* centre in Glasgow.) But such is the nature of our profession. Perhaps I, too, will have to answer the call one day.

Other things have changed in the last six months. Sonia and her husband have separated. Temporarily, she says, because he's been offered a job in the north of England. That's what she says. Not wanting to hurt the children's feelings, probably. She hasn't been to the reading group since Christmas. Having said that, our numbers are up, thanks mainly to Cerys, who's recruited the parents of some of her workshop pupils. Siân and her husband, Ben, for example: they are among our most dedicated members now. Buttered Hot Dogs and a Pair of Crimson Socks, to adapt the old mnemonic. Yes, Tŷ Dedwydd is a splendid place for meeting like-minded folk.

Sue is going out with someone else now. Brian. I say 'now' but I have no idea when the relationship began. I saw them in town one lunchtime in April. I was standing in a queue at Boots, waiting to buy my contact lens solutions, when I heard them behind me, talking animatedly about their holiday plans. I recognised Sue's voice and, despite myself, despite knowing it was a foolish thing to do, I turned. Sue recognised me. Of course she did. They were holding hands.

Brian seems an amiable chap. Taller than me but a little older, too, I think. He did his best to ease our discomfort, fair play to him, although he need not have expounded quite so volubly about the bargains he'd seen in the Electric Goods department. Is that his line? I thought. Is that what Sue wanted all the time – an elderly electrician? 'We'd invite you for a coffee,' he said, after showing me his new electric toothbrush, 'but we've got to get back to work.' Which led me to conclude, rightly or wrongly, that Brian and Sue worked together. I did not ask, perhaps because that question might have led to other, more forensic, more pointed questions such as, How long *exactly* have you been seeing each other? No, Brian, what I mean is, how long *precisely* have you been screwing Sue? Because I can see now that she's put on weight. That her cheeks are unusually pale. Are you pregnant, Sue? Are you expecting Brian's baby? Mm? And other awkward, unworthy enquiries of that sort. I reached the head of the queue and bade them a hearty farewell. Heartier than was appropriate, perhaps, so great was my relief.

Good luck to you, Sue. I begrudge you nothing. But be careful, Brian. You have taken on something of a queen bee here. And the queen bee, in case you don't already know, is very partial to a bit of aerial copulation. Way up in the blue, blue sky, that's where she likes to do it. Her privilege, you see. Nothing mundane about the queen bee. Maybe there's a little thrill in it for the drone, too, for a second or two. Until he sees his betrothed dashing back to the hive with his penis and testicles and intestines hanging down between her legs. She won't have much use for him then, will she? No, Brian, you watch out. I had a lucky escape. You might not be so fortunate.

As for myself... Well, I am full of sweet anticipation that, sooner rather than later, yes, perhaps during the next few days but certainly, I'm sure of it, before she goes to Glasgow, Cerys will ask me to move in with her. How bleak, she said, after our holiday together, to return to the loneliness of her house. I am a little surprised that she has not asked me already. I must say that the idea appeals to me more and more. I have purged Sue from my system. I have immersed myself thoroughly in my new career. And I am exceedingly fond of her: more than fond, I am sure, given the chance. But I must be cautious. Although she has said nothing on the matter, nor have I asked, I cannot be certain that she, too, if only subliminally, is not thinking, Yes, here's my chance, perhaps my only chance, to build myself a little nest. And it would be cruel to awaken maternal instincts that I cannot, that I will not, satisfy. Perhaps she'll ask me tonight.

I cannot say that the girls have made much effort to get to know Cerys. This, I'm sure, is merely the indifference of youth, rather than an active hostility. They are simply too busy with their friends, their clothes, their hair. That said, I must note here, for the record, how indebted I am to Nia for sitting with me and her grandmother on many occasions while I related my stories: I do not think they would have taken half so well had she not been present, contributing her own natural, unprompted responses and queries. Stories are Nia's delight, of course: she was required to do nothing but follow her instincts. In truth, I believe that Nia's little interventions, her willing surrender to my mother's improved life-story, brought the two of them closer together. Both have been the beneficiaries of my project, and of that I am proud.

I have not introduced Cerys to my mother. Not because of the risk that my mother might start talking about grandchildren – although that would be reason enough – but because she is convinced that Sue has returned, that we are reconciled, that she has, in fact, called round to see her two or three times in the last week alone, to have a cup of tea, to pass on messages from me and the girls. From me, Mam? Surely not. But I must be patient: it would be cruel, as well as futile, to remonstrate with her further on this matter. Nothing can be gained by dealing too roughly with her delusions.

So, then, my mother. How is she? you ask. Well, I have told her thirty-eight stories to date. I had not intended telling so many, but it could not be helped. Some fell ignominiously at the first fence and were replaced without further ado. Others, often through the curiosity of Nia, spawned interminable sub-plots of their own. When I mentioned the chest in her grandmother's bedroom in Llanelli, it was not enough to be told that a teddy-bear lived in it, a teddy-bear that Mam-gu had had from her own grandmother, and to hear a few recollections about her, too. No, Nia had to know what else was in the chest and, on hearing that it housed more toy animals, insisted on asking questions about them, too, the sorts of questions that only little girls can ask. Did all the animals get on well together? What did they do when they weren't in the chest? Did Mam-gu play with them? Did she give them names? Where are they now? And so on.

The best of the stories, however, struck a happy medium between the sprint and the marathon. Occasionally, when I was on top form, there was no need for any preamble about the Gaudy

Welsh or the sideboard or the old chest, because, for whatever reason, my mother seemed content to ride on the wave of the new memories I had created for her. She would repeat details, as though trying them out for size, savouring them, making them her own. In the end, if the story were sufficiently vivid, she could do this even without the aid of thiopental. I had only to plant the roots deep enough and feed them with copious circumstantial detail, and my story seemed to acquire a life of its own. This was most satisfying.

I have, by now, given Wncwl Wil a rest. The truth is that I have run out of ideas, or rather of *mises-en-scènes*, in which I could credibly situate him. I wrote to my brother a month or so ago, in an effort to gather more raw material, to expand my portfolio, as it were, but he did not reply. I was not surprised: John rarely concerns himself with our affairs. Perhaps I shall ring him. He has access to memories from before my time, and to whom else can I turn? But I must not labour the point or he will become suspicious. It is possible that I have already burned my boats in this regard.

I fear my stories have become a little bland of late. Between preparing my lecture (the lecture on beetles which Dr Bruno has asked me to deliver) and the demands of translating Wallace, there has been little time for creative endeavour. I have also become rather tired of the old houses and it is, I think, no coincidence that, in preparing my lecture, in devising my *aides memoires*, I have used not a single house to store my specimens. Nor a cemetery, either, despite Dr Bruno's shining example in that regard. Cemeteries and houses are, after all, merely conveniences and I am glad to say that I have discovered an alternative convenience that better suits my purpose. I have determined to store all my beetles – that is, the twenty common species which I have agreed to discuss – in the art galleries of the National Museum. This is a much more congenial place than a graveyard, I'm sure you'll agree. It is, moreover, a place with which I became well acquainted during my long service in that institution. No, I can claim no special knowledge of art, of its history or its practice; I did, however, when the weather was wet, when I was tired after a morning's cataloguing, enjoy many a pleasant lunchtime standing in front of Cézanne's *Provençal Landscape* or Turner's *Day After the*

Storm or Hogarth's *Children's Tea Party*, losing myself in their rich colours and images. And although paintings and insects have little enough in common, I believe that my scientific training – particularly my capacity for close observation, for noting tiny variations – put me in good stead when I came to consider the works of the great painters. Be that as it may, memories of those pleasant hours of retreat stirred a little pang of nostalgia in me as I considered how I might best harness these masterworks for the purposes of my lecture.

Aside from the nostalgia, my choice of 'convenience' also had hard-headed practical benefits. Using only one of the sixteen galleries, I could devote two different paintings to each species – one each for male and female – reserving the larger pictures for those families that have within them a number of sub-species. Take, for example, the three varieties of horned beetle that breed in Wales: *Lucanus cervus, Dorcus parallelipipedus,* and *Sinodendron cylindricum.* I have placed a specimen of each on the walls of a building in Naples in the famous painting by Thomas Jones. (As I say, only the males are to be seen here; their mates are sunbathing in the adjacent picture: a similar study by the same artist.) By visualising the specimens in this way, the memory can move easily and naturally from one to the other. And insects are, by and large, adept at adhering to walls, even walls as smooth as these. I do this all in my mind, of course. The beetles are already there, as are the galleries and the pictures. They simply need to be introduced to each other.

Beetles on a painting by Thomas Jones

34. Excerpt from an Autobiography

Had to keep a list in those days, see. In a book. No computers then, Sue. Just a list. The name and address over here, on the left. The date and the time, then, over the other side. Yes. Two names, there'd always be two. The one selling the house and the one buying it. The vendor and the... and the... No, not the one buying it, not the...

Where was I?

Not the one buying it. The
one who was going to

The one who was going to view the house. That's it. There was another book for the ones that were going to buy. Yes. And I'd write my initials down, on the side of the page. Or Geoff's. Depending on who was going to do the viewing. I was the first woman to drive a car in our street. Did you know that, Sue? Had to, see. To drive people about the place. People didn't have cars in those days. Not like now.

No.

S. Allchurch. P. Clements. Fifty-six Dinas Terrace. Sixth of February. Three thirty. That sort of thing. That's how I'd do it. And M.R. in the margin, then, to show it was me doing the viewing. M.R. for Mari Robson.

Yes.

Daniel

Called him Daniel then, not Dan.

Daniel didn't like it at all. Thought it was common, poking about in other people's houses. That's what he said. Poking about. Didn't like it at all. Told him, Your mam's got to work, I said. How do you expect to eat if your Mam doesn't go out to work? Don't know where he got that from. Did a viewing in one of his friends' houses. Hated that he did. Hated it. Good job, though. Estate agents. Tidy wage in those days. I was manager then, see. Yes.

John?

No, John's in Canada, Sue. Set up his own business there. Did you know that? That's his picture over by the jug, him and Helen and the children. Take it down, have a proper look. It's an old one, mind. Children have grown up by now. Yes. A little sherry?

You sure?

Ah, on duty, is it?

Gaudy Welsh Daniel calls it. The jug. Gaudy Welsh. Don't know where he got that from. Funny name, that. Ugly, don't you think? Swansea China Mam used to say. Daniel couldn't stand it. Too old, see. Couldn't stand old things. Bit spoilt he was, see. Yes. His Mam-gu saying, Eat your pudding now then, Daniel bach, there's a good boy. Come to your old Mam-gu for a *cwtsh*, now. By herself by then, see. By herself, needing the company.

Yes.

Swansea China.

Yes.

Sold properties up in Llansamlet and Birchgrove as well, mind. Did you know that, Sue? Not just Morriston. No. Over in Glais and Mynydd-bach as well, sometimes. Biggest office around, see. People thought, put your house up with Pritchard's, you've got a better chance of selling it. Busy. Very busy. Not that I'm complaining.
Treat to see them come in, the little families, looking for their new homes. Yes. Made you feel glad when you found something tidy for them. Daniel didn't understand that, see. Never did. That's boys for you. Too busy, see. Yes. With this and that. This and that.

Not to worry.

Back together now. That's what matters. Back together. Yes.

Mm?

Daniel said.

Yesterday.

Yes.

Where was I?

The beetles.

That's it.

Busy with his beetles, see. Barely saw him from one day to the next. Daniel and his beetles.

Ha!

What kind of hobby's that for a young boy, Sue? Mm? Wouldn't let me into his bedroom. No. Into his bedroom! Can you credit it, Sue? Put NO ENTRY on the door. Made me mad, that did. Couldn't go where I wanted to in my own house. Had enough of that sort of thing with his father. Yes. Quite enough.

Kept them in boxes.

Specimens.

That's what he called them. His specimens.

Kept them in shoeboxes. Said that's how you do it, Mam. In boxes. Him and his NO ENTRY. Had to go in, see, to do the dusting, to get his clothes for the wash. Young lads don't think. Spoilt, see. That's what it was. And there's a stink there was on the stuff. 'To keep them fresh,' he said. 'To keep them fresh.' Meaning the beetles, see. Turned my stomach. 'Make you ill, that will,' I told him. 'Make you sick.' Chemicals, see. Couldn't understand it. Couldn't understand why he didn't want to go out and play with his friends. Daniel I called him then. Not Dan.

Little sherry, Sue? Cup of tea?

Later, is it?

He'd take me out to the garden and say, Look, Mam, look at this. And show me a dead mouse then, something the cat had got hold of, you know, like they do, but not eaten it. Yes. A mouse. Tried a bird once, I'm sure he did, but it was too big. Yes. And he said, Look at this, Mam. And I had to sit there. He'd bring a chair out from the kitchen so I could sit there, in the garden. Half an hour I'd be there. An hour. I've got the dinner to do, I'd tell him. But no, he'd say, hang on just a minute, look, they've got the scent now, Mam. And I'd say, Got the scent? What d'you mean, got the scent? And he'd say, they can smell it, Mam, they can smell it all the way from Trebo'th. All the way from Trebo'th, Sue. Yes. Got the scent, see.

What were they?

Don't know, Sue.

No.

Don't remember.

Well, beetles they were, I know that much. Yes. Daniel would have some name for them. Some big name. Yes, very likely. If we asked him.

Where was I?

The beetles?

Yes.

The beetles had got the scent, see. And it had gone before you could blink. Not eaten, mind you. No, they don't eat it. Bury it. That's what they do. Bury the mouse so they can come back later, see. Lay their eggs on it. That's what Daniel said. Lay their eggs. Yes. Can you credit it? Lay their eggs on the mouse.

Turned my stomach it did.

His Nan? Daniel's Nan?

Oh, yes. Daniel would go and stay with his Nan in those days. Weekends. Yes. When the weather was good. Daniel we called him then. Yes. Liked to go to his Nan's.

A photo?

No, I don't think I've got a photo. Not here. Looked like me, though, Daniel's Nan. Bit stouter. Carried a bit more weight. The old *sachabwndi* Dat used to call her. Not nice, that. Calling her names. Bought that music box for me, my dad. Can you see it, Sue? Up by the… No, it's gone from there… Where's it got to, then? The one with the pearl inlay, you know the type, Sue? The little lady dancing when you open it up.

Must be in the bedroom.

Saw it in Sam Pope's shop in town. In Llanelli, I mean, not in Morriston. Llanelli I was living then, see. Sixteen Ebenezer Street. That's where I saw it. And I thought, yes, that's what I'd like to be, just like her, with her little white toutou, spinning around on her one leg, everybody watching her, everybody clapping. And I came back from school then one afternoon and Mam said look, I've got a present for you.

What did you say, Sue?

No, no, *Dat* bought the music box. Not Mam. That's what I said. Yes. I told you that yesterday. Up by the Swansea China it was.

Yes, yesterday.

When you called by yesterday.

Yes, Sue, that's John. In Canada now, John. Got his own business now. Yes. And the children. That's Rebecca on the left. And Sam's the little boy. Not a boy any more, of course. No. Works with his dad now. Yes. Sam. Samuel.

Like his father? Who, John?

Yes, I suppose he is.

John was about to go into the big school when it happened. Boy needs his father, that age. The little ones cope better. Funny, that, isn't it, Sue? Don't understand, I suppose. Don't remember, then. Daniel didn't remember a thing.

Broke his heart when the cat died.

Yes.

Ha!

Not his father, though. Not his own father. Just think.

Yes.

Been away, see. Away at sea. Out in the… Out in the … Out in the what'd'you-call… And Wil said, He's got a right to know about his dad, Mari. That's what he said. Got a right.

Fair play.

Aden. That's it. Out near Aden.

Used to give him little picture cards. Trains. Ships. Cars. That sort of thing. Wil, I mean, not his dad. Daniel didn't know his dad. Gave him little photos. Got them with his fags, I think. Didn't know anything about the sea, mind.

No.

And he'd tell him, he'd say, Daniel, your dad's been on that ship. And that one. And that one. Drove them round the world he did. America, Brazil, Australia, Africa, everywhere. Because he was the First Engineer. Most important man on the ship, Wil said. Never met him, mind. No. Never met Jack. That's what I called Daniel's dad. Jack. No, never met my Jack, but wanted the boy to know, see. Be proud of his dad. Wil showed Daniel his photos and Daniel showed Wil his beetles. Oh yes, he didn't mind showing his beetles to Wil. 'Knows how to handle them,' Wil said. Daniel liked that.

He'd come over

He'd come over and help me in the garden, do a few odd jobs around the house. Awful state on the house, Sue, when we moved in. Never been there, have you? Just heard about it, is it..? From Daniel..? Yes, there you are, then. But he wasn't a real uncle. No. Wncwl Wil we all called him, but not a real uncle. Met him through work, see.

No, no, he wasn't moving, not Wncwl Wil. Had a little farm, over by Neath. Just a little place. Farmer he was, see.

Yes.

Lived there with his mam, too. Yes, I know, with his mam. Can you credit it? Over fifty and still living with his mam? Been there all his life, see, didn't want to move. Couldn't move, maybe. Had to keep the farm going, see, had to make do.

His sister.

What was her name again?

His big sister. Husband had the dust. She's the one was moving. His big sister. Selling her house over in Pantlasau. Gelli Wastad Road. Fifty-six Gelli Wastad Road. Yes.

Terrible, that, the dust.

Yes.

Came over to help me in the garden the day it happened. Do a couple of odd jobs about the place. He was good like that, Wil. Clearing the muck out of the gutter he was. The leaves. Lost his balance.

Yes.

Yes.

Spent four years dying, poor dab. Over in Bryn Coch. His mam looking after him.

'I told him, Mari,' he'd say. 'I told the lad… I asked him...' 'What did you tell him, *bach*?' I'd say. 'What did you ask him?' But he'd gone by then. Couldn't remember a thing. Lucky he didn't, perhaps. Not a thing.

What do you think, Sue?

Was it for the best?

It's not something you want to remember, see. No. Not something like that. It just comes back, and there you are, what can you do? But then, you remember the other things as well, the nice things. And you wouldn't want to forget them, would you? No.

So I'm lucky, in a way. When it comes down to it. That I've got the memories.

What do you think, Sue?

Acknowledgements

The author is grateful to Wales Literature Exchange for its award of a translation grant and to Mick Felton of Seren for his support and editorial help. Thanks are due to the following for permission to reproduce pictures in the text: National Museum of Wales (painting by Thomas Jones on p.222); Andrew Syred/Microscopix (photographs of insects superimposed on Thomas Jones's painting); and www.museum.woolworths.co.uk (picture on p.114).